...AND SNOWFLAKES WILL NEVER TOUCH THE GROUND...

TANYA RAKOS

Print information available on the last page.
Rev. date:
To order additional copies of this book, contact:
Maple Leaf Publishing Inc.
3rd Floor 4915 54 Street Red Deer, Alberta T4N 2G7, Canada 1-(403)-356-0255

CONTENTS

Introduction

Like the universe, the human brain will never be fully understood. Anything can be proven right and wrong at the same time. All you have to do is to ask yourself, "Which answer do you prefer?" Isn't it true that everything in the universe including the human brain works in mysterious ways? Yes and no are just the snow that comes from nowhere. And only the human brain decides if the snowflakes create drifts or never touch the ground and twirl through the air forever.

In this book, I tried to show how people's extraordinary skills might be looked from a quite simple point of view in a combination with rules of the universe.

Being raised in the family where both parents and us children were receptive to any anomaly as to everyday events, I tried to figure out why "the strange things" seemed not so strange to us, but were strange to the people around. Thirty years have passed in the constant research that did not bring any results, but only a hypothesis. Dealing with my life's constant adventures and at the same time helping my son to find his true life's path, I stopped my research and decided to take it easy.

In this book, I combined my educational background in physics, microelectronics, psychology, and philology with my work experience in children's education and mental rehabilitation services.

All the extraordinary events in this book have never taken place.

All characters of the book are not real and have never been prototyped from actual people. The only real features that were described are the beautiful parks across Canada, particularly in Alberta, and my parents' inspiration.

The developing events take place in a Canadian town of Gray Stone (fictional name) in the province of Alberta in the twenty-second century.

The world becomes a paradise. There are not any conflicts on Earth anymore. Was it a good idea to give people all they wanted? The universe itself opens up with the answers.

PART 1

The Conversation

"Do you think they are ready to define the purpose of life? Sorry for such a cliché.

"They should by now…Humans are creatures of language. They create, use, and misuse words, symbols in order to comprehend the world as mediated by their senses. At this point, they don't need to concern themselves with controversial and widely divergent views on events. Let's just make it as a presupposition that is at least somewhat tenable. The knowledge of the purpose of life has always been in conjunction with the other vital forces in human beings as an essence from the very beginning. They don't need to look for it, but 'axiomize' out loud, if you wish…How many generations have already gone since we gave them happiness and security?"

"You mean the promised Paradise?"

"Paradise is quite a strong word. Let's call it security—life without worries for their future…"

My dearest reader, if you are trying to visualize those two who are responsible for the conversation, I will try my best with the description.

Let me start with the location of the conversation. Umm…it could be the very universe somewhere beside the blue planet or on the blue planet or anywhere we can't even imagine. And how can we imagine something we have no idea of? There are endless debates going on about the dimension we live in: three- or four-dimensional world or both options are clearly acceptable. Obviously, those two participants in the conversation don't fit in a three- or four-dimensional world. As the author of this book…and a human, I assure you that no Earth creatures could describe their appearances or hear their voices. To proceed further with the reading, you have no choice but to consider the information I am giving to you as the only source we have for now. The closest description I came up with was the two energies were communicating with each other in the space that three- or four-dimensional beings cannot locate.

"My dear Junntie, I have put you in charge of human's world since your spirit completed the cycle of twelve generations. I observed your evolving as a human but have always been with you as your adviser. Now you run the Earth by yourself. Are you sure that the choice you have made was the right finding for this mission? I understand that your attachment to humans is pretty strong, and you would do everything to save their kind from self-destruction. No wonder you think as a human. You refused my way of renovating the Earth and the human race a century ago. An outcome would be the same with the only difference—a matter of time. To be precise, a couple of centuries, that is all. For you and me, it is nothing. For humans… They would start from the very beginning…You would start from the very beginning with them."

The communication paused for some time. If we talked about people in the conversation, we would say, "It seemed like as if he was wrapped up in a cloud of nostalgia." Here in this situation, it was some kind of flickering in the space, exactly for a length of the paused time.

"But you have chosen your own way, the way of saving mankind from their mistakes. You are creating a balance by destroying the Balance."

Another pause reigned, with playing all the colors of a rainbow in the night sky. The dark space was reflecting its sparks, catching bypassing asteroids and endless stardust, carrying it away into some other unknown universes.

"No doubts on Your words, Bohg. You are the essence of everything. You created me for the purpose known exclusively by You. I can only try my best, which is not even one hundredth of Your perfection. How would I know without a try if something I do is good? I have been created by You but developed among people of the Earth. My logic is 50 percent of a mankind logic. I have known the best minds of human civilization, observed their work techniques, and learned that nothing and everything can be proven right or wrong at the same time. I know, Bohg, that from Your perspective, my arguments now look naïve and sound like baby talk, but hear me please.

"This is a simplistic example, but it is the basic idea behind science. The universe continually throws experiments at people. And some of them could be the ones that break the pattern, no matter how carefully they have observed it and no matter how well their theory has held up so far. Speaking of humans, until they have examined the entire Universe over all of space and time, they can't really see beyond a shadow of a doubt, there isn't some contradiction out there. Speaking of Earth, gravity is an excellent example there. People though had a really good theory that was working out great for about a few hundred years. Then came a brilliant mind, who figured out a set of circumstances under which that theory would fail. And later, people found it. I could say that the old theory was superseded, but remained as a special case or various other formulations of the same idea, but the key lesson was that even something as obviously universal as gravity could turn out to be incorrect in some extreme circumstance. And here I am with my new theory, which is worth a try…"

My dear reader, if you lived in Canada, northern part of Russia, or Norway, you could have witnessed a set of huge Northern Lights like flashes across the sky at the very moment of this conversation. Two Energies were having a discussion that was visible to the whole universe, but not everything or everyone in the whole universe was able to understand what it was about.

Along with the green waves of the Northern Lights, the sky lit up with such a perfect brightness. The color…it was visually hard to describe the color. I am sure that you, my dear reader, occasionally have experienced a confusion around two completely opposite things in your life when you tried to understand the right meaning out of them. Remember when you walked outside wearing sunglasses? The sunlight was so bright, shining through your shades, making you lose sight in complete darkness. Have you asked yourself how the bright light could cause darkness in your eyes? Or when your ears got hurt with a sound of silence. Or when you used the facial mask made of dirt to clean up your skin pores. Or when your face was burned by the frostbite. Or…okay, okay, you've got the picture.

"Junntie, I am glad that you are experimenting, trying to find the right way to do your job. You are about to come up with the solution, which has already been unveiled to me. I am giving you freedom of your choice. Create! Think as a human. Know as a Spirit of the universe. Keep the universe spinning with any kinds of vibes!"

For a few seconds, almost half of the sky flashed with a crystal-bright light, pulsing with transparent teal and green in the spots with clouds. Shooting stars, magnifying through the space dust, looked like flying fireballs made of liquid glass carrying rainbow tails. Their flame reflected the hymn of Glory of the universe back to the dark space and became very noticeable from the Earth. This magical moment of nature stopped unexpectedly, in the same way as it started. The flashing colors of the sky slowly dissolved into one color, quiet teal, which was sparkling with billions of golden dots looking like pixy dust. They were slowly falling, twirling in the clear air of the night sky, trying to touch the Earth and…a couple of people on the Earth, who were stoned by this phenomenon of nature.

One Second—Whole Life

It was getting dark outside, but the summer evening was still giving away all the fragrance of blooming trees and flowers to those who were still able to notice this simple and forgotten phenomenon of nature. With the twenty-second-century busy life, only those who were born in the last century and were free of cyber diseases and money chase could appreciate this magical appearance of nature. Some of us would say that the evening came from the very Paradise. Some would just smile. Others would simply enjoy the complete bouquet of nature's aromas and pheromones of fresh feelings.

When two people are attracted to each other by the invisible forces, there is something in the air that makes those two forget about everything and everyone around. They see only each other. They feel only each other. This is the very magical time in a fresh innocent old-style relationship. Just feelings…

Nicolas has been waiting for this moment since he saw Marsha for the first time one year ago, in the same park where they were walking right now. Even the weather was exactly the same. The only difference was the time of day.

One Year Earlier…

It was a usual morning when the majority of Canadians were about to dedicate another eight hours of life to society's well-being. I wouldn't talk for Canada as a whole country because of the huge size of the land, but if we focused our attention on a certain province (let's say Alberta) and a certain city (Gray Stone, I am sure it was the name), the following narration would start to make sense.

Unfortunately, not all people of Canada were so diligent in their work performance that day. Apparently, two of them, who lived in the same city but far from each other, were woken up in the early morning by the cheerful chirping of birds through the opened windows and, without opening their eyes, decided to postpone their contribution to the society's well-being until tomorrow. Right after the decisions have been made, those two people confirmed their choices with sweetest smiles. They stayed in beds, stretching and savoring a beginning of the extra free day for a few more minutes, making plans on how to spend this wonderful bonus day.

Those two people would never imagine how much a one-second spontaneous decision could transform their entire lives.

The best way of spending any bonus day is to fill it up with things we never have time for in our carefully planned everyday life. Wouldn't it be nice to start the day with walking in a park? No? Because it is nothing special? I totally disagree with you, my dear reader. Let me represent you with the greatest creation of the country—Canadian parks of the twenty-second century.

The Wild Nature Trails Park in Gray Stone of Alberta. You are there now. Can you see the people with their best friends (dogs), and just their best friends, passing by in both directions, strictly conducted by the bright yellow line painted in the middle of a walking path and offering them a beautiful view of nature on both sides? It is a lot to offer regardless of a short summer in Alberta. Where else on Earth could you find such an integration of wild nature and civilization? Only here in the numerous parks of Canada. Obviously, there are no palm trees or exotic animals. No one can hear the hypnotic noise of an ocean or falling coconuts. Let me ask you something. Would you be able to find a pine tree or a reindeer in Hawaii? Maybe in the local Hawaiian zoo. So…big deal! It is all relative.

Nicolas loved jogging in the Wild Nature Trails Park. Unfortunately, with his busy school hours and volunteering work in the Gray Stone Immigration Center, he had only one day per week for exercising. Apparently, today was the day when he decided to step away from the perfectly organized schedule.

"It's a perfect day for jogging!" Nicolas threw off his blanket, jumped up on his feet, and, smiling, marched to the kitchen.

No shower! It's only one free day! Straight to the park! Water on the face. Water in a bottle. Runners on the feet. Excitement in the heart. Car...Drive...Park...Sun through the branches...Up and down...Run...Stop.

Trying to catch his breath, Nicolas slowed down. On a side of the walking path near a pine tree, he spotted a young woman standing still and observing something through the camera in her hands.

"Wow..." Nicolas stopped completely about five meters behind the girl, forcing himself to get rid of that noisy breathing.

Long strawberry-blond hair covered her shoulders and back, touching her rounded hips. She looked awfully short but unusually captivating...

This is the only one free day...Anything that happens, happens for a reason.

Nicolas decided to go with the flow.

"What do you see?" Nicolas asked quietly.

The young woman turned her face. A moment of silence conducted an invisible route through two pairs of eyes, punching hearts, conceiving one more task for the young people—to carry on with their prime responsibility of mankind on Earth.

"Everything of nothing..." she quietly replied.

For Nicolas, it wasn't a voice but music...

A month later, Nicolas and Marsha were walking together in the same park, holding hands and talking about the magical morning that brought them together.

"Nicolas…" Marsha looked at the man's left jawbone because that was all that her height could offer when she usually walked beside Nicolas. She hated this feeling of being so short compared to this tall and skinny young man. It was alright to hold hands because in that time, all young people were doing so, especially when a relationship was still innocent and exciting.

"Yes, my dear." Nicolas turned his face to his left. A wavy ash-blond lock of hair touched his forehead.

Marsha looked at him with a rascal squint in her teal eyes. Her lips were slightly opened with a smile, showing a row of perfect teeth that looked even whiter compared to the golden hair moving across her face. "What's that my dear about? And why are you wearing those fancy clothes here in the park?" She stopped but still held Nicolas's hand, then made a half step back and looked at him up and down, slightly tilting her head to the side and giggling.

Nicolas felt like being stroked all over his arms and shoulders by a brush with very tiny but rigid spokes and automatically touched the chest pocket of his jacket. Then he took Marsha's other hand and said, "Come with me. I'll show you something." He pulled Marsha's hand, dragging her along, and accelerated his steps.

Marsha kept joking and mocking Nicolas's fancy look. A mix of the fast walk and excitement made her voice tremble. Her short legs moved way faster compared to Nicolas's walk. She was talking about nothing and laughing loudly. A feeling of upcoming surprise from the man in charge worked out its magic.

Happy couples on matching bikes, athletic singles in spandex, families with children and dogs, birds on the professionally trimmed trees…all were enjoying this warm summer evening in the trails of the Wild Nature Park of Gray Stone. For some of them, a harmony of the perfect evening got distracted by the ridiculous run of two youngsters jumping across the yellow-lined pathways. Diving into the bushes and out, they were crossing multiple walking paths. Nothing about them was making any sense—neither their divergent look as a couple nor the way they were dressed.

The girl was very short, almost developed as a woman. She was wearing tight leggings and a hoodie. Blithely laughing, she followed a man who was dragging her to God knows where. Tall, skinny, in his teen age, he was dressed in trousers, shoes, and a fancy jacket. With a serious look on his face, the man was pulling that girl behind him with one hand and clearing the branches in front of him with the other.

The night sky was about to wake up, blinking with myriads of stars, when Nicolas and Marsha arrived in the place where the park verged on the Blue Mountains outside of town. They stopped, trying to catch their breath. They looked at each other and exploded with laughter.

"I bet you have a damn good explanation to this marathon, young man." Marsha touched her knees with both hands, bending her torso forward. "You're crazy…" She dropped her head down, making a couple of short inhales and long exhales. Golden almost white hair was hanging upside down, looking like ripe kernels of wheat pouring out of an upturned pot that never touched the ground.

Nicolas used this moment of distraction and took an engagement ring out of his chest pocket and quickly put it on his pinkie. *It is dark enough to notice the ring*. He smiled with satisfaction at his brilliant idea. A sudden panic attack swept over of his whole body, *Oh god… What's next? How should I start?* His hands began to shake.

Marsha straightened up with a sigh of relief and a calm smile, looked around, up at the sky, and then at Nicolas's face.

Nicolas caught her eye and felt something warm and cozy begin filling his body. He looked into Marsha's eyes. For the past month, Nicolas had studied those two magnificent tranquilizers very well. He could tell exactly how many eyelashes or hues of teal were in the irises of each her eye.

The glance of enjoyment changed into prolonged passionate

staring. Out of nowhere, Marsha's eyes began to change color. Instead of calm blue, her eyes started to fill with a yellow-green light and kept changing into violet and other tones of a rainbow mix. Marsha's gaze slipped from Nicolas's face and got lost somewhere behind his face, in the sky.

Nicolas momentarily turned in the same direction Marsha was looking and became astonished with a very bright play of the Northern Lights.

Nicolas embraced Marsha's shoulders from behind, putting his chin on her left shoulder, and shared this wonder of the world.

The sky, illuminated by the unusually bright Northern Lights, was pulsing with multicolored waves.

Nicolas and Marsha were enjoying the view and each other in silence for some time.

It was hard to measure the length of happiness. Probably a mountain harbour and a couple of crows on a pine tree knew it better.

When hugging Marsha's shoulders, Nicolas felt a slight shivering in her body. She must be getting cold. He took both her hands and locked them up in his, still embracing her shoulders from behind.

"Are we dreaming?" Marsha turned her head and kissed Nicolas on the cheek. "I don't want to wake up."

Two crows on a pine tree began to caw.

Nicolas's heartbeat accelerated. His eyes were still looking in the same direction as Marsha, but his thoughts were with the tiny ring that was almost on the tip of his pinkie. He turned his head and softly whispered into Marsha's ear, "I don't want to wake up either. Would you like to stay with me in this dream forever?"

For a moment, Nicolas felt that Marsha stopped shivering and breathing. Immediately, she turned her whole body toward Nicolas, placing her hands on his chest, and looked into his eyes without a smile. "Yes. I would."

The crows on the pine tree started cawing louder. Out of nowhere, the people's best friends—dogs—immediately reacted on this crime of nature with barely heard barking. A highway behind the park was trying to send a noisy reminder to people that somewhere there, outside of this piece of paradise, was an existence of a hi-tech civilization. I cannot talk for all the people who were in the Wild Nature Park at the moment, but two of them, for sure, didn't hear or see anything around but the beats of their hearts and warmth in their eyes.

Nicolas took off the ring and kneeled before Marsha. "It's yours if you marry me and share this dream with me forever."

"I will...I will..." Marsha's voice and her entire body trembled with pleasant feelings.

Nicolas put the ring on Marsha's tiny finger and, looking into her eyes, kissed her. For a moment, he could not see any difference between the color of Marsha's eyes and the sky behind her. He lost all feelings of his physical body. All he felt was diving into the freshness of the teal ocean and being carried with its strong streams deeper and deeper. He did not want to resist but go with the flow as far as the moment was taking him.

Lights in the sky have spread farther and become brighter. From the other point of view, thunder worked on aiming arrows of lightning into the glory of the Northern Lights, trying to make the sky rain. And so, it has been done. Nature has presented the act of conceiving something new and nurtured all the existing.

Creating a New Society

My dear reader, I bet you wonder about your future. If you think of a super-advanced technology and people's explicit intelligence in the future—think harder. The assumption that people's intelligence would evolve proportionally with technology was a simple mistake of all generations.

Speaking of intelligence, we are not looking at the knowledge experience of a human mind collected through the centuries, but the ability to navigate in the surrounding reality, particularly being able to recognize where we are standing in this very moment—why we are here and for what purpose. In other words, we are talking about consciousness.

It is paradoxical that the greatest knowledge in modern science and an ability to control keyboards do not guarantee enlightenment of consciousness but creates a complete opposite.

The year of 3020. According to the Great Book, mankind is supposed to become happier and live in a society based on absolute love and kindness. But before this achievement or…let's say *the gift from above* would have taken place, something very devastating was supposed to occur to people of the Earth, and only a certain number of us would survive…

It has never happened. All the credits of a peaceful action mankind should have addressed to Junntie, the Highest Spirit, the creation of the Creator, of course, if we had any knowledge about his existence. The process of renovating of humankind has started slowly.

In the beginning of the twenty-first century, the Earth became a huge transmitter of a negative energy spreading far into the universe. Countries began to fight aggressively against each other over sources of gas and oil. Major world religions tried to prove their domination with endless humiliation toward each other. Most of the media subliminally brainwashed everyone, especially the young generation, implementing unhealthy messages and actions, creating negative energy that was spreading with the speed of light everywhere.

For a couple of thousands of years, humanity lived in such a division where people became richer by using others, fighting for peace with deadly weapons, treating illness by sacrificing the health of millions, twisting the true meaning of words and proclaiming the idea that it was our own choice how to interpret them, exalting on a pedestal negative reinforcement to entertain people.

The value of kindness, absolute love, happiness, and helping others was switched into evil, hatred, sorrow, and wars. All this negativity escalated so fast, people started to lose their ability to see the difference between good and bad.

The blue planet was choking in a thick layer of chemicals rotating around it, bleeding with hot lava of volcanic eruptions out of numerous empty oil wells. The Earth was defending itself from endless wars by terrible Earthquakes. People were destroying themselves and their children's future without noticing it. All this and much more turned into a great turbulence for the planet and began to spread destructive frequency into the universe, creating chaos.

From Biblical stories, we all remember how a similar situation was fixed by a fellow named Noah, and for hundreds and hundreds of years, we kept expecting the same things to happen.

In the year of 2037, Junntie, the creation of the Great Creator, received an assignment to fix all unhealthy destructions on Earth. He was the spirit or soul of the very first intelligent man on Earth, who possessed human bodies twelve times, from the moment of conceiving until the time of each death. Are you calculating the length of each life right now? The mathematics refuses to match up, doesn't it? My friend, please do not forget that a length of a human life in the Biblical period was way longer than present time...let's say around eight hundred or one thousand years!

Twelve human lives as one cycle of a universal life...Ah, it sounds so cold and uncomfortable, just like in those nightmares where you were stuck somewhere between galaxies. You lost your way home to the Earth. You were so small and alone, surrounded with all the glory of the universe, staring into your eyes with meteorites, pieces of space junk, countless Milky Ways that looked like dust from the Earth. And you thought, I want to belong...It doesn't matter how to belong or where, just...to belong... When you belong, you feel like you are noticeable, valuable. You consider yourself as part of something. You feel yourself as the center of the universe. And it doesn't matter how big the universe is; you are looking at it from your own universe that can fit in your heart, and nothing can make you feel less than any of the biggest galaxies in the entire cosmos because you...belong.

Blessed someone who has never felt lonely, who is at home in any place he goes, who is accepted easily by people, without any problems and consequences, who looks in the world with wide-open eyes, who doesn't have a sense of fear because there are no enemies or crime for him, who finds the way out of a difficult situation without even looking for it, who is just an ordinary person without any layers of burden such as lies, selfishness, greed, stubbornness, betrayal, manipulation, gossip, enrichment at the expense of others, violence, or aggression.

This kind of person would never have been popular in the world of monarchy, but remained at the very base of the Pyramid, helping the starving, ill, poor, or the hopeless. This type of person is still very seldom on Earth. Some of us call them touched by angels, others saints or mentally ill. But if the person has mastered all twelve lives by being "popular" in almost every level of the existing society, the spirit of twelve generations would not need to come back for another twelve spins. This spirit is ready to face anything and fix everything everywhere.

Junntie, the first creation of the Creator, was the one out of many other spirits who fit in this description. Two centuries were about to pass by when Bohg assigned Junntie to restart the civilization on Earth.

Junntie and all the spirits have created the Parallel Dimension Society. This society kept the universe in order, avoiding any unexpected shifting that started destruction of their work in the Parallel Dimensions with peoples' spontaneous actions because only the Earth was sending chaotic signals into Space and unbalancing the work of the entire universe.

Junntie came up with the decision not to restart the civilization but to develop a formula that would keep the universe in order without any effort.

After a cycle of twelve human lives, new evolved souls/spirits become part of the Parallel Dimension Society. The highest ones are back in human bodies to start from the very first life spin of another twelve lives' cycle and find the right solution to the formula, using all knowledge and experience as human beings.

"Junntie, I am giving to you the authority to run this meeting."

"Bohg...should everyone expect your presence?"

"My dear son, you know that it is not necessary for me to be at a place to hear or see what is going on. Anyway, I don't take human appearances, which is a strict requirement in Zaclear Dimension.

23

You know that I am always around, guiding you, but in Zaclear, my celestial presence will create only a chaotic interference."

"Isn't it ironic? We are trying to avoid chaos, but the perfect solution of your decision will lead to a bigger chaos. I am sure, Bohg, you know the answer. Why does it have to be so complicated?"

"My dear Junntie...It has been created this way. Everything in the universe has its own purpose. I will try to explain it to you from the human point of view. Imagine a young man in his teen years. His physical needs dominate over his spirituality. When the same person reaches fifty years old, he doesn't care much about his physical appearance, but evolves mentally and spiritually. Imagine what would have happened if a ratio of physical and mental development of humans goes in the same proportion?"

"Our world would not exist anymore..."

"Let me stop you right there, Junntie."

"Does this metamorphosis even relate to a human being?"

"I am afraid we have to come back to this conversation someday, Junntie. Xahrns are waiting for you."

Kondrat and Rasara

Rasara was standing in the middle of a big round auditorium. In about fifteen minutes, this room would be filled with all Xahrns of the Parallel Dimension. She was a spirit who had just completed the twelve generations' cycle as a human and now was ready to start her new spin on Earth.

As a spirit who transported into Zaclear Dimension, Rasara had to take a human form and communicate with the voice of her last "soul mate" on Earth.

She belonged to R-Xahrns. R-Xahrns could be recognized by the golden ring in gray-blue eyes, creating the visual effect of a green spark.

She liked the body type of the female from the last life spin: tall, skinny, a very narrow waist, long blond-ash wavy hair. Ah…how many times had Rasara wished for this girl to be dressed up every day as a queen or a model. Unfortunately, every generation on Earth had to follow a certain style of the century they belonged to. For the last 150 years, she had to wear comfortable clothing because she worked as a teacher in an elementary school.

Rasara smiled with the satisfaction of her reflection in the crystal walls, then moved her eyes along the quartz ceiling, down to the sparkly white marble floors, and back to her dress, feeling its texture with her palms. Here in Zaclear, she could choose any clothes she wished to wear. And her choice was a long tight dress made of thousands of rose petals. To be exact, the roses were glued to her upper body, and beginning from under the belly button line around the hips, the white rose petals gradually changed into rose color, connecting to each other with tiny diamonds. On the bottom of her dress, red roses were flowing around the floor with each step she made. Rasara did not want to wear shoes. She liked the sensory feeling of the cold marble floor under her feet.

Humans don't realize how lucky they are to do this every day or night. Rasara was walking slowly, touching the uneven surface of crystal walls, trying to focus on the sensation only. She really enjoyed the last journey on Earth and looked forward to the next life spin.

She glanced at her reflection again and sighed. "What will the next life bring to me? How will I look? Hope not fat…"

"You will always look amazing, Rasara."

Her spirit sense came to the fore, detecting a very familiar energy flow.

"Shouldn't we communicate human in here?" Rasara turned her head a little, looking to her side with a smile. "Zaclear will not be happy about disobeying its rules." She smiled into the emptiness and turned her whole body toward the detected vibes. "Welcome back, Kondrat. You are always following me in your journeys."

Noctilucent cloud insensibly appeared in front of Rasara and started to take the form of a middle-aged man. He was almost the same height as her, but looked shorter because of his slouching. The bright light reflected from the crystal walls pierced a materializing but still transparent figure, distorting its outlines. O-shaped legs that were barely noticed on Earth seemed very bandy and skinny through the light. Curly black hair was dissolving in the brightness, creating an illusion of a completely bald head. Dots of light blue eyes vanished completely from his face. Only big lips, an aquiline nose, and a low forehead were left untouched by the light.

"It is amazing how much the perfect light can blindfold people and at the same time reveal unnoticed-before imperfections." Rasara crossed her arms in front of her, relaxed one leg, slightly leaning on the other, tilted her head, and acting human, squinted her eyes up and down Kondrat's body.

"I thought you loved all this..." Kondrat made one step toward her, smiling and straightening his posture.

"No. I was just sorry for you. Never loved you." Rasara became amazed by her own words. She couldn't lie here in Zaclear. On Earth, she would never let herself make such a hurtful comment to any human being, even to her worst enemies like Kondrat.

Kondrat stepped back. His smile vanished from his face. Silver dots of eyes became bigger, showing a blue color. Invisible eyebrows jumped up, creating the facial expression of a puppy that has just lost his chasing rabbit. "Why didn't you say so back there? Even in the end of our relationship, when me and my family were humiliating you so bad...you...you were so quiet, just crying in your room, where nobody could see you?" He lost his cool look and stuttered. "I need to say s-so much to you...I...I..."

"Kondrat." Rasara touched his shoulder, looking in his eyes. "You've just left the Earth. Your emotions are so fresh right now. You still act and feel as a human. Trust me...tomorrow you'll forget about all the feelings. After tomorrow, about your whole journey. The day after, you'll be looking forward to the next spin."

"When did you die, Nicole?" Kondrat looked up at Rasara. His eyes were clouded with the veil of silver tears, looking like liquid mercury. He swallowed them, trying to hide unacceptable weakness.

"Three days ago. I didn't wake up the next morning. It was a simple and beautiful transformation, just like a continuing existence in a dream." Rasara looked nowhere with a smile, trying to remember that last moment of the past.

"It was much different for me. Committed suicide. I became mentally ill after my niece was gone."

"I thought your niece had changed your life for the best. You trusted her blindly…" Rasara looked at her nails, trying to dust them.

"When you and our daughter left the house, my life became hell. I was supressing my real feelings until my niece passed away. After that…" He turned his back to Rasara, wiping away tears.

"It is all gone now, Doug. Nothing exists anymore. Now your tears are for nothing. Pull yourself together, man!" Rasara forcefully turned Doug's whole body back by grabbing and shaking his shoulders. "That's why I have never loved you, only was sorry for you, because you've always been such a mama's boy. You've never had willpower. Didn't you see what happened when your niece died? You became helpless. I was ready to sacrifice my life for you, but you have made your choice. So shut up and be a man…hopefully, in your next life!" Rasara's eyes were blazing with green flames. Wavy hair fluttered with each of her words and looked like each hair lock was conducted by a separate remote control.

One of the crystal walls started to move apart like a two-door elevator. Xahrns began to enter the auditorium.

Rasara stepped back from Kondrat, looking at Xahrns and smiling with the excitement of a new journey.

Before the Conference

The crystal walls of the auditorium began to reflect the glow of arriving spirits. It was fun for Rasara to observe their appearances.

Explosions of bright white-and-blue lights were showing randomly around the place, breaking up into rainbow spectrums through the edges of crystal walls and ceilings. The entire room looked like one giant brain made of glass, where its neurons were transmitting signals to each other, exploding in synopsis.

Rasara immediately forgot Kondrat's existence and sank into the ocean of flowing colors. This colorful prelude was one of the favorite parts of Xahrns' conference for Rasara.

Observing the arriving spirits, she could recognize K-Xahrns and R-Xahrns by their luminosity.

K-Xahrns were the spirits with light complexion and very light-blue dominant color in their nonactive mood. The spirits preferred reassurance in every action. Most of the time, their Earthly and universal life experiences kept them on the right path of anything they did. They were good advisers and always had a reasonable solution at the end of each discussion. As all the communication lovers, K-Xahrns were excellent consultants, but regarding themselves, they were afraid of action. It would take a great amount of time for them to consider and reconsider any decision before turning it into a deed, which was typical for all communicators, not doers. The big part of their energy came from their socializing. When they take the form of a human or other Earth creature, they have a light blue, almost silver spark in their eyes. From a human point of view, it would look like a person with this spark in their eye suddenly got hit with some brilliant idea. Generated by the human nature, this spark would stay for only a moment in the person's eyes. Generated by K-Xahrns, this metallic gleam would remain as long as a spirit stays in a human shape.

Like Rasara, R-Xahrns didn't have a certain basic color. Their energy spectrum had all the possible colors. If R-Xahrns were in a tranquil mood, they would have been swimming slowly in pastel tones with a gentle touch of all hues. R-Xahrns were free spirits with a strong, intuitive nature, supported by the knowledge of Earth civilization and law of the universe. They were open to any changes and obstacles coming their way, embracing challenges. When frustration occurred, R-Xahrns illuminated a golden aura and played with strong rainbow colors in their presence. In order to describe R-Xahrns' emotions, I would say that they had a "child's way" to express themselves. R-Xahrns didn't rush to take shapes of living creatures on the Earth to create or remove obstacles when helping humans to find the right way of thinking or acting. They preferred not to interrupt people's actions and let them go with the flow, observing events and learning from them. R-Xahrns didn't like big socializations. Their colors became pale, identifying exhaustion. The spirits could easily lose their energy by being together with their kind for a long time. They were strictly recharging their energy from Space alone in a certain dimension. If R-Xahrns had to turn into somebody or something, they could be recognized by the golden ring around their pupils of gray-blue eyes, looking like a little green spark…

With a big smile and wide-open eyes, Rasara was enjoying the magic of colorful play in the auditorium. Soon the rainbow divided into large areas of light blue, indicating groups of K-Xahrns, and myriads of single golden dots randomly thrown around, showing R-Xahrns' presence. The crystal walls of the auditorium were not visible anymore. They kept their existence somewhere far away, behind all the attendees.

Rasara's big smile slowly dissolved by metamorphosing the lights into human shapes. She sighed with a satisfaction when the last blink of the rainbow disappeared. Her sensory abilities have activated into the human-looking spirits around her. Hearing men's and women's voices turned a smile back on her face. How wonderful it was to see people dressed in their preferred clothes and hear their happy talks. Just like back on Earth!

Suddenly, Rasara felt a very warm sensation on her back and shoulders, like the shawl made of down that kept her cozy during cold winters. She turned around. Her heart started beating fast, blocking emotions that rolled up to her throat. At the speed of light, Rasara appeared beside a woman, standing and quietly looking at her with tears in her eyes. Her lips were twitching from holding up a great avalanche of human feelings. She looked like Rasara, but much older. Very short and skinny, the woman was wearing a blue knitted skirt and cardigan. With her casual look, she would be easily lost in the crowd of young-looking people-spirits.

"Mom…" Rasara, barely squeezed out the word and, trembling, touched the woman's hands folded together in front of her chin. Kissed them. "I've missed you so much…"

The woman touched Rasara's face, and with tears of happiness, she started kissing her eyes and all her face. "My little girl…Look at you. You have become even more beautiful."

Both women froze, embracing each other, kissing and touching each other's faces. It was hard to say whose tears belonged to whom. They both were covered with this holy nectar.

"Thank you for not changing your appearance for the younger look," Rasara whispered into her mother's face. "Even if you did, I would always find you here."

Marisha's light-blue eyes filled up with tears again and looked even bigger in the magnifying liquid. She wiped them quickly and gave Rasara an optimistic smile. "I've never doubted you, Nicole. I hope you forgave me for ignoring you as a child and giving away all my love to your brother. I want you to know that I have regretted this since you were gone."

"Mom, please, don't. You know I loved you very much and always missed you, no matter what. It's all gone. We are together again. I don't care how long we are going to be this close, but you are here with me right now, and the rest is not important." Rasara took Marisha's hand and locked it up very tight between her hands, looking at the most beautiful face in the whole universe with a happy smile. "I will never let you go anymore."

"And I...am not going anywhere..." Through the tears of happiness, Marisha's eyes released a spark of something that was known only by her.

Rasara noticed it. She could read her mother very well since every childhood of numerous life spins and didn't want to interrupt this moment of reunion by asking silly questions. She simply let it go because Marisha's facial expression was hiding only good, and the good was always welcoming anytime.

The Conference

If it was only Rasara and Marisha who have reunited here in Zaclear after heartbreaking loss in the endless mourning back there on Earth… For all Xahrns, each conference in Zaclear was the only place where they could have one more chance to see the dearest people in the whole world to whom they once said goodbye forever. Exclamations of happiness with the purest liquid in their eyes were flying in every possible direction of the auditorium. Children meeting lost parents, parents embracing lost children, lovers, spouses, siblings… The spirits glued to each other with the strongest force in the universe called human bonds. None of them cared that in a while, they would begin their new journey and would not remember any of this.

All those valuable moments were happening right before each conference. The spirits in human forms were still strongly attached to their last journey on Earth and the people around them. They all knew that this moment wouldn't last for long, only two or three Earth days, but it would be worth a whole life. They were enjoying the moment.

Lights in the auditorium went down very slowly and flared up with fireworks of the brightest refulgence. It formed an enormous cloud hovering above everyone. Billions of happy faces in their best emotional state were turned toward the light.

Silence reigned momentarily.

Rasara and Marisha looked into each other's eyes with a fear of understanding that this was the beginning of the end. The end of the memory of the present family connections. They grabbed each other's hands, squeezed them strongly, and said at the same time, "I'll be with you forever."

The light in the air started to show sparkling bids. Each bid projected a beam beside each spirit gathering.

Rasara and Marisha looked at the beam of dazzling light right beside them. It started taking the shape of a man. In a few moments, they were looking at Junntie, the Highest Spirit of all.

The huge auditorium had vanished. Rasara and Marisha appeared to be sitting in the comfortable armchairs in front of a cozy fireplace. A coffee table with a porcelain china set and a just-baked apple pie brought the very happiest déjà vu from the neverland of their previous life.

Junntie was pitching firewood with an iron poker. He turned to the table, smiled at Rasara and Marisha, and started cutting the pie. "Welcome back home, Xahras." He passed plates with pie to Marisha and Rasara. "How did you like your last journey?"

Flavor of jasmine tea in a big teapot and three cups filled the room, creating a relaxing environment. Junntie sat in an armchair and took a sip of tea. He closed his eyes for a moment, savoring the aroma, and remained quiet, giving Rasara and Marisha a chance to speak.

"Thank you, sir." Marisha took a teacup in her hands and touched the painted convex of each flower on the cup. Then with a smile, she inhaled the scent of tea. "It is too bad we can't carry on the memory from our previous journeys." She looked at Junntie with a glance of hope and right away turned back to the teacup with the understanding of the impossibility of the request. It was worth a try. She waggishly smiled, paying extra attention to a little flower on the teacup.

"It was a pretty memorable journey." Rasara touched Marisha's hand. "We are both under nostalgia and the hope to save these feelings for as long as we can. From the point of view as a spirit of a daughter and then a mother, I can assure you, sir, that it was wonderful to live without any problems. Speaking on behalf of humans…the forgotten truth about *the meaning of life* rises more often now. If we look back, let's say, about two centuries ago, each person dreamed of a happy life path without any challenge. People tried to earn 'a ticket to the paradise' by helping the less fortunate. Even those who have lost any hope began to turn their faces to God and begged for forgiveness at the end of their path. Sure, some of them have never heard the voice of conscience, never cared for anyone, even themselves. Still, they were looking for the solution to survive and let their imagination go wild.

"All I am trying to say is that people weren't afraid to make mistakes, improvise, learn, pushing the civilization forward. All this has stopped a century ago, when Earth has been provided with the life without worries by an immediate redirection onto the right way. Has it made people's life easier? Maybe. Has it moved people closer to their destiny? Yes. Their dream of living in a paradise came true. Still, something didn't feel right.

"Marisha and I are spirits. Our world here in Parallels is perfect. We have anything that imagination is capable of, but…look around, Junntie. For some reason, all the spirits come here in Zaclear not only for the conference, but mostly for reconnection with the life that gave them emotional and physical pain. Why? Because happiness doesn't exist without pain, and satisfaction without disappointment. How can you appreciate something without being challenged? Challenge is the energy that helps people to identify feelings of happiness and satisfaction. And for us spirits, to feel this happiness even for a few days here in Zaclear is worth a whole life.

"You think people's problems have been solved now? We are dealing with humans. Their life built on their connections and relationships. How can you fix the problems of one over feelings of the other? What if a conflict involves a third person and so on? If we are showing humans the right way of solving their problems without hurting them, they will become more fragile, and at the end of this experiment, they will not be able to handle any situation physically or mentally. I am talking about the complete degradation of mankind. Our mission to support the civilization is going to fail. Look around… All you see is hurt spirits. The more we protect people, the more they get hurt…"

Kondrat and Kanna were standing on the deck of a house, leaning their elbows against handrails and sipping bottled beer.

"Why are we here in this house?" Kanna looked around and turned her attention back to the bottle in her hands. "Aren't we supposed to discuss our last journey at the happiest places of our last life spin?"

"Seems like it has never happened." Kondrat took a sip of beer, holding and savoring the taste in his mouth. Looking around, he stopped his gaze on bedroom windows. A very deep wrinkle formed in the middle of his forehead.

"You know they aren't there anymore. Right now, the house is just a stage decoration." Kanna looked into Kondrat's eyes, easily recognizing his thoughts. "Anyway, thanks for staying with me."

"Huh?" Kanna's voice pulled Kondrat out of his nostalgic dream. He gave her a vacant look. After a couple of silent seconds, with a distorted smile on his face, Kondrat lifted his beer bottle as a cheers gesture and headed toward the back entrance of the house.

The door unexpectedly opened, and Kondrat bumped head-to-head with Junntie, who was holding a six-pack of beer in front of him. The box hit Kondrat's chest with a clinking sound.

"Here you go, my friend." Smiling, Junntie pressed the box of beer against Kondrat's chest, giving him no choice but to grab it.

Kondrat got confused with the sudden change of his plan to enter the house. He waited for a moment, hoping that Junntie would step away and clear out the path.

"You've had your chance. It's all gone now." Junntie touched

Kondrat's shoulder and slowly walked him back to the plastic table on the deck to enjoy the beer in his niece's company.

"It's good to see you both again." Junntie took one beer from the box, popped the lid open, and gave it to Kondrat. He did the same with the second bottle and gave it to Kanna. "Well, my dear friends… Obviously, you both are still in a deep relationship as siblings, which will help us to analyze the journey of Doug and Hellen by their spirits Kondrat and Kanna. Start shooting." He opened a third bottle and made himself comfortable on the plastic chair, listening to the story and enjoying the drink.

"It was the most incredible spin I have ever had." Kanna took the initiative in speaking. "Going through the humiliation and total control in her childhood gave Hellen built-up, strong self-esteem in her future life. I know that it doesn't work well for everyone, but for Hellen, it worked perfectly. She had an understanding and supporting family, her good looks, eager to explore the unknown, and anger for the kind of people who used to make fun of her. Of course, there were some romantic and financial failures, but her family was always there for her, helping as much as they could. With all the support from Hellen's family, I, as a spiritual guide, didn't have to make any changes or redirections for her. Hellen was in very good hands." Kanna put her hand on top of Kondrat's hand and smiled, looking at him. "I had a good uncle and loving relatives." Kanna moved closer to Kondrat and put her little head on his shoulder. A smile couldn't come off her puffy face. "If I could, I would live the same life one more time." She closed her very blue, almost colorless, eyes and sighed.

"Sure, my dear. If we had to go through all of this again, I would support you even better." Kondrat patted Kanna's hand a couple of times and kissed her very blonde, almost white hair. His words were carried by the waves of Kanna's emotions, but his thoughts were locked inside the granite box of the past.

Kondrat's face was serious. His eyes looked nowhere but in his very soul, trying to find an answer for the question known only by him. Suddenly, his face lightened up. He looked at Junntie, freeing his hand out of Kanna's tiny fingers.

"I think, what Kanna just said makes sense. What if the spirits who have made mistakes and had a strong eager desire to fix them would be put in a similar situation in their next life spin and were given one more chance to improve themselves? Do you think it would be a good idea?" Kondrat almost jumped from his chair and hugged Kanna. "You are genius, dear!"

"You like my idea? I am so happy!" Kanna got up and, holing a beer bottle, wrapped her arms around Kondrat's waist. Tipping her head back, she smiled, trying to catch Kondrat's facial expression, but got the view of her uncle's chin and nostrils.

Kondrat hugged Kanna for a moment, then very slowly redirected her back to the plastic chair. He kissed her forehead and sat on the chair beside her, slightly leaning toward Junntie. He was ready to speak.

"Dear Junntie, I left my last life with a broken heart. I loved my two families very much. Unfortunately, I kept forgetting my role as a husband and a father. I got trapped between love to my niece and love to my wife and daughter. I wish I had a good push into the right direction, the direction I wanted..." He paused, probably imagining what life would be if he had enough strength to change it. The left corner of his mouth slightly pulled up. His eyes became bigger and showed some excitement and hope. "Every one of us has our loving families to whom we always come for advice. But they are only humans. Like every human being, even the most loving parents think about themselves first while giving parenting advice to their children. As a spirit, I know that people shouldn't take any advice from their loved ones if their loved ones are young souls. Unfortunately, humans don't know anything about it. Just imagine, if I were a mature soul with the strong connection to my spiritual guide, but was still looking for advice from my mother who was a very young soul, I would have been easily misguided by her. She couldn't act as the true decision maker because of her poor spiritual connection. Even if I followed my own instincts, I wouldn't be able to express my disagreement to the woman who gave me birth. It would take only a second to turn my whole life into hell and suffer the rest of it from oppression of conscience. Family members of young souls must receive stronger connection and constant control from their spiritual guidance. That way, they would manage their life better. No one would be hurt..."

Since the creation of the Parallels Dimension, there were no souls or any other creatures who have witnessed the wonders of this sudden decoration's change and had no comments or curiosity how it was happening and who was behind the curtains. It was normal for every soul of the Parallels to see it right before each conference in Zaclear, just like for people of the Earth to see how day comes after night.

Marisha and Rasara were standing in the same conference room holding their hands tightly as they had never left the place. They looked around and noticed that all the spirits in the room were acting the same way. It was another change of decorations that brought everyone back to the conference room to continue the meeting.

The entire room became a one hologram-like area, expanding its reflection in the crystal walls. All the breathable space was glistening like snow on a very sunny day, visually creating density. Somewhere between the floor and the ceiling, in a few visible places, the air started thickening. In ten seconds, the light of the multiple spaces took the shape of Junntie. The hologram was visible to everyone in the audience. It appeared everywhere: in the center of the room, in the middle of each gathering, beside each pair and a single person. The great silence reigned in the audience.

The tall, perfectly built man in the long gray coat, narrowed in his waist, looked at everyone out of each hologram. He didn't have a smile, but his facial expression looked captivating. Since the creation of all and everything, those who had the chance to speak with Junntie became possessed with an understanding of any doubts they had once.

"Once again, we are all here in Zaclear."

Junntie looked around the audience. His face was so white and glowing, it was hard to identify the exact color of his hair and eyes through the glow. Brown or black, maybe blond hair looked a little messy and touched the dark eyebrows on the side of his face and protruded in all directions on the other side. Very bright whites of his eyes made his pupils and irises undivided solid black. Everyone in the conference room felt the look of those eyes penetrating the very depth of each soul.

"The last interviews helped me to get closer to our goal in modifying the formula that was supposed to keep our universe in the complete order. We will start to fix mistakes of humanity by simplifying their life paths by redirecting them onto the right ways. As a spiritual guidance for each human being, you are all doing an amazing work, but for some reason, the Earth slowed down its energy transmission into the universe. The deficit of energy has created an extra suction of the outsider force. Space is trying to balance itself with a harmful friction for the Earth. With this suction, the universe can get any unwanted energy that could create a chaotic input in everything we have achieved. At the same time, the spirits who have completed twelve life cycles came back to the Parallels without any new knowledge of humanity, which was supposed to become a major part of our goal in the improving of the formula of the universal self-adjustment. It is up to us whether we continue to support mankind. If we learn how to increase the Earth energy flow that has the same frequency with the entire universe, we will achieve our goal in balancing universal energies without harming the Earth. Everything that has been created would automatically maintain the Great Balance without any harm to anything. On Earth, it is called a perpetual motion machine. Here we are dealing with the energy of an intelligent spirituality. I want you to continue everything you've been doing with applying maximum force of your involvement into the people's life. We are remaining in the large spectrum of emotional instability, which creates selfishness. Selfishness leads people to the very low level of spirituality and a high level of materialistic desire." Junntie paused. His eyes became bigger and darker under the veil of countless centuries. Only God knew what was hiding behind that veil. And this something must be pretty heavy. Slowly, his head bent downed, and his eyes disappeared under a layer of his hair. After a few seconds of dealing with his thoughts, Junntie lifted his head and continued in a serious tone of voice.

"We all have very strong attachment to people and ready to make their life easier regardless of any conflict situations they are dealing with. I ask you to remember that each conflict involves another human being and usually works against their interests. Our goal is to solve any conflicts without hurting anyone. You are given the greatest power to turn any negative energy into positive. Use this power wisely. Look ahead before making any change."

Junntie paused again, stopped his eyes on Kondrat, and, with a fast glance at Rasara, turned his attention to the audience.

"I am giving a chance to those who recognized their mistakes of their previous lives by willing to correct them in the next life spin. Only one thing I cannot guarantee is the memory of your previous experiences. If you are really willing to make serious changes, you will feel only déjà vu. When you assist couples with creating a new family, make sure they both are being matched with the maturity of their souls. This will avoid any conflicts in their spiritual growth. Only people with mature souls can represent a top of society or any positions in management, education, health care, media...Xahrns! We have to work together in order to achieve our goal. And now...please, enjoy the time before your next journey begins."

After the Conference

Marisha and Rasara were standing still, holding their hands tight, when Junntie's hologram began to vanish gradually. Spotlights of tranquil colors started moving slowly throughout the conference room, gently touching everyone. Quiet music set up the relaxing mood. Some spirits spun in waltzes, and the others talked to each other or wandered with the hope to find those who have gone through the centuries.

The conference room started showing its crystal walls and marble floors. Some spirits were leaving, carrying away the joy of long-awaited reunions.

Marisha and Rasara gave to each other one big squinting smile and at the same time shouted out, "Tea time!"

They walked toward the exit door of Zaclear, smiling and looking forward to the most desirable thing in the world—having tea with each other and chatting about nothing right there, in the wonderland of their happiest times together.

"Nicole…"

Rasara slowed down. This very familiar voice wiped off the smiles from both faces. She gave Marisha an anxious look and caught the muted "No" coming out of her mother's lips. Both spirits stopped and turned toward the voice.

Kondrat was standing right in front of them, excessively catching his breath after following the ladies in "marathon style."

Using Kondrat's "recovery time," Rasara tried to guess the possible subject of the upcoming conversation. "Kondrat, you understand that the time we are having right now is valuable, and every second of it I want to spend with my mother. We can be called at any moment. So please, do not waste my time."

Rasara and Marisha turned around and walked away with the smiles of satisfaction.

"Forgive me if you can…I am taking a second chance on you, Nicole. I'll find you…" There was not enough time for Kondrat to overcome after the run. His one hand was still on his chest, feeling the heartbeat, and the other one touched the crystal wall to maintain balance. Rasara was leaving fast, and Kondrat was afraid that she would not hear his last words. He didn't have enough strength to run after her, but made his voice heard by Rasara. Exhausted, he slid down to the floor.

My dear reader, if one of you had the "all-seeing eye," you would be able to catch some very invisible details around the room, such as Rasara's speed-of-light-glance toward Kondrat when she stepped out of Zaclear's gate, or Kanna's full-of-hatred look at the leaving Rasara, or Kondrat's stubborn tears that he was trying to hide under his fake smile. Oh, how Marisha hugged her daughter, kissed her cheek, and proudly whispered, "That's my girl."

So do you have the "all-seeing eye"? No? Well…it's too bad. Would you feel happier if I told you that a couple of beings in the Parallels did have "the all-seeing eye" and were able to catch all that and more? But…we'll talk about it later.

Reunited spirits were absolutely safe from calling back to Earth for their next life spin. They stayed in Zaclear, visiting their happiest places of the past life. Marisha wasn't worried at all when she saw Rasara glancing at Kondrat through the closing doors of the conference room. She was sure that Rasara wanted to know if Kondrat stayed longer in Zaclear or was ready to leave the dimension. Kondrat's departure from Zaclear would help her to calculate the age difference that would have been between him and Rasara on Earth. This technique worked well for Marisha each time before entering her next life spin. It helped her protect Rasara from Kondrat's negative influence as a human.

Out of previous life experiences, Marisha knew that her relation to Rasara on Earth would be inevitable. Marisha loved this little spirit as much as a mother loves her child. The secret she was carrying through the centuries was that she could remember each of her journeys from the very beginning. And in all of them, Rasara was beside her.

PART II

Tia

"The rose, sleeping inside a bud,
Wrapped up in the silk of her own petals,
Is not a rose yet."

"As a matter of fact, I disagree. I believe that people with disabilities have to be treated the same way as fully functioning individuals. And what's that 'fully functioning' mean? It's just a majority of the population. Can I ask you something, sir? What if we lived in the world where people had disabilities, and only you and I didn't have any? What would it look like? It would be…like you and me had disabilities of being without disabilities!"

A very young woman in her twenties was standing right in front of the executive director of the Gray Stone Rehabilitation Center and was passionately expounding her thoughts. A million times Serge was trying to figure out what went wrong with this kid. Why did she keep coming to work instead of getting her degree done and then proceed with her career? Long straight hair scattered over the girl's shoulders and touched her skinny elbows. Her long saggy T-shirt committed a crime of covering her slim body and long legs in tight jeans. Her folded arms talked of strong confidence.

"Tia, our agency has developed a very specific system of work that continuously provides an excellent quality of life for the individuals in service. Look at the rating…the number speaks for itself. What exactly are you proposing? And don't get me wrong, don't you think it is too early for you to push for the policy change? You work here, what, three months per year and already try to rewrite the book? I am happy to hear all of your concerns, but we are not changing anything. We have people who've been working in the agency for decades. All their knowledge and experience, everything we have achieved, has been reflected in this book. Tia, you've probably noticed that the agency is the biggest one in the province, and yet, we have an endless waiting list of the prospective individuals who are looking forward to becoming part of us."

Serge liked Tia's visits in his office. Her fresh way of thinking worked as an amusement for him. Tia's passion for her work reminded the old man of his youth. How many times had Serge caught himself just looking at Tia without hearing any of her words? He liked the way Tia talked—full of energy, trying to change the whole world, great passion, without raising her voice or using fancy words. She had a way about herself that was very easy to understand. The slight body language that was usually helping her to activate words conducted a serious conversation, which had never matched with the facial expression of a child.

"Our individuals receive the best medical treatment—"

Tia interrupted the executive director, making one step forward and pointing her finger toward Serge. "Bingo! That is exactly what I am talking about…"

Her eyes sparkled with a green flame, and her smile was about to soften the wrinkle between her eyebrows.

"Why are they receiving the best services ever? Because of their disabilities…Because they are different. You see now? We are trying to help our individuals to be accepted by society with creating an even bigger gap. Each of us have disabilities. Can I ask you, sir, what medications do you have in your pocket? Some. And it was your choice to use them and keep searching for different ways to manage your well-being or become dependent on the verdict given by your doctor and legalize yourself as a 'person with disabilities.' I understand that some people cannot speak for themselves. That's why they need our help, their parents' help, the help from doctors and government services. Here comes the work of our agency with providing the most wonderful services the individuals have ever imagined…"

Serge leaned forward and, without noticing that he was being dragged into the interesting conversation, started to pay attention to each of Tia's words.

"I am proud to be a part of these services. My concern is about people who can control their disabilities without realizing that they have some." Tia continued, "Some people prefer meditation for stress relief over taking psychotropic medications. We educate new staff about valorisation. Aren't we trying to recognize talents in the individuals' disabilities and take them as special abilities? If their family doctors or psychiatrists don't educate the very people with disabilities and their families in nontraditional ways, let's say, for stress relief…what if we do? It is never too late to hook them up with psychotropics and make them believe that only those medications and our services would keep them fully functioning. Sir, you've just mentioned how big this agency was and is about to become bigger. Shouldn't we work on the opposite outcomes of our beliefs? If we help people with disabilities become accepted by society and get comfortable around with their lives, shouldn't we look at the goal of our work to minimize the number of individuals with disabilities? That's what we want: to see more people being able to manage their lives independently. Isn't it? We work for them, for the people, who don't have a chance to realize that nothing went wrong with them. They are perfect as they are."

Tia stopped talking. She was looking at the executive director and trying to figure out if she was clear enough in her endless arguments. She slowly straightened her posture and backed up to the chair behind her, maintaining eye contact with Serge. For some reason, she was sure that even a tiny disturbance, such as a sound of her breath, could interrupt his thoughts.

In a very slow motion, Tia made herself comfortable in the chair and kept staring at the executive director.

The sixty-five-year-old executive director of the Gray Stone Rehabilitation Center was sitting behind his desk and trying to maintain overwhelming work on making a connection between his thoughts and words and recognizing the reflection of his young self through Tia's speech. How old was he when came up with the decision to dedicate himself in neurobiology? Hmm…he was about her age. What went wrong? Just got more comfortable with the symptoms of schizophrenia. Learned how to live with the illness without letting it poison his life. How many authorities he went through to get a subsidy for the research… None of them showed even a slight success.

Forty-five years ago, psychotropic medications had kicked out all the nontraditional therapies for depression, bipolar disorder, schizophrenia, autism…almost all mental illnesses. All Serge could do was to complete his education for work in the med-rehabilitation field and grow up as the executive director of the Gray Stone Rehabilitation Center, which was built on his sweat and blood.

Serge felt an invisible outreached string between his and Tia's eyes that was trying to connect their thoughts and reflect guesses back and forth. The feeling of being amused around Tia's presence has vanished without a trace. *She sees through me…Can't be true…What does she know? Okay, I'll let her speak.* It wasn't the first time in his life when Serge thanked God for creating him as an African American. His skin was able to hide any emotions that usually involved flushing blood up to his face. The only sign of the great worry was a couple of sweat drops on his forehead.

"Speak."

It was the shortest and clearest word the executive director could say without his voice trembling while organizing his thoughts. He locked his hands together in one big fist and guarded it safely under the tight zipper of ten fingers. It was the only physical exhaustion Serge was trying to fight with. Mood swings and anxiety kept his movements disorganized. He needed some time to get rid of this wave of emotional disturbance and pretend that Tia was granted with all his attention.

Tia didn't show any expression of the received satisfaction, and with a calm tone of voice, she started talking, leaning back on her chair. "We all know how important antipsychotic medications for people with mental illnesses are…Let's say with schizophrenia…"

The sound of the fallen stapler made Tia pause. The executive director immediately disappeared under his desk, obviously trying to find the stapler. Tia patiently waited. Surprisingly, Serge's reappearance at the scene took much longer compared to any other person who would have been gone on the same quest to pick up a stapler from under the desk. Finally, he was up and seemed much happier holding the "trophy" in his hands. With extreme care, he put it on the desk, looked at Tia, and with barely a noticeable smile, he let her continue.

Tia caught this smile and interpreted it as a welcoming sign.

"Also, we know that there are endless debates in psychosis regarding antipsychotic treatment. When individuals start taking those medications, their emotional and physical well-being begins to change. Of course, everyone is different despite of the same diagnosis, and the side effects of the medications they take will be different as well. If you look at the individuals in our agency, you'll notice how unique they are with the same illness. Not all the individuals are gaining weight, becoming constipated, dizzy, or showing other side effects when being put up with the same treatment. What if we focus our work on the minimizing the side effects they have by observing people who are using the same treatment and didn't have similar side effects? I know that we have to consider many factors such as age, severity of illness, the generation of psychotropics…What if we involve doctors in this process? For example, David is skinny but has bad body trembles. He is smart with lots of learning potential, but he cannot even hold a pencil to draw or pick up puzzles to create a whole picture. You can see in his eyes how much he wants to be involved in this kind of activity. He can't because the side effects bring him uncontrollable body movements and muscle spasms.

"Now, look at Tiffany. She is a pretty big lady who is exercising whole days long without a stop and gaining even more despite of all the efforts to slim down. That's all she dreams of: to get rid of those extra pounds and be happy, maybe to meet a man and fall in love. Sir, what would you do if one of them were you or a member of your family?"

Serge didn't put Tia on the wait list and spit out, "I would definitely do some research and then go see my doctor in order to meet my goals."

"Exactly!" Tia got up from her chair and started measuring the office with steps, keeping the invisible string between her and her boss's eyes. "What if we ask their doctors to make a change in the prescribed antipsychotics? According to the side effects, David is taking first-generation antipsychotic medications that makes his body experience uncontrollable movements. It works against his well-being goals in self-determination, intellectual growth, self-esteem, and emotional well-being. If we switch his medications to second-generation antipsychotics, he would be able to enjoy the activities he likes and participate in them without the spasmatic movements. His self-esteem would get higher. He would become happier. When David starts to gain weight, we can always switch the medications back if he is alright with that.

"The same technique we can use for Tiffany by switching her second-generation antipsychotics that poison her life with excessive weight gain to the first-generation treatments and see if it reduces her weight gain. Sure, she will have uncontrollable movements, or… maybe not. Like we have talked before, every one of us experiences the side effects differently. Speaking of the well-being of each individual in the agency, it is worth a try."

Tia quietly sat on the chair right beside Serge's desk and kept eyeballing him.

Serge looked at Tia's eyes as well and made a surprising comment in his head. *Hah, why did I think that she had blue eyes? They are more like some kind of…amber? Weird…* Serge felt relaxed. *Actually, all she said made perfect sense. I've been using these techniques for myself, and they worked well.*

"All that you are saying is very innovative, Tia. You are the outside-the-box thinker. Your mind is very fresh. It will help us start working on the agency's goals from different perspectives. The only thing I disagree with is the minimizing of a number of individuals in the agency. Tia, I see you are thinking only about the people we serve. Please don't forget that this is a workplace. Over seven hundred employees make their living here. You don't have to worry about anything because we can serve our individuals with disabilities by helping them as much as we can. If people master independent living, we will be happy to release them and accept those who need our help. I find your considerations valuable, and because of that, I am inviting you to the next Service Management Team meeting. Let everyone hear what you've just said in this office."

Tia smiled, showing two rows of perfect teeth. "It sounds good, sir. Thank you." She stood up.

Serge came from behind his desk and was about to shake Tia's hand for a final goodbye. He politely looked in Tia's eyes and froze. A pair of gray eyes with purple hues all over her irises looked back at Serge in a smile. His first thought was that his illness started kicking off, creating hallucinations.

The executive director pulled himself together and said goodbye to Tia, squeezing her hand pretty hard and trying not to look in her eyes anymore.

Tia grabbed her jacket and left the office.

The executive director returned to his desk and picked up a tiny container with anxiety tablets from the floor under his desk.

Changes in the Air

- A beautiful summer day. Too beautiful.
Not even an ethereal breeze.
- Why not?
- Because the day is too beautiful.
No birds are singing,
No butterflies are flying.
- Not to disturb
The beautiful day?
- Yes. The most beautiful day…before a storm.

What an unforgettable feeling when riding a bike! It is almost like flying in dreams. You have no rules and speed limits while cycling. If you want to look like a driver, use a road, and all the vehicles will give you a lot of space. If you are in a hurry and don't have time to make a stop on the red lights, use all the sidewalks around. Wait a minute… You are almost late for work! Here comes the shortcut. Maximum speed! You are barely touching the ground…from a sidewalk to a lawn. Jump! Fly! Jump again! Dust and gravel are beneath the wheels. The sun and wind right under your wings. Your mind is free, so is your body. You can do anything…even get to work on time.

The twenty-one-year-old blonde stepped hard on the bicycle brakes, drifting forty-five-degrees on gravel with the back wheel. Only two crows on the handrails of a group home porch were able to identify what disappeared first: dust beside the bike wheels or the girl behind the back door of the house.

Tia was standing in front of five females seated at the kitchen table of the residence. Immediately, she sensed some tension in the air flowing between four air conditioners in each corner of the kitchen. Tia's hair was still messed up from the sun and wind. Dark blond strands scattered randomly on her face and shoulders. For a moment, she froze, trying to understand what went wrong. She started breathing slowly, working on the perceptiveness, as if she had the sixth sense on catching the mystery in the air of the kitchen. Her nostrils were slightly moving, indicating fast breathing. Beads of sweat after riding a bike tinctured an extra glow to Tia's pink cheeks and puffy red lips. Was she late for a staff meeting? The clock showed one spare minute. So it's not that. Once Tia left to the living room to get a chair, she heard a whisper behind her back. She noted to herself, So it's me. *OK, Tia, confront the situation. You have nothing to hide.*

The five women got quiet again when they saw four pointing legs of a chair moving toward the kitchen. They didn't see Tia behind the chair, but even if they did, the attention would be focused on the pair of those long legs that were walking the chair. Tia momentarily understood what was going on. They all were fighting the same enemy—hot flashes and jealousy of Tia's youth.

She put the chair down and, with a smile, opened a window. "It's so hot in here, isn't it?"

A big dark red face spread out around the kitchen table started showing its eyes. A pair of brown eyes looked at a pair of blue eyes across the table and, with a sigh of relief, said, "Oh, I thought it was me...hot..."

A pair of blue eyes released a smile. "Same here. Thank you, Tia, for opening the window."

The tension that was pushed around by four fans in the kitchen a minute ago immediately escaped through the open window.

"No problem. Happy to help." Tia put her chair behind the kitchen island, far enough from the piercing wind of the four guardians of "kitchen hell," and sat on it.

A tall conservatively dressed lady, the residential supervisor, entered the kitchen. Staff meeting had officially started.

"Good afternoon, everyone. Thank you for coming in such a short notice." Paulina's gaze slightly touched everyone at the table and disappeared inside the blue binder in front of her.

Tia immediately stood up and offered her a chair.

Paulina graciously accepted the chair with a smile and sat far from the table, crossing perfect legs coated in shiny pantyhose. "Let me start the meeting with the agency update and then make a transition straight toward our group home news. If you get tired of my accent, please, let me know, I'll try to involve some other activities in the meeting besides the talking…"

Tia giggled from out of the kitchen island, dipping a teabag in a cup. The red exhausted faces spread around the kitchen table turned, five pairs of brown, blue, and other-colored eyes on Tia, giving her "the look."

Tia held the teabag above her cup and, with a smile, said, "Tea? Everyone?"

The faces immediately redirected their eyes back to the kitchen table and just missed a nonprofessional smile in the supervisor's eyes.

"Some of you have already known that for the past two weeks all the rehabilitation services across Canada started accepting lots of new individuals recently identified with mental disabilities. Our agency has accepted five people…"

The big red face slowly started showing outlines around each pair of eyes, forming five separate faces. A spirit of curiosity dislodged the spirit of boredom in the room.

"Oh yes…I've heard the news on the radio. They said that lots of people got affected by some kind of solar wind or excessive radiation or by the possibility of a new virus."

Trista and the other four women at the table looked at each other with arising interest to the subject of the conversation.

"I think my sister got affected by this virus too. She acts strangely. She calls everyone in our family by different names…weird names. She hallucinates with seeing creatures, as she said, hiding in all corners of the house. Sometimes she is back to normal. We are taking her to a doctor tomorrow. It is so hard for us to see her like that." Trista cleared her throat and wiped unwanted tears. "I hope they find the cure soon. We don't have a history of mental illness in the family. All this is very strange…"

Trista became quiet, but her lips couldn't stop trembling. In a few seconds, the last drop of tension in the kitchen had been neutralized. Nobody cared anymore about who was skinny or fit, who suffered from excessive hot flashes in the fine summer day, or who couldn't get enough hot tea to warm up. And definitely, nobody cared of the supervisor, with her perfect manicure who spoke with some European accent. One more time the human nature showed how a critical situation brought people together.

Everyone at the table was thinking the same thing: What if this illness was not over yet? What if their loved ones would be affected by it?

A slight touch on her shoulder interrupted Trista's unsettled thoughts. She turned her head up and saw Tia standing beside her and holding a cup of chamomile tea in her hands. Trista accepted the tea with a sad smile on her face and thanked the girl.

Paulina used the pause to organize her papers on the table and continued the meeting.

"I am really sorry, Trista, that your family was affected by the illness. It is very sad…We are expecting a new individual in our group home tomorrow. His name is Noah Fjusher. He is thirty-five years old and has been diagnosed with schizophrenia. Noah used to live with his mother. One month ago, his mom found Noah adjusting a rope to commit suicide. I wish to get more information on Noah."

"Does he have a public guardian?" Tia paid attention to every word of the supervisor. She was responsible for community outings with the individuals in the group home and needed to know everything about them.

"Noah has a private guardian, his mother, who is also his trustee." Paulina made some notes in her papers. She lifted her beautiful green eyes to Tia. "Tia, do you think you could do community outings with Noah as well?"

"I wouldn't rush with the community outings right now. It is a big change in Noah's life: leaving his family and facing unexpected health conditions. I bet he is confused. It seems like there is something else going on. Noah was about to commit suicide. Of course, it is none of our business, but it is better if we set up a meeting with his guardian and get more information on both of them."

Tia was talking seriously. She got a feeling that something big and unexplainable was about to intrude into her life.

We have all had that feeling of an upcoming excitement when some tickling waves were flowing up and down in our body, squeezing, and right away releasing the very soul in our stomach. Some people call it butterflies. This very feeling suddenly possessed Tia when she was listening to the resident supervisor. She couldn't explain what was going on with her.

It's just a job, nothing else... She tried to analyze this weird excitement. Maybe working with Noah would help me make a breakthrough of the century in neurobiology! I guess...We will see...

Paulina let Tia share her opinion with everybody and agreed with her completely.

"All we need to do is welcome Noah into his new home and show our support and patience. The first month or two, we will observe him and make, as many as we can, notes to help each other work with Noah productively. Gradually, Noah will learn his new daily routine in the house and become acquainted with the rules of the agency."

Paulina looked at everyone with a comforting smile.

"Any questions? I understand that right now the information is not clear enough, and it takes some time to process it." She paused and focused on everyone around the table. "I just want to hear your concerns and suggestions regarding this change in our group home. Please, address all questions to me. I am sure that all of us would rather work in a positive environment rather than pull gossips out of the bushes."

Paulina knew about all conversations that were circling in the house. Most of them were about her and Tia. As an immigrant from one of the European countries, Paulina was working so hard to get into the residential supervisor position here in Canada. Despite of busy work in the residence, somehow she always managed to look her best: elegantly dressed, with perfect makeup, fresh manicure, exquisite hairstyles, high heels, no matter what. If you were not familiar with the European culture and traditions, you might say that this woman was nothing more but a show-off or a stupid lazy gold digger (pardon my language).

As a matter of fact, Paulina was the complete opposite to all that. Even after becoming a Canadian citizen, Paulina didn't forget her European roots and proudly spoke with a very noticeable accent. If someone didn't like it, it would be their problem to deal with, not Paulina's.

The residential supervisor patiently listened to all the suggestions on how to provide the right service to Noah Fjusher. She was glad that despite the problems in their personal life, people at the table were trying to give their best suggestions on how to improve the life of the less fortunate.

Soon, all debates were paired up with best solutions. The rest of the staff meeting took its usual way. With the supervisor's request of choosing a subject for the next meeting, it came to an end as everything under the sun.

Tia couldn't wait to share her excitement with her parents on the upcoming research in neurology. The way back home was laid only through shortcuts, countless speed bumps, and any kinds of bumps.

My dear reader, for sure, you are familiar with the fact of how fast obstacles arise on the way toward your most desirable goals. They appear from out of the blue and at the least expected moments.

Tia's mind was 99 percent focused on sharing the excitement with her parents. Only 1 percent of her cerebral cortex was trying to solve the shortest and safest way back home.

Tia's bike counted every single chip of gravel, sharing the sun's reflection in her eyes. The sound of upcoming traffic merged in resonance of two cawing crows, flying low and trying to disturb Tia's attention. Should we care about all those interruptions around? Good question. As a writer, I would say, "Yes, we should." The girl on the bike, however, she was far away from thoughts like that. She trusted her "1 percent safety guard," which she activated once and had it forgotten completely. All she felt was the bike fueled with her excitement and sunlight. She didn't even hear those crows or notice the reflection of the glare that was supposed to distract her riding because all her senses were serving the near future reality thirty minutes from now, at home, with her mom and dad.

Metamorphosis

When clouds play together in the sky
The game of calling rain,
They have no time to realize
What would create this game.

The outcomes could bring strong hail,
Mudslides or wind to blow.
Just think and visualize the end
With crossing skies, rainbow.

"It is very unusual. My search results came back inconclusive. I wasn't able to find any scientific explanations to this phenomenon. What should we tell her?" Nicolas took off his reading glasses and put them on the kitchen table. He rested his eyes for a moment, massaging his nape and then forehead. He looked exhausted.

For a moment, the smell of strong coffee took his mind off his thoughts. A relaxing smile pushed up his tired eyelids. A pair of the most beautiful eyes in the whole wide world looked at him with a soft, calming smile.

Marsha sat beside Nicolas and gently touched his cheek. "Tia is a wonderful girl with an outstanding personality that doesn't fit in any of the psychological categories. She is unique inside as well as out. Maybe that is the only explanation to this phenomenon?" Marsha paused. "Your eyes are gray-green..." she whispered and kissed his eyes.

"And your eyes are sky blue..." Nicolas kissed Marsha's eyes and touched her hand on his cheek.

"Do you remember the color of the sky that night?" Marsha's smile became wider.

For a moment, Nicolas thought that he saw a golden spark in Marsha's eyes, or perhaps he was too tired to see clearly. That night... Nicolas remembered every detail of it. How many times he lived through that night again and again. Twenty-three years had gone, but the spirit of that night became younger with each day. It was not necessary for Nicolas to close his eyes to rewind the color of that sky because the first time he saw it in Marsha's eyes as a reflection was twenty-three years ago. And now, those two portals to the past were right in front of his face, inviting him to make a tour into the neverland...

A metal sound of keys in the front door of the house successfully achieved two goals at once: the goal of opening that door and the goal of closing the portal into the neverland.

Nicolas and Marsha were waiting for this moment for at least a month and, as always, were not ready for it.

With a comforting smile, Marsha stepped away from Nicolas. Nicolas put his reading glasses back on and attentively focused on anything at the kitchen table that, at this moment, would be considered as readable.

"Hi, Mom! Hi, Dad!" With a flying gait, Tia flitted up from the entry stairs to the kitchen and, without looking, turned on a kettle.

"Hi, honey. What's the good news?" Smiling, Marsha kissed her daughter and put apple pie on the kitchen table.

Tia sat beside her dad and passionately started showering both parents with the news of an upcoming opportunity to study the unique case of schizophrenia.

A strong wind of her fresh energy filled up the kitchen. Tia twitted like a bird with pretty complicated words that she immediately defined to her parents.

Marsha couldn't stop smiling every time she heard a fancy phrase. She adored this little creature and thought that this "smart talk" was making Tia cute. What a powerful energy this kid was possessed with! Each of her movements and words were counted.

For the past ten years, Marsha watched her daughter closely, discovering something unusual in Tia. She had never shared her observation with anyone, not even with Nicolas. Today was the day when the family got together and talked about it, only just about only one visible "complication." The rest of it...Marsha and Tia would discuss one-on-one.

Tia was washing her hands in the kitchen and at the same time nonstop talking about her day. She liked to see both parents at home at the end of each day. It made her feel cozy. A big kettle made of blue glass finally ascended on a pedestal of the kitchen table, complementing aromas of apple pie, lots of fruits and vegetables from the backyard garden, and homemade bread.

The family was about to start supper. Golden sunlight streaming through the branches of a big apple tree behind the kitchen window created the vision of a dancing crochet on the dining room wall. August didn't want to give up its hotness yet, pleasing everyone and everything with its gifts: fruits and vegetables, long days and short nights, the clearest skies of all seasons, the feeling of a possibility to do anything and be anybody, or making families enjoy the simplest pleasure in the world, like getting together in the dining room and having a good time just chatting and eating...just like this family at the kitchen table.

A short, properly fit, forty-seven-year-old woman was sitting at the kitchen table with her family and managing a few tasks at once. Her ears, hidden under nicely brushed very blond hair, heard every word of her daughter. No present or past could hide from her teal eyes that only with one glance could turn a soul inside out.

Marsha was rewinding a memory film from the past over the present recording. She was looking at Tia and remembering the day when she was born, when she started walking, talking, managing her first task at school. Her daughter had changed completely in such a short period of time and kept changing since.

Tia came to this world wearing an amniotic sac wrapped over her tiny body. Only her little head was sticking out. "You've got a princess in a gown. All you need to do is find the crown that fits properly." Those words of a midwife made Marsha forget about the pain of birth.

Tia was three years old… "Tia, you can't give all the toys to your friends. Your daddy would need a second job to buy things for your friends and not spend so much time with you. Do you want to play with your mommy and daddy or with a babysitter?" Marsha was holding her little one on her knees and tried to find the answer in her daughter's big gray eyes.

"I like to see my friends happy. It makes me happy too." Tia's eyes became very sad. That was the first time when Marsha noticed a tiny blue dash in the perfectly gray iris of Tia's left eye.

Age of seven…Tia got a bike for her birthday and, together with her mom, went for a ride in the Wild Nature Trails park. That day, both of them shared the happiness of freedom and speed. Wherever the trails led, they followed with endless screams of excitement. Tia's favorite features of the Wild Nature Park were countless shortcuts and bumpy deer paths that wandered on both sides of the trails. Marsha could barely catch Tia's disappearance from the perfectly paved pathways into the green wall of trees and bushes. When they finally arrived at the lake, they stopped their bikes and sat quietly beside the waters. Marsha couldn't stop staring at Tia. Somehow her eyes became green. She looked carefully and noticed the bright amber circles around her daughter's pupils that merged with gray irises, creating that green hue…

Sweet sixteen. Tia was so excited about her first date. She was flying around the house, tweeting about the boy she was going on a date with. As faster the time passed, the quieter the bird became, transforming its flight into a walk. When waiting time was far behind and nobody picked up Tia on a date, the spirit of a desert reigned around. For the first time in Marsha's life, she got scared to death when she saw a stranger's eyes looking out of her daughter's face. They didn't have any color but were flat emptiness that couldn't become a subject to any description…

And so on. Marsha knew that her daughter was not an ordinary child. She had gotten her father's young soul that maintained her curiosity, and her mother's soul was on the last circle of completion. The nature of Tia's old soul kept her from repeating the mistakes she had made once and the ability to get out of any difficult situation safely.

Marsha completed serving the table with a crystal bowl full of honeycombs. She sat across Nicolas and Tia and quietly observed them with a smile. Nicolas has always been Tia's soul mate. Those two have never been apart since the first day of Tia's birth…

This little girl, using scientific language, tried to explain to her father the work of the human brain. Nicolas was listening to his daughter speaking while wearing a serious facial expression, and from time to time threw some questions at her.

"…lack of ketones in a diet affects the speed of thinking."

"What are ketones?"

"They are proteins that help neurons process the information fast. That is why low-carb diet is very important, especially a ketogenic diet. If we follow this diet, our brain will be fueled by ketones. Our body starts to produce the proteins by itself."

"Okay, Tia. Now I understand. The low-carb and ketogenic diets are the same thing?"

"They are similar. Ketogenic diet has lesser level of carbs..."

"What about if you stay without food at all?"

Marsha raised a teacup. "To low-carb diet!"

Nicolas and Tea turned their heads toward Marsha and froze for a couple of seconds, adjusting the interaction.

"Five seconds are gone. You both need some extra ketones to process the information faster. So...start working on it." Marsha picked up a coconut butter toast and had a bite. "I heard that coconut butter is full of ketones." Marsha began to chew the toast slowly, squinting her eyes and looking closely at the coconut butter. It seemed like she was trying to taste the very ketones in the toast. Her facial expression was very serious, but deep, deep in her eyes, a frisky sparkle of inevitable laughter was searching a way out.

An explosion of great laughter came up with the solution to start dinner. As always, Marsha's word saved the moment.

The shadow crochet on the kitchen wall sank in a deep golden light of the sunset. The whole room filled up with gold. Even the food on the table looked amber with all hues of the color. The family was still sitting in the kitchen. Here in the house, dinners were not about food, but about being together. This evening looked usual, but aura of unfamiliar energy has been sensed by those three at the dining table. Same people, same food, same time, different subject of a conversation.

When Tia quenched the thirst of sharing her academic plans with her parents, a cup of green tea and a honeycomb became quite welcomed.

Marsha and Nicolas looked at each other with an agreement to begin "the talk."

Nicolas cleared his throat and took the book that was previously left at the table. Looking through the pages, he started the conversation that had been planned a long time ago.

"Tia, honey, have you thought about getting a driver's license?" Nicolas was talking to Tia and still looking in the book. He tried to sound casual, as if the conversation he started wasn't very important.

Tia didn't rush with the answer. Closing her eyes, she enjoyed tea with honey. "I will, Dad...I will. Not right now. It will not be necessary until the graduation. Gray Stone isn't a very big city. Everything is so close to home. I enjoy riding my bike, and it is healthy."

"When you are right, you are right." Nicolas paused, focusing even more on his reading. "It is not necessary to get a vehicle right away. Sooner or later, you'll have it. I am talking about having a driver's license. It is good for ID as well. What are you using for ID right now?" Nicolas put the book away, took his glasses off, and placed them beside the book on the side table. He poured tea into his mug and picked a honeycomb from the crystal bowl.

Tia opened her eyes with a smile. She liked tea with honey and the company of her mom and dad. She also liked when they were giving advice to her. She felt loved and protected. So many times, Tia thought about living separately from her parents. For some reason, those thoughts made her sad. Almost all her friends got married or lived with their significant others. Tia has never understood why she was so different and didn't want to start her own life as an adult yet. She rushed home after school or work to see her parents, talk to them, have supper and tea all together. She has never understood her friends who were dreaming to get their own place as soon as they graduate from school.

"Hmm...Actually, it makes sense. I think I can start studying for the written test. Sooner or later, I have to do it. By the way, it is not really comfortable to show my passport for ID all the time." Tia poured more tea but didn't rush to drink it. Obviously, this part of supper called for a conversation.

"Well…you are going to have one more plastic card in your purse…something like this…" Marsha came back with her driver's license and gave it to Tia.

"Are you really only five feet tall?" Tia tried to give a good tease to her mom. "Well…your weight matches your height. You are safe!"

The family shared a good laugh.

Tia loved the "after dinnertime" and tried to make those minutes last longer. She continued to inspect her mother's driver's license. "Eyes, blue…" She looked into her mother's eyes. "They are so blue. Just like the sky." Tia turned her whole body to Nicolas with the obvious purpose to see his eye color. If Tia had 360-degree sight vision, she would notice a smile of satisfaction behind her on Marsha's face.

"Gray…Green…No…gray with green…" Tia got back on her chair, still looking into her father's eyes, and became a little confused. "Dad, can I see your driver's license please? What eye color did you put in there?"

"Help yourself, honey." Nicolas pulled a wallet out of his chest pocket and gave it to Tia.

She opened the wallet with a smile on her face, found the driver's license, and pronounced, "Green!"

"What are you going to put in your driver's license?" Marsha started to clean the kitchen table, taking away plates and forks and leaving only tea and all sweets related to the tea-drinking ritual.

Tia chuckled with the obviousness. "Gray! What else!"

"Are you sure?" Marsha gave Tia a little mirror.

"What do you mean, Mom? Of course gray. It's in all my documents…" With a smile, Tia took the little mirror and was ready to uncover the upcoming joke. Yes, everything was alright, except…

The reflection on the other side of the mirror started losing the smile of the original girl.

"Where did you get this mirror?" Tia immediately got up and rushed into the washroom, holding the little mirror.

Nicolas and Marsha waited in silence, trying to catch any of Tia's vocal expressions.

"What is going on?" The chirping bird that was flying up and down the stairs a couple of hours ago turned into a scared baby bird that didn't know how to use her wings to fly. "What?!" This time, Tia's voice came out from her bedroom.

Nicolas and Marsha patiently waited for their daughter's reappearance in the kitchen. They both turned their heads toward the stairs.

The little baby bird looked restless and confused. "I sense you both know what is going on." Tia looked at her mom and dad with a begging face. "Please, tell me why are my eyes constantly changing in color? Here in the kitchen, they were green. In the washroom, brown. In my room, they were covered with pale spots. I am scared." Tia sat beside her mom and said in a quiet and trembling voice, "Did you adopt me?"

"Oh, honey, no…Of course not! Don't be ridiculous." It was Marsha's turn to talk. "You were born with perfectly gray eyes." Marsha was stroking Tia's hair and touching her face. "They started changing when you turned three years old. Your father and I hoped that sooner or later your eyes would keep one color. We even started betting on it. Your dad wanted green color, I was waiting for a gray—"

"You were betting on my eye color?!" Tia jumped out of her chair with indignation, ready to express all the negative emotions toward her parents.

Marsha took the little mirror out of Tia's hands and placed it right in front of her daughter's face. She smiled.

"Ah! They are almost black now! What is going on! I am a freak! What if people noticed it already? It's awful! They would think about me like I was…some kind of…witch or something…"

"Honey, you are not a witch. Walk with me. The fresh air will help you calm down. I'll tell you a little story." Marsha kissed her daughter, wiped a tear off her face, and affectionately smiled at her.

Tia followed her mom to the backyard garden, constantly wiping tears from her "out of order" eyes.

A few more minutes, and the sun would be resting on the green mattress of countless gardens covered with gold-burgundy blankets of the skies. A few more minutes, and trees would fall asleep, sheltering hundreds of birds on their branches for the night. A few more minutes, and another night would neutralize the stress of the passing day.

The two women were sitting on a swinging bench surrounded by white roses. The young girl looked upset. Her long dark-blond hair was falling over her shoulders, chest, knees. Skinny arms grabbed the edge of the bench on both sides of her body. Her head grew into shoulders and down. The girl's mother did not seem to be upset. She was watching the magical transformation in the sky and smiling.

Marsha put her hand over Tia's shoulders and intruded in her daughter's lost thoughts with a poetic voice. "Twenty-three years ago, two young people were walking in a park. It was dark already. The young man decided to propose. He looked in his girlfriend's eyes and froze. She was staring somewhere behind him with her eyes wide-open. Why do you think he froze? What did he see in her eyes?" Marsha started stroking Tia's hair, trying to flip them back out of her face.

Tia stopped sobbing and remained quiet. "I don't know what he saw..." She finally looked at her mom. "Love?"

Marsha chuckled. "You silly goose. How can you see love in darkness!"

Tia turned her head away and smiled. "I don't know..."

"Tia, baby, look at my eyes..." Marsha touched her daughter's chin and slightly turned her head to the opposite side. "Look at me, Tia."

Tia looked in her mother's eyes and froze. All colors of the Northern Lights were flowing in Marsha's irises—just like in that night when Nicolas opened his heart to her. Tia couldn't move. Her eyes became big and round.

Marsha noticed the reflecting sparks in a couple of sweat drops that protruded on Tia's forehead. For a few seconds, it was hard to say which pair of eyes had the source of those lights and which ones were reflecting. A mother and a daughter were sitting and staring at each other for some time. Gradually, green, yellow, and purple blended into one color—teal.

Marsha slowly touched Tia's hand to make sure she was alright. Tia immediately jumped away from her mother. Her face was completely white as if she saw a ghost. The whole body was shaking, teeth clattering. Marsha got up from the bench and tried to make a step toward her daughter. Tia stretched out her arm in defense and jumped back from Marsha. Then she accidentally stumbled over a garden stone behind her and fell on her back. That was the last memory Tia had when she woke up next morning.

"I hope it was only a dream." Tia looked around, trying to turn her head. Dull pain in the back of her neck stopped the movement. *"I don't want to think about it right now."* She closed her eyes a little, but could still see the room through her eyelashes.

The bright morning light coming through the waving tree branches behind the bedroom window invited Tia to play hide-and-seek. For a moment, she closed her eyes completely and could feel a strong beam of sunlight on the back of her eyelids. She smiled. *"What if the sunlight were a hundred times brighter? Would it give people an ability to see with the eyes closed? Haha...freaky..."* She opened up one eye, adjusting her head in the right angle to avoid the direct light. Did the same with the other eye. Opened both eyes wide. *"No hiding from irritations anymore...Face them instead!"*

The sun in its whole glory involved itself in the game with the direct hit in Tia's eyes. She defiantly looked at the sun. For a few seconds, she couldn't see anything. Then a nature of the human eye started to adjust its vision to the brightness. Dark and red spots paired up in a dance, creating something beautiful. Then Tia started seeing the sun as a black disk blinking in the light red and yellow sky. Her eyes did not hurt anymore. *Apparently, you are not so scary, Mr. Sun.* She smiled with satisfaction and looked at the wall clock. She didn't see anything but the same black disk on the red background printed in her eyes. *Too bright indeed.* Tia relaxed her eyes again until she started seeing clearly. *Can't see when it's too dark. Can't see when it's too bright. Interesting, but adjustable...*

With those thoughts, she sat up on the bed and noticed one pill of Advil and a glass of water on the nightstand. She took it with a smile. "What would I do without you, Mom."

"Poor girl. She was so upset." Marsha was wiping the kitchen table after breakfast and thinking that it would be better if Nicolas didn't know all the details of yesterday's talk in the garden. All he knew was that Tia got upset and fainted.

For some reason, Marsha wasn't worried about Tia's well-being. It was clear that her daughter was a special child whose abilities were just starting to open up for her own comprehension. At the same time, she had to maintain the worried look, keeping Nicolas's attention away from the truth and acting as an average human being.

"What if I spend the whole day with her today? We can go hiking. Tia likes nature." Nicolas put away a newspaper and glanced at Marsha over his glasses.

"I don't think so. She hurt her head badly. She is probably having a headache right now. I pray to God that he would spare her memory. We'll see how she is. We might need to take her to the hospital. I better check on her." Marsha took off her apron and was about to go upstairs to see her daughter.

Tia's bedroom door opened, and the worried parents saw their darling daughter walking down to the kitchen with her hand on her forehead.

Nicolas rushed toward Tia to help her with the stairs in case she lost her balance. "Are you alright, dear?" He anxiously gave her his shoulder. "You should stay in bed today."

"Thanks, Dad. I am fine. It's just a headache." Tia rejected his help and successfully reached the kitchen under her parents' watch. She sat at the dining table and took a bite of the toast that was left after breakfast. "I am so hungry." She got up to start the kettle.

"Take it easy, darling." Marsha touched her daughter's shoulder to sit down. "I'll make tea for you. What else do you want?"

"A coconut butter toast with raspberries and honey, please." Tia helped herself with a glass of water.

"My poor baby. She is in such pain." Nicolas looked at his loved one without hiding his worries. There was nothing left from yesterday's chirping bird who was flying and tweeting around the house. Dark blue circles around her eyes clearly showed a bad headache. "Honey, do you want to see a doctor? We can go after breakfast…"

"I think I am fine, Dad. I am not dizzy or nauseous. It's just a headache and muscle pain. I'll be alright tomorrow." Tia had almost finished the toast. She picked up all the crumbs from her house robe and reached for the next piece.

Marsha carefully observed her. What an appetite! Something was not right.

"Did you sleep well, Tia?" Marsha placed a teapot with freshly made green tea and coco-butter toast in front of her daughter. She sat beside her, staring right into Tia's eyes.

"I don't remember anything after my fall yesterday." Tia was eagerly biting off the bread, totally focusing on the meal.

"Do you remember our talk in the garden yesterday night?" Marsha glanced at Nicolas.

Tia stopped chewing for a moment, looked at her mom, gave a meaningful smile, and calmly said, "Yes, I remember the talk, Mom, and I am alright with it. Sorry for my childish behaviour. I want to talk to you more about it, if you don't have any plans for today." Tia looked at her mother with a questioning look in her eyes.

"That's my girl!" Marsha patted Tia's hand and poured tea for herself as well.

No Name

> Forgot the way home—
> no worries—look at the stars.
> Forgot how to smile—
> Lift up your eyes to the sun.
> Forgot how to forgive—
> Take your dog for a walk.
> Tired to live—no one can help—
> You are immortal…

Maria, Marisha, Marsha. She remembered all the names she had since the Creation. All the names, all the people and souls around her, all the patterns of numerous life cycles. With enormous memory baggage and lives' experience, Marsha was living her perfect life now. None of the spirits in the Parallels, none of the people on Earth, had a clue about Marsha's little secret. She wanted to know if some of the spirits had the same experience and, at the same time, didn't want to open up in front of Junntie, continuing to spin on Earth with the Earth.

In each lifetime, Marsha smiled when she heard people saying, "If I were this smart ten years ago, I wouldn't make such a mistake." Oh, how bad Marsha wanted to say, "Ten years is nothing, how about ten centuries?"

Marsha loved to walk in the Wild Nature Park with her dog Chana. This golden retriever like all dogs kept those walks as one-on-one with nature and maintained a good company to Marsha. Today was the day when Marsha decided to take some time off from work and dedicate it to herself.

The Wild Nature Park...The walks in the park have been as a sanctuary from day-to-day-life stress for Marsha. Even Chana, regardless of her fat belly, had never risen her voice against walking in the park.

Fresh air and the friendly rustle of leaves immediately proceeded with their duties of the physical and emotional healing to all visitors in the park.

It was early morning when Marsha and Chana arrived in the park. The intention was to spend the whole day there. Marsha took a deep breath, closed her eyes, and smiled. Chana got free and rushed to sniff at all the familiar objects around.

Ah...even bad events did not seem so bad when there was such a freshness everywhere. *Okay, Marsha, clear up your thoughts and start reviewing yesterday's conversation with Tia. That's why you are here. Right?* She pushed away the relaxing mood and replaced it with the work of thinking.

"Yes, Mom. I remember everything, and I am alright with it. We can talk more about it if you don't have any plans for today."

Heading toward a lake, Marsha sorted every word of yesterday's dialog with Tia.

"How did you sleep, honey? Did you have any dreams?"

"I don't remember...There was one word or a name that stuck in my head...Sara...Rasara... It didn't want to leave me. For some reason, I feel like this Rasara wanted to control me. The more I paid attention to this name, the stronger this weird connection became between her and me. I hope there is no development of schizophrenia."

"Tia, honey, you hurt yourself badly. You are an intelligent creature and know better than me that sometimes, after some physical or mental traumas, people develop unusual abilities such as speaking in different languages, or seeing invisible things, or…remembering something from nowhere…"

"Mom, do you believe in previous lives or…existence of guardian angels?"

"I don't know. Why?"

"Maybe Rasara was my name in the previous life, or it is my Higher Self who wanted to talk to me?"

"Do you want to talk to her?"

"Sure…I am curious, but don't like to be controlled. I am afraid if I focus on this thought, I'll become dependent."

"Listen to yourself, and you'll be fine."

"I am sure that you know much more about this nonsense, Mom. I figured it out when I saw your eyes yesterday. You've passed this on. It is obvious. Now, tell me, why do we have this? When was the first time you noticed it yourself, and why haven't I noticed it in you before that night?"

"Tia, I had the same pattern in physical development as you are having. I was born with light blue eyes. When I was young, life didn't have the same fast rhythm as it has now. People, especially children, paid more attention to the world around rather than to themselves. They looked at everything with wide-open eyes with no ability to hide any emotions.

"So kids at school noticed that I was different and told their parents. Parents instructed them to stay away from me because 'Who knows what disease this girl has?' Kids in my class avoided me without saying why. I've figured out that they thought I was a witch. One day, we had a new girl in class. She and I became friends. She was the one who told me about my eyes. Her family moved to Canada from Sudan and needed friends to help them with a new life in this very different country.

"Dew's father was an optometrist. He helped me get contact lenses with the original color of my eyes—light blue. I was using those contacts until my graduation. The very next day of graduation, I promised myself to make dramatic changes in my life and march forward without any fear, only with strong confidence. I threw away the contacts and learned how to maintain the same eye color.

"Now, I want to share it with you. I am sure you'll find your own way of dealing with this. My experience will help you to start. I began to carry a little book with a tiny mirror inside. After experiencing a certain mood change, I looked in the mirror and made a record in the book. It amused me for a while. Soon, this project became boring. By that time, I'd come up with the understanding what I should do in order to keep my constant eye color. All I needed to do was to suppress any emotions that caused the color change, such as anger, fright, sadness, disappointment, even tiredness or excitement. Almost all emotions."

"I think I can do it, Mom. Studying and working with mentally challenged people gave me good knowledge. I can use this uniqueness as a benefit or some sort of advantage in my life. That is exactly what I do at work every day. I teach my clients to accept their disabilities as a gift and redirect them into a significant way of using it."

"No doubts, honey. I understood it right away when I saw you at the kitchen table next morning. You were so calm and confident. And when you said to me that you were alright with it, I stopped being worried at all."

"Thank you, Mom. I am so glad we talked it over. I even feel closer to you right now. At this moment, I understood why Dad and I were like good friends all the time. He wasn't afraid to express his emotions in front of me, which was very important to a young child. He was very spontaneous, and therefore, I preferred to spend more time with him. Now I am becoming more like you—rational."

"No…wiser. You will keep both your parents in your heart, Tia. You will find your own way of dealing with any situation. Listen to yourself. That's all you need."

Marsha reached the lake with a smile on her face. Chana was circling around her, barking at crows and almost scared all of them, except one crow that landed on the rails of the lake deck a few meters away from Marsha.

Regardless of the ridiculous look of the round belly and bandy legs, blinded by the successful fight with the local bird army, Chana headed toward the crow on the handrails. After a couple of lazy barks, she expected the complete triumph. The bird didn't even move a feather. The poor dog started barking at the crow, vocalizing its outrage. The bird turned its tail to the furry bully. Bandy Legs was almost choked in its endless barking. Suddenly, the crow turned her head toward Chana and croaked very loud at her. Frightened, the dog ran away immediately, dragging its tail between its legs.

Marsha grinned without looking at the bird. "It's nice to see you too, Rasara. I sense that you are not by yourself today."

"Not in this moment." The crow's gray-gold eyes looked happy.

A lonely woman was standing on the lake deck right beside the waters, looking down. That was exactly what the people in the park would see if they glanced at Marsha. What they wouldn't see or hear was the conversation between the two.

"Some development in your family!" A third person has become involved in the conversation. "Finally, you've decided to confront her."

Marsha immediately straightened her back and looked around. "Good morning, Junntie. What a pleasant surprise! This is the first time I feel your presence on Earth."

"Our experiment looks promising. The Universal Bank of Energy has indicated a jump in the yellow wavelength."

Marsha paused her thoughts for a moment and continued. "I am confused right now. Hasn't it been our goal to keep the energy of the Earth in the same level to avoid any kinds of interference? The past two hundred years showed such a good result. There was no major catastrophes on the planet. Political systems of all countries have reached their golden peak by working together, helping each other. All religions are being equally respected. There is no hunger, poverty, or epidemic diseases in the world. All this became as a brilliant alternative to the Biblical Flood. People's mentality changed tremendously when the Parallel Society started working on your plan, Junntie. The project of helping people to find their significant others by maturity of their souls has saved millions of lives. Finding a soul mate is a first step in absolute happiness. Happy people are kind people. Positive energy attracts the same energy. Yes, people still experience stress in life, but this stress is nothing compared to the global destructions of wars. Doesn't it prove that we are on the right path? Why are you changing your project, chasing some results of a new experiment?"

This conversation didn't require any muscle movement, but Marsha became exhausted. She sat on a bench, preparing herself for a brainstorm.

"Life is more balanced among people, I absolutely agree," Junntie replied.

Marsha looked around again in vain. Junntie's voice was coming from nowhere and everywhere. She felt that it had occupied her thoughts pretty tight.

"If we looked at it from the humans' point of view, if we talked of the entire universe, we would notice a gigantic energy shift that has contradicted to all our expectations. Since people started receiving the spiritual guidance for their right decision-making, the energy flow from the Earth to the Universe has decreased dramatically. Two hundred years have gone without bringing any new discoveries in the scientific world.

"Technology stays the same. Medicine loses its use. Which is wonderful because there is no need for all of that. People don't get seriously sick anymore. We have created almost a Paradise on Earth by destroying the Great Balance. The Universe has started to shrink toward the center of decreased energy, sucking in the anti-energy from out of the other side of the Universe. And this very center is the Earth.

"One hundred years ago, we have indicated a slight energy leakage. Therefore, we started that experiment with your family. The experiment of allying two different souls: the old one as you are, and the young one as Nicolas. As a result of the union, we've got Tia. I believe that she is the answer to all our questions. Her energy spectrum contains unbelievably strong outburst. Only her energy has increased the energy of the entire population of the Earth by 5 percent."

The crow on the handrails flew up to the pine tree, under which Marsha was sitting.

"Junntie, can you explain me something, please. Why can't I work together with Tia anymore? She doesn't let me in. She and I are supposed to be a whole one. Tia knows how to reject me or involve herself into anything she chooses. This is my job to 'manipulate.' She is a few steps ahead of me. Right from the day she was born, Tia created some sort of cocoon around herself. She is developing her own spiritual guide, I feel it. When Tia hurt herself a couple of days ago, I finally felt a connection with her. The cocoon gave a crack in the head area. She'll get better soon, and the channel will be closed again."

"This is a part of our project, Rasara. To be precise, everything that is happening around Tia is a part of the project. A lot of unpredictable events are ahead of us. All we have to do is to observe and learn, protecting Tia from the destroying energy. Tia became an easy target to the attacking energy flow when her aura was damaged. Rasara, get inside of her head if it's not too late. Do not rush to identify your presence until it's necessary." Junntie paused.

Marsha felt a feathery touch of the summer breeze over her hair and face. She closed her eyes and became less tense. "I don't want to be controlled. I hope it is not a development of schizophrenia..."

The echo of Tia's words slapped Marsha's face right after the pleasant feeling of the summer day.

"Helping Tia might create a bigger problem. If we decide to give freedom to her new soul development, we should stick to the plan. Tia possessed a young soul at the moment she was born. According to the energy parameters of Tia's soul maturity now, her soul develops proportionally with her physical age. In her twenty-fifth year of the first life spin, the maturity of her soul hits a mark of the third life. She will be able to complete the whole twelve-life cycle in a single lifetime. I am sure there is no coincidence with the excessive energy outburst from Tia's direction. If we keep her safe, we'll never find out about her full potential."

Marsha didn't believe what she just said. She was throwing her own child into a fire. Two beings were fighting inside her: a human being and a spiritual being. As a mother, she wanted her daughter to be protected. As a spiritual guide, she wanted to find a solution for this project. Deep inside, Marsha felt that Tia's physical and spiritual developments were taking the same path as Marsha had in her very first life spin. What she didn't know and was curious about, that if Tia develops something new, then that "something new" should be achieved without any help, but by Tia only.

Junntie's presence disrupted Marsha's thoughts.

"I am afraid that you are right, Marsha. We shouldn't step back from our experiment. We should give Tia freedom. Rasara will continue to be Tia's spirit, but without guiding her. This decision of mine is not subject to discussion. The extraneous energies are here already. Their intake is strictly proportional to the energy leakage out of the Universe. The energy from the other side is not an intellectual substance. It's working according to the law of balance. They are balancers. Their goal is to find hosts, i.e., humans with weak or damaged auras and start to transform their energy into the balancers' energy. This process will go on until the source of energy deficit, which is the Earth, is replenished. Unfortunately, the balancers that have already entered our universe cannot be kicked back out to the other side. All we can do is stop the incoming forces by increasing the energy of humans' brain activity. Once the balance is restored, the portal from the other side will be closed by itself. The balancers will remain here, creating chaotic turbulence among humans. It has begun. More and more people became mentally disoriented. We have at least three months before the final decision making. In three months, three of us will get together for the resolution, and Xahrns will hold an emergency meeting."

Marsha pulled up the hood of her jacket. A wave of cold air went through her entire body. The presence of Junntie and Rasara had vanished.

Marsha rushed from the bench toward the water. *So much for the relaxing time.* She turned her back to the lake, leaning on the handrails, and tried to find something positive in this situation as she usually did when some problems arose. *Well…we still have three months until the 'end of world.*

The day had given away its half to the sun, pleasing people with the wonderful weather. Constant cries of the seagulls interrupted the laughter of children chasing Chana. Park trails gradually filled up with the fans of a healthy lifestyle. What a perfect summer day!

No. Not perfect at all.

Sooner or later, all pluses will be neutralized with minuses. It doesn't matter how much we try to avoid their presence; negatives and positives will always march side by side through infinity and beyond.

Deflected Reality

Look at me with your eyes wide open.
Let me jump in your soul through them.
It's not true that we are two strangers,
We are here for each other again.

You're repeating that you don't know me.
I can call all your names from the past.
I am back just for you to forgive me.
And bring true all your wishes, please ask.

Why are your eyes so cold and empty?
And the voice doesn't sing any song.
Please, my darling, wake up and remember
Who I've been in your life not so long?

My dear reader, remember that day when suddenly you came to the realisation that you have grown up? Yes, it is true…some of us couldn't wait to become adults. Obviously, our mind has been set this way from the very moment we lost the physical connection with our mothers. Some of us didn't want to accept it for quite some time and fully enjoyed being a child, even in our twenties. If you are falling in the second category, you would never forget the most disturbingly uncomfortable feeling of being noticeable as an adult by "strangers" attracted to you. You understood that you were supposed to react to the situation like all grown-ups usually do—with a possible flirt or playful facial expression. Instead, you became busy with stepping on slightly frozen paddles and getting excited by hearing an amazing sound of the broken ice under your feet, or just publicly wiping your nose because it was only itchy, not runny…and this lifestyle suited you much better at that time. Then you were back home after school, and your parents noticed dirt on your jacket after the fun with the paddles. After giving you "the look," they asked you to sit down and have "the talk." With tears in your eyes, you ran to the washroom and threw up. You refused supper and locked yourself in your bedroom. Yes…the best time of your life has gone. You became an adult, and you hated it.

Fresh morning wind was playing with the curtains through an ajar window when Tia opened her eyes. She gave herself a good morning stretch and smiled at the dancing sunlight scattered by multicolored rainbows on the walls and ceiling of her room.

"Every morning, look at this crystal jewel and remember how unique you are…"

Last night, Marsha adjusted the faceted crystal bead in the middle of Tia's bedroom window, kissed her daughter good night, and left.

Oh yes…multicolors…

The smile gradually vanished from Tia's face. A wave of worry flashed around the room. She felt as if she were not at her ease right now. Déjà vu was painting a picture of the similar mood when Tia was fourteen and climbed on the old poplar tree in the backyard. She loved to sit on the top branch and swing with the wind. Her mother was looking at Tia in the kitchen window. Tia waved at her. A few minutes later, before dinner, the mother and daughter had "the talk." With each word, Tia felt that she was losing piece by piece something unbelievably valuable inside of her, something that was going away irrevocably—her childhood.

Feeling miserable, Tia picked up a little mirror from a drawer and looked at her eyes. They had a very dark gray color with a few light gray stripes. She put the mirror away and sat in the lotus position on her bed, trying to relax. "I've got over this once. Will do it again. All people deal with awkward situations, and everyone turns alright. This is my awkwardness. It is a bit different compared to other people, but it's mine, and I will manage it. Besides, there is nothing that can affect my health…" She was breathing in and out.

Morning sunshine and fresh breeze from the open window caressed Tia's face. It felt so right and accommodating. "God gave it to me for a reason. It is mine now. All I have to do is accept it and like it. If I fight, it will fight me back. Now I have to find the cause. Okay, my eye color is changing because of emotional state. It means if I want to keep the eye color constant, I have to be in charge of my emotions. How can I do it? Well…the answer will come because the question has been placed."

Tia opened her eyes and smiled with satisfaction. "Hah! Apparently, it is not the eye-color-change problem. It is a mood-change problem! It all depends on how you look at it. And I look at it with excitement of accepting this challenge!"

She looked in the little mirror with complete satisfaction. A girl with a green spark in her gray eyes looked at Tia from the other side of the mirror. "That's my girl! Green it out!" Tia threw a robe on her shoulders and marched with triumph down to the dining room. She was ready to embrace the day.

Tia's bike was doing its job every morning for the past three summers. Every time it looked like an extension of the skinny rider who rushed to work. As always, the bike was the last link in the chain of receiving a signal from the rider's brain, passing it to the muscles responsible for her every movement and momentarily performing the required work of pedaling in any direction with any speed.

This morning the bike felt that motor neurons in the rider's spinal cord didn't make the usual connection with her muscles for pedaling the bike. Some unfamiliar impulses were irritating the rider's brain or wasn't irritating it at all. This morning the bike was sharing a road along with other transportation, using the very street. Only the trees on sides of the street could notice how much the bike wanted to make a turn on a footpath or cross the road on a red light and act as a pedestrian while all vehicles were waiting and staring at the bike with jealousy in their headlights. Hey, Tia! There are some speed bumps over there! Are you ready for a jump? I am! In your dreams, dear bicycle. Jumping time is over. From now on, Tia followed the traffic rules, training herself for a driving test in a vehicle. She was going to pass all the tests available and receive a driver's license.

It was a usual morning. The same grass, sky, and a crow on the pine tree beside the group home where Tia arrived for work. As always, the night staff was peeking through the closed blinds, waiting for Tia, and as soon as she arrived, Lucie would be gone home. Finally, she saw Tia parking beside the porch from the opposite side of the house. Lucie kept observing. There was something that didn't feel quite right today. Lucie glanced at the pine tree right beside the window. Every morning when new staff arrived, the crow cawed, identifying the arrival. Today the crow was sitting quietly on a branch.

Lucie smirked at the bird. "Are you getting old today?"

She kept observing Tia's arrival, which was different as well. The girl wasn't rushing today. Yet she arrived ten minutes before her shift start.

Tia slowly proceeded up on the wheelchair ramp to the back door of the residence. Lucie sat at the kitchen table and waited. The back door opened. Tia entered the house.

"Morning, Lucie. How was the night?" Tia slowly took off her shoes and jacket.

"It was alright. Pretty quiet. Noah slept well. It was his first night in the new place. He seemed a nice young man. Yesterday evening, he was watching TV and reading his books. Went to bed at midnight. Asked me to go with him to a bar. I told him that I work at night, and night staff don't go out with the residents. I let him know that you were coming next day to work with him. He said, 'Alright' and stayed in his room since."

Lucie talked and kept looking at Tia, trying to catch what was different in that young lady this morning.

"You look different today, Tia."

"It's just the hair and clothes. If I take Noah out today, it is better if I look more professional, less girlish. The first meeting with a new individual sets up the boundaries."

It was true. Despite riding the bike, Tia was dressed as office staff: black pants, tight in hips, slightly loose in the ankle areas. White blouse showed its collar and low edges from under the blue sweater. Tia's hair was tightened in a knot. Today she was wearing shoes with sturdy heels instead of fancy high heels.

"I am thinking of getting a vehicle as soon as I pass my driving test. I am done with the bike riding." Tia smiled.

Lucie got up from the kitchen chair. "It's a strong decision, Tia. Good luck with your plans, and have a wonderful day with your new client." She picked up her backpack and left the residence.

She is an attractive woman. Tia looked at Lucie through the kitchen window as she was leaving. *A little short and chubby...Actually, it would work in her favor. Those legs would look perfect in high heels and tights.*

"Thinking of how to make the world more beautiful?" Paulina, the residential supervisor, opened the fridge and put a couple of oranges inside.

"Oh, I didn't hear you coming, Paulina." Tia stood up and greeted the supervisor. "Good morning."

Paulina casted a quick glance at Tia. "You look very nice today, Tia. Is there a special occasion?"

Tia wanted to share her thoughts with Paulina about her new starting point in life, but changed her mind immediately, remembering the cold reaction from her coworker a couple of minutes ago. It was understandable. Who cares about others' life-changing ideas? It was not a work-related subject anyway.

"No. Just trying to get ready for a new day with a new client. I've heard that Noah was here, and the first night in his new home went well. He is still in bed. This week I am going to observe Noah and collect as much information as possible about him. Maybe we'll go for a walk or personal shopping together. Lucie said that Noah asked her to go to a bar yesterday evening. I am telling you right now, Paulina, this bar thing is off the table because I don't go to bars, even for work purposes."

Tia lowered her eyes because she wasn't sure if their color stayed the same. Her mood had changed a bit. Then she realized that from Paulina's point of view, it wouldn't be noticeable because the light from the window behind Tia's back would blind up Paulina pretty well during the conversation. It meant that Tia's eyes remained in the shadows.

With the satisfactory thought of how to deal with "the problem," Tia smiled and proceeded further with planning her workday.

Every morning Paulina and Tia worked as a team. Each of them was doing their duties and at the same time successfully discussing possible approaches to arising problems in the residence.

Tia got quiet for a few minutes, concentrating on last week's staff meeting notes. Her fingers were flying across the keyboard of a tiny laptop, barely touching its surface. Suddenly, the computer symphony paused for a few seconds.

"Paulina, I have an idea for the next staff meeting. It would be helpful for everyone to get a better knowledge of our work. The agency does so many wonderful things for the individuals in service and provides lots of trainings for the staff to perform excellent work. In other words, the well-being of our individuals depends on staff work performance. Right?"

Paulina stopped typing and looked at Tia with curiosity. "What are you saying, Tia? I don't quite follow."

Tia moved away her laptop and tried to keep her mood steady during the conversation.

"After the last staff meeting, I got a little bit sick because of the excessive wind in the house. You probably have noticed it." Tia turned on an electric teapot and gave a couple of seconds to the supervisor to think of what she wanted to say next.

Paulina tried to smile, but only one corner of her lips went up. Her eyes didn't want to follow the lips and stayed still.

"Again, I would like a little bit more information. How is your cold anyway?" Paulina focused on a computer screen, pretending that she had no idea of what that young lady was talking about.

Tia made two cups of green tea and brought one to Paulina. "It's gone. Thank you for asking." She sat closer to the supervisor, holding a teacup in both hands. "It is not about my cold. It is about…let us say, 'the middle age crisis' in women. I hope I was wrong, but it seemed to me that there was an embarrassment with this particular health condition that day. When I tried to play along, pretending that it really was hot in the room and opened a window, some of the ladies felt more relaxed, even joked about the elephant in the room. Every woman sooner or later will go through menopause. There is nothing to be embarrassed of. What if the next staff meeting, we invite a professional to talk about it? I am sure everyone would be happy to get a doctor's opinion, maybe find a way of dealing with hot flashes. The happier we are at the workplace, the better our work performance."

Since the beginning of the conversation, Paulina hadn't moved a muscle. She was looking straight into Tia's eyes, trying to understand why this child happened to care that much about the old nonrelated women in the group home. Was it her study project? Perhaps. *Well...it wasn't the first time when she tried to help others. And anyway, why is this perfectly built human being coming back to work as a casual staff? Her looks and smarts could open up any doors for a successful future. Ah, if I were only born in Canada...my life would have looked much different by now...*

"What do you think, Paulina?" Tia's voice made a ripple in the pond of Paulina's thoughts.

"It is a very good idea, Tia. What if we expand it up on the whole agency level? Ninety-five percent of the agency's employees are females. All of them, including me, would participate in this kind of lecture. And it would be easier to find a professional who agrees to speak in front of a big audience than for six employees in a small kitchen."

The sounds of opening bedroom and then washroom doors verified the awakening of a resident. Those two in the kitchen couldn't see the individual but realized that it was Noah. They heard the flushing toilet and running shower.

After ten minutes, a man in his thirties walked into the kitchen. Loose jeans on his short x-shaped legs were making rubbing noises with each step. Long skinny arms sticking out of his fat shoulders looked grotesque. He ignored or perhaps didn't see the women at the kitchen table and tried to reach a cupboard door, showing a bald spot on his head hiding under combed straight yellow hair. He was too short for this quest and realized that he needed something to step on to reach the cupboard door. The man looked around and spotted two people sitting at the table, quietly watching him.

"Oh, hello..." Noah winced. Two dots of red eyes looked

surprised, almost frightened. Pink spots of uncomfortable feelings covered his pale face.

"Good morning, Noah. Welcome to your new home. My name is Paulina. I am a manager of this house. This is Tia. She will be your keyworker. If you want to go somewhere, she is your company."

Noah remained in the same spot. Stretching out his neck, he tried to gaze intently into Tia's face through the shadow of the bright light behind her.

Ignoring Paulina's welcoming speech, Noah swished with a set of quick tiny steps toward Tia, keeping his eyes on her. Finally, with his trembling voice, he said, "Rasara...It is you..."

Tia glanced at Paulina with bewilderment and right away focused on Noah. "Hello, Noah. My name is Tia. It's very easy to remember. Just like tea. Can you say Tia?"

"Rasara...It's me, Kondrat...Remember me? I missed you so much. Can you forgive me for everything I've done to you? I miss you and our little girl. How is she? Please, forgive me. It wasn't my fault. I was trapped between two families and made the wrong decision... Please, forgive me." Noah grabbed Tia's hand and started kissing it, covering it with tears. His cry became louder.

Paulina slowly stood up and was about to get a sedative.

Tia touched Paulina's arm with her free hand and mouthed a no.

Paulina stopped with hesitation.

Tia looked surprisingly calm. "I forgive you, Kondrat. But...you have to promise something to me in return." Tia looked at Paulina with a smile and right away focused on Noah with a serious facial expression.

Right after those words, Noah stopped crying and released Tia's hand. His eyes remained widely open and very red. He wiped tears with his tiny hands and smiled. "You do remember me, my Rasara. Thank you. I knew it. I am here to fix all my mistakes...You'll see it! Nobody believed me...even my mother. You are the one who took my words seriously. I am not sick, I just…remember. They are here after you too. I am the one who can help you. We have to stick together to fight them. Listen to me, and you'll be safe."

"Noah…" Tia stared into his eyes and, in a harsh tone of voice, repeated, "You promise me…"

Suddenly, the man became quiet and maintained eye contact.

Tia slowly got up from a chair. Noah straightened his back as well. Tia repeated very slowly.

"You promise me to forget the past."

Noah repeated, "I promise, I will forget the past."

Tia continued. "My name is Tia. Your name is Noah."

Noah repeated her words as well.

"You are forgiven." Tia paused.

The flame of unconditional emotions in Noah's voice started fading away. Movements of his lips lost the power of sound. In a few more seconds, his eyelids became heavy. Only Noah knew how much energy he needed to keep his eyes open. Finally, he gave up and fell asleep, standing in front of Tia.

Tia exhaled with relief and looked at Paulina.

The residential supervisor seemed to be glued to her chair. A look of consternation had affected her face.

A million thoughts flashed through Tia's head. *Eye color change… Noah fell under the hypnosis…Rasara…Kondrat…What is going on? Why does Paulina stare at me? What should I say now?*

"Paulina…" Tia touched Paulina's hand.

Paulina flinched. "How did you do that? And your eyes…they went red…" Paulina jumped closer to Tia, trying to get right into her eyes.

"Paulina, please, don't be ridiculous. They were not red. It's just… play of light. And this…hypnosis was just a simple psychology trick. All students know that. Come on, Paulina. You are an intelligent human being. Stop looking at me like that." Tia acted naturally and was quite surprised about it. "Let's walk Noah into his bedroom and let him sleep a little. When he wakes up, he'll feel much better."

Noah was transferred into his bedroom, and right after that, the residential supervisor and Tia decided that a week off would work beneficial for Noah and his keyworker.

Tia took a walk home. She walked beside her best friend, her bicycle, gently holding its saddle with one hand and a handlebar grip with the other. She didn't remember how this friendship began. They were growing up together, changing in size, helping each other with riding techniques and any experiences on bumpy gravel and bumps all over their bodies.

Pieces of memory tape with unforgettable moments of childhood, youth, and early adulthood were sweeping past. When Tia was learning how to make her first steps safely, her friend, the bike, gave her an idea how to move in space faster without walking. Since then, family members and neighbors could catch only a blink of golden hair and silver tinsels instead of a slow-walking girl. She was clumsy with walking. He was helpless with no movements. Together, they were exploring the universe.

The little baby grew up, and so did her bike. The golden-haired child became a dark-blond teenager. The tiny pink bike turned into a skinny metal structure with two trusted wheels. They were happy and free. All Tia's friends soon became obligated with vehicles in high school and began to make jokes about her still riding a bike. She was only smiling and saying, "I love my bike." The same verbal response led her through the first couple of years in university and part-time job.

Happiness…freedom…Why doesn't it last forever? Unfortunately, one day you wake up and make a statement—I am an adult. It's time for a change…

They walked hand-to-handlebar beside each other, a young woman and her old friend, her bike. The last walk was made by thousands of slow steps. With each step, a veil of time tried to cover and then vanish the best event of a human life—a childhood.

Noah Fjusher

> \- What is real?
> \- All you can touch.
> \- What about the Moon?
> \- O-o… It is very real…

"I hate my life…" Noah sat on the twin-size bed and looked around his new room. Two suitcases stared at him with huge purple flowers from the middle of the room. "Whole life fits in two suitcases, and those suitcases are not even mine." He grinned. "What a loser…"

Sighing, Noah took off his runners and stretched his short legs down to the floor. Round toe heads tried to feel the rough surface of the carpet, but a layer of socks prevented them from the desirable sensation.

Noah was tired and didn't want to move a muscle to take off his socks.

Why am I here in a group home? He relaxed his back, leaning on the wall behind him.

The sunset has already passed a baton of light to the street poles, visually distorting the reality.

A projection of traffic nightlife was rolling its movie across the bedroom walls conducted by the window blinds. Noah began to count the shadows sliding on the walls. A minute later, this activity turned into a game of guessing what vehicle is passing by the window without glancing outside.

In a few minutes, Noah was able to recognize each passing by vehicle by their sound and headlights' brightness.

"Wow…this is a huge one…probably some heavy-duty truck." A sharp combination of light and shadow stripes sliced the walls up to the ceiling. "And this one…I hear something, but nothing's on the walls. Wait a minute…Here it comes…"

A pale shadow was slowly dragging along the floor line.

"It's a motorbike! Hah…Fun! Stupid fun…"

Noah got up, shut the blinds, and hit the light switch. The reality became real again. Blue bedroom walls welcomed a new resident with an invitation for décor. A big corner desk was ready to be fulfilled with valuable and not-so-valuable belongings of the new tenant. A huge walk-in closet patiently waited for lots and lots of Noah's clothes and a possibility of a hide-and-seek game. A tall red oak bookcase wanted to know immediately how bad Noah would need its shelves.

"Not bad. Not bad at all…I have to get out of here…right now!" Noah jumped in his running shoes and let himself out of the depressing room.

Bright light from the dining room stopped Noah for a few seconds with the request to adjust his visual perception. A woman at the kitchen table paused her writing in a logbook and surprisingly looked at Noah.

"I am going out." Noah headed toward the front door.

Lucie jumped out from the kitchen table and quickly followed Noah. "It's almost midnight, Noah. Do you think this is a good time for an outing?"

"The Night Bar has just opened." Noah touched the doorknob.

"It's downtown," Lucie said in a calm voice tone, but the blush of worry was pumping over her face. "The city buses stopped running a couple of hours ago. How will you get there?" She remembered the training at work. *How to help an individual with decision-making.*

Lucie visually reduced her fast breathing and vocal anxiety, switching her own concerns as a caregiver with Noah's concerns as an individual in service.

Noah stopped for a moment and, keeping his hand on the doorknob, turned around. "How far are we from down-town?"

"About forty minutes walking."

"Do you drive?"

"Yes, but I can't go out with you right now. I am night staff. There are two more residents in the house, and I can't leave them alone. What if you wait till tomorrow? There is a lady who will go out with you every day or evening, depends on her work hours. She'll be here tomorrow morning. You can talk to her about the places you want to visit."

Noah paused for a few seconds and left the doorknob alone.

Lucie invited the new resident to the kitchen table and offered a glass of milk. Noah politely rejected the invitation, took a glass of milk in his room, and said good night to Lucie.

"It is actually not bad at all!" Noah took a sip from the glass and put it on the shelf beside his bed. Then he unzipped the side pocket of his suitcase and pulled out a book. "Maybe living here is the best thing of my life. I don't have to worry about rent or mortgage. Staff will cook meals for me, drive me in their cars. I will have a girl to go out with. Hope she is pretty. Not sure if I even have to work! It's a government problem now! Hah! Hello, Paradise!" He brought the book closer to his mouth and whispered into the text block, "There is only one thing I need to figure out: why am I here in the group home?"

Noah opened the book. Perfectly lined words of pencilled handwriting greeted him from the first page. The words were placed apart from each other with microscopic precision, and each letter of the words maintained its right size. Noah smiled with satisfaction and felt the paper with the tips of his fingers. He began the ritual of invoking a spirit of the narration by reading each word with a trembling voice.

Suddenly, Noah stopped reading. His pleasant smile disappeared from his face. The dot of a letter i happened to jump a half-millimeter higher from its usual location. Noah pursed his lips, pressed that self-liberated letter with his finger, and pulled a nightstand drawer with his other hand. Then he grabbed an eraser from the drawer, carefully removed the uneven dot, and placed a new one a half-millimeter lower. After the examination of his work from all possible views, Noah exhaled with satisfaction and continued his reading. The rest of the letters and words learned a good lesson after the incident with the jumping dot. They obediently remained in the perfect order until their master got to the lower right corner of the page.

Noah flipped the page. Empty rails of blue lines were waiting for the story train that would pull forward lots of carriages—words of Noah's meticulously organized handwriting.

Noah straightened his back and closed his eyes. The rebellious feelings he had been experiencing for the past couple of years cried for escape. And the best way to get rid of them lay through the numerous pages of this thick notebook where the train, full of unwanted emotions, would carry them away.

A heavy-duty truck slushed the bedroom walls with its bright shadows and made Noah open his eyes. Led by the moving lights, his gaze stopped on the still-unpacked suitcase in the middle of the room.

"Right…" Noah quickly got up and unzipped a side pocket of the suitcase, pulled out a book, and opened it. He sat on his bed, totally occupied by reading. Then he took his notebook and began to write out from the book.

"…Then who are you?
—I am the Energy,
That always will evil
And does forever good…"

(The writer's translation from German)

Noah put the book back into the suitcase. He closed his eyes and smiled. He stayed like that for a minute, picturing something in his mind.

So many times, Noah visualized himself in the palace of Haon, the Arbiter of Mazaria. What would it be like?

A pencil in Noah's hand began to work on his imagination and rope him into a new narration. Soon Noah couldn't recognize where the line was between written and real. Noah was falling asleep, whispering...

The mistress placed a few branches of blooming jasmine in a huge vase painted with gold and glanced at the terrace. Her face lit up when she saw Haon, the Arbiter of Mazaria, emerging into the palace.

"Wow...It seems like I am there in the palace with the Arbiter. Wait a minute...I am there—I mean, here. I see Haon! Look at him... his clothing...so different from what we wear on Earth. I can tell that the Arbiter is preoccupied with some heavy thinking...just like in my book. And...who am I here in this scene?"

Noah tried to look at his hands and body. Couldn't see anything. He didn't have the visible body.

"I am a spirit!" As every single person who has just become a spirit, Noah tried a few "cutting through his body" movements and, with the satisfaction of being invisible, wondered, "Whose spirit am I in this book?"

Noah left the Arbiter alone for a while and redirected his attention on the magical garden outside of the palace.

Aromas of exotic flowers and blooming trees hung in the air by an invisible luscious cloud. There wasn't a slight breeze to dilute the heavy scent.

"Yep, the storm is coming." Noah was about to come back to the palace scene, but his attention got captured by the unusually big crow that flew by. "Those creatures are everywhere, even on this planet, planet Mazaria. This one is so big! Two or three of those flying around the garden, and no wind needed."

With a smile, Noah watched the bird that suddenly landed behind the acacia bush, shaking it hard, and again, no movement.

"Is it dead?" Before trying to make any motion or decision if he should go and check what was going on with the bird, Noah found himself soaring in the air toward the acacia bush. "Wow! The power of mind. No muscle use, just thinking! That's how spirits move! Awesome!"

Noah got down right beside the acacia bush and saw a young woman sitting on the grass surrounded by flowers. Her head was turned away, resting on her bent knees. Her light-ash hair was scattered all over the silk of her gray dress and disappeared in the grass. Noah couldn't see the woman's face, and it didn't bother him. He knew that it belonged to an angel.

He moved closer to her. "It is so cool that she can't see me. I can get as close as I want…"

Noah appeared right in front of the girl's face. What a peaceful scene it was. A child was sleeping in the garden surrounded by flowers. Her huge eyes were locked up under her heavy eyelashes. Buttoned nose harmoniously wheezed with each breath. Tiny bow-shaped lips were so red and puffy that even a slight touch of makeup would destroy the innocence of the whole picture.

"A young woman with the face of a child. It must be one of God's angels…" Noah couldn't take his eyes off her. He felt like being under hypnosis and forgot how bad he wanted to witness the dialog between Pontius Pilate and the accused One.

The angel-child stopped wheezing and yawned, twitching her shoulders a little. Noah held his breath. A pair of huge blue eyes got unleashed from under the heavy chain of her curly eyelashes and looked straight at Noah. The creature lifted her head from her knees, keeping eye contact with him.

"She is seeing me…She is not a human…"

For a moment, Noah felt like his whole existence began to diminish in size. Only the blue of her eyes remained the same. Everything around them—gray dress, ash hair, graceful figure—everything had washed out in the blurriness. Noah's presence smoldered away with countless golden dust around the crystal blue.

Suddenly, he began to feel unconditional love and comfort. He wished to remain as a part of the golden dust forever and move in any directions of its streams. Here he was, going around of the blue in the dance of the golden tornado. From the top of the spinning funnel Noah whirled down in the center of the great dance, conserving an angular momentum. He felt safe in there, in that vacuum of glory. Everything was moving and glowing around him. In the moment, Noah could see each separate spark of the golden dust. Every single particle had a unique shape. "Just like snowflakes…Billions of them and no identical one…"

One by one, the dust particles started changing their spinning route, passing by Noah very close and disappearing in the great flow. Soon, Noah noticed that every dot began to stop for a moment in front of him, deluging with a pleasant memory of a familiar smell, sound, unforgettable state of mind, feeling, taste…

All the treasuring recalls from Noah's past were visiting him one by one right now. Somehow, he knew that if he wanted to stay with them, he had to choose one of the "snowflakes," follow it, and be happy forever with living again and again through the same moment.

"Which one? There are so many of them…What a smell? I know that smell…ah…it's Christmas baking! Mom used to make chocolate cookies every Christmas for me. I am definitely going back into my childhood!"

Noah moved toward the spark of his childhood memory, but the sound of a familiar voice stopped him. He started listening and recognized the source. It was a conversation.

"I will never hurt you, Nicole, even if something goes wrong between us. Please, trust me. I love you…"

"I believe you because I love you too, Doug."

The moment was taken away at the same time when a new one took its place as a footage of film.

"Sorry, honey. I will always love you, but I am choosing my family over you and our child."

"We *are* your family, Doug. Sandra is your little girl. I don't understand…"

"I love you both, but my niece needs me more…"

Something suddenly shifted in Noah's memory perception. Gold-colored sparks started showing more of orange. The vibes of pleasure and comfort neutralized to the point of zero. The golden tornado stopped, then started moving again in the opposite direction, changing its color. Gold…orange…red.

"Mom, why did Daddy leave us?"

"I don't know, sweetheart. He needed some time to be alone. I am sure he'll be back."

Noah felt the pain of those two and immediately recognized his wife and daughter from the very deep past. "Nicole? Sandra?"

The orange flake switched with a red one. Another strangely familiar voice whipped by his ear.

"What if the spirits who have made mistakes in their past lives would be put in the same situation for their next life spin? They should be given one more chance to improve themselves…"

The fire tornado sped up its rotation, pulling Noah's existence in all directions. The safe spot where Noah found his shelter no longer was safe. On the contrary, it was the ugliest position of all existing and nonexisting matter in the entire universe. All physical and emotional pain has centralized in Noah's entity. He was flouncing from side to side in the flaming walls of the tornado, hoping to find a way out.

"I am ready to prove my love to you, Rasara!" Noah screamed and cried in despair. "I am ready to meet with you again! Come to my life! I will recognize you in any appearance…I promise! Nobody will stand between us this time! Come to me, Rasara! I am ready…"

Noah's scream resonated with the tornado and pushed his substance out of the flaming funnel. He looked around, hoping to cool down in the crystal blue, but couldn't find it. The creature's eyes still remained blue, but more with frozen dead-white tincture around the pupils.

After burning and being torn apart, Noah felt that his entire body became pinned through with hundreds of invisible frosty needles. He couldn't move, hovering in nowhere. Dead eyes of the angel creature stared at him.

Noah heard her voice, reaching him from everywhere: "Kondrat, listen to me. If you want to avoid the same mistake from your previous lives, this is the very time. You've been granted with the chance to correct them. All you need to do is to listen to my voice. It will guide you to the right direction. Tia is in danger as well as all mankind. Only you can help her because only you can hear me. You are the Called One. Listen to me…listen to my voice…listen to me…"

Noah woke up, repeating, "Listen to my voice…Listen to me…" He was shaking. Cold sticky sweat reminded him of the frosty needles around his body. Noah tried to move. It worked. "Oh…it was just a dream. I have to stop reading in bed." He looked at the book on his pillow and moved it to the night table drawer. "It is time to get up, take a good hot shower, and begin to investigate why I am here in the group home."

Blinds up. Welcome sunshine. Become one day wiser.

A Stranger

If I could only tear apart the veil of time
From my memory…

Is it possible to accomplish anything meaningful in five or six days of our free time? Some would say, "Everything!" Some say, "Nothing."

Let me guess…Isn't it up to us? If you are mighty and planning to create life in the universe, a six-day period would be just right. If you are a laid-back individual, it is impossible to fulfill a one-week timeframe with all the laziness that possesses you. Anyway, it is not of my business to discuss anybody's free time, but one thing I know for sure that my current position as a writer gives me the consent to chat as much as I want about any characters in this book…

It froze in a position of uncertainty. She was about to leave it forever. It tried to remember this moment in all possible details, but the life of the pedal-powered bike lights is very short. From the moment she stopped the bike and started walking away, the headlight was able to capture the very few last seconds through its dying lens: the pair of long legs under conservative black pants that was taking away the most desirable creature of its life. Slim figure covered with a shawl of straight blond hair disappeared behind the License and Registry door, and then…total blackout sealed with the handwritten sign "Free."

"Mom, I am taking Chana to the park." Tia ran down the stairs to the kitchen and kissed her mother on the way out.

Clumsy Chana recognized her name and stumbled along toward Tia's new car. She didn't need a master's degree to learn quickly her place in Tia's car on the blanket of the back seat or, if she doesn't behave, on the floor of the back seat.

"It is actually cool to be a driver." Tia took off slowly and headed straight to the Wild Nature Park. Everything around looked different when you are in charge of your own vehicle. The very first feeling was security and comfort. In a couple of days, security and comfort became habitual and got replaced with a new feeling—seclusion. There wasn't any presence of the wind that used to touch your face… No bumpy gravel that kept you awake in the early mornings when you were pedaling to work or school… No sound of the wing strokes from the birds that accidently crossed your way and carried something against your slow biking. The chance to cheat on red lights was gone as well. And where are all those connections with Mother Nature, for goodness' sake..? Changes…it is always tough to accept them…

Tia parked her car under a pine tree and looked at Chana in the rearview mirror. "Well, my dear girlfriend, let's thank our Lady-Bug for bringing us safely and quickly to the nature. I hope soon we all become friends." She petted the dashboard of her new orange Honda and let herself and Chana out.

Two girls of different species got busy in the park according to their mission on this planet: a dog, to sniff and bark without any purpose, and a human, to think and analyze her thoughts.

"Today is the last day of my one-week holiday. I did well, had straightened all pros and cons regarding a big change in my everyday life. Still fighting with the acceptance of my new self, but feel like getting on the right path. Succeeded with both driving tests. Got my license and a new car…Made a first real step toward being an adult."

Escorted by the cloud of thoughts, Tia walked down to the lake and slightly bent over the water deck.

"What does it mean to become an adult? I am so confused with the concept of being mature. To be responsible? For what? Family. Job. Future. What's the responsibility good for if you don't have enough knowledge or experience? It is impossible to be totally knowledgeable and experienced if every moment we learn something new. How can we become mature enough to be called responsible? What is the answer?"

The cloud of thoughts flew down the waters and spread its marbles beneath among the existing flora and fauna.

For the moment, Tia's physical presence lost its value, vaporized, and, with invisible particles, reconnected with her own thoughts, making the lake water glow. She was swimming between each possible and impossible idea, looking for the right answer.

"Intuitiveness!"

A voice behind her shoulders momentarily returned Tia into the lost physical body and shoved all the "marbles" back in the place they belonged. She flinched and turned her head toward the voice.

A man in his thirties was rushing toward Tia. His khaki pants and beige jacket didn't match with the lay-back environment of the park. She pricked up her ears. The man appeared right beside her. "Intuitiveness!"

"Pardon me?" She inquiringly glanced at him.

The man pointed to the puppy right beside Tia's feet. "Intuitiveness…my dog…Always hides in places I never look."

"You named your dog Intuitiveness?" The inquiring expression of Tia's face turned into the expression of bewilderment.

The man was trying to grab his puppy and at the same time kept talking without looking at Tia. "Yes, *Intuitiveness*. You know…the comprehension of truth by direct contemplation of mystical penetration without scientific analysis."

Tia stepped back, giving more room to the catching game, and observed those two with curiosity. "I am familiar with the definition of intuitiveness. It's just an odd name for a dog." Tia relaxed her face and left only a smile.

"Odd? Like the color of your eyes?" The man finally got his puppy on a leash, straightened up his back, and gave Tia a prolonged gaze. His black eyes deeply penetrated her soul.

She shivered and turned away. "Whatever..." Pretending to be bored, Tia put herself together pretty fast and was about to walk away, but "her constantly working brain marbles" sent a signal to the inner voice. *He said that without looking at my face. How did he know my problem?*

For half a second, she tried to figure out how to get back into the conversation without looking desperate.

When she was about to turn back and ask the man if he had seen her dog, she heard him say, "Miss! Is that your dog?" The "malicious man" was pointing toward the lake where the snarling and roaring Chana was trying to catch something in the water, stepping and jumping back and forth.

"Chana! Come here!" Tia tried to distract the dog from whatever she was doing in the water. The shrilling yelp of Chana scared off all ducks from the lake when she started to get rid of something from her nose, making big splashes around.

"Chana!" Tia was about to step in the water, but the dog, wriggling and screeching, ran to her, carrying a tiny crayfish clutching her nose with one claw.

"Hold the dog." The stranger in a beige jacket picked up a stick. Tia grabbed the distraught and muddy Chana by the collar and pressed her to the ground using her knee and hands. Immediately Chana stopped resisting and seemed like she fell asleep. The man in the beige jacket touched the tiny lake warrior with a stick. The little guy opened up its claw, left the poor dog's nose alone, redirected his close grip onto the stick, and right away was thrown back into the lake.

Tia looked at the stranger's face with a "thank you" expression and stopped blinking.

A pair of light-blue eyes were looking back at her with a smile. All she could say was "Thank you."

The man helped Tia to get up and walked her to the nearest bench, holding her elbow for a few seconds.

She didn't want to talk. They sat on the bench in silence, looking at the lake and probably into the deepness of their souls, trying to remember something. Something that was familiar to both.

Thick fog began to spread over the lake and the trees. All birds sheltered themselves in the branches. All the existing sounds were swallowed by the fog. Hypnotic silence started its creative process through the veil of time.

Rowena was awake for a while but didn't want to open her eyes. She thought if she kept her eyes closed, no tears would come out. She turned on her back, forcing the annoying liquid to go in reverse. The trick didn't work. Something very powerful was pumping the water from inside.

She squeezed her eyelids against each other as much as she could. Even so, salty streams found their way out. Rowena stopped fighting and burst out in tears, flipping over her little body and burying her nose in Maleen's pillow. She was choking by the endless tears and the smell of her mother's hair preserved in the pillow. And then...there was nothing. No tears left.

She looked around with empty eyes. Sorrow had painted everything in strange colors...dead, unnatural colors, like reused decorations on a stage.

A nine-year-old girl came back home last night after a year of staying in "the witch hole" together with her mother.

Maleen Andresdotter was accused of practicing sorcery, and a year after the endless trials, she had been acquitted and released. Because of being kept in unbearable conditions for a human body, Maleen became very ill and died the same day of being released. Rowena came back home alone.

The small house outside of Norway's tiny village of Vardo sheltered an orphaned child away from people's eyes. Only the Barents Sea knew how many people's lives were ended by the fire, water, or torture in the year of 1662…

Rowena opened her eyes, looking nowhere. This "nowhere" was dark, shapeless, cold, and sounded like the hiss of a snake. She covered her face with a blanket, leaving a little gap, just in case. For how long she was lying like that, she didn't know. Blank.

The smell of bread disturbed Rowena's sleep. A touch of something warm on her forehead and then her cheek pulled out a smile on Rowena's face.

"Mom…I am hungry…" Rowena opened her eyes and realized that it was the end of a very desirable illusion that lasted half a second.

"Rowena…baby…I brought something to eat." Hilde was sitting beside the girl and touching her face and hair.

Rowena didn't make any moves and looked through Hilde, trying to rewind the recent events.

"Come on, I'll give you a bath. You'll stay with me now. I promised your mom to take care of you." Hilde tried to uncover Rowena, but the girl gripped the blanket tightly.

"I am staying home."

Those were the last words Hilde heard from Rowena that day. The good woman had opened her heart to that little girl. All was in vain. Rowena remained in bed, looking through the air blindly. The only sign of life was her soundless breathing.

"Alright, honey. I will visit you sometime. If you change your mind, you are always welcome to live with me. Here is clean clothes and some food for a few days."

Hilde got up and left the house. The tall woman dressed in a tight blue linen cotehardie beneath her gray cape proceeded to the gate. She glanced one more time over her shoulder, waited for a few seconds, covered her hair with a tailed hood, and closed the gate behind her. A bunch of crows got scared with the presence of life around the abandoned place and flew up, releasing sounds of confusion.

Tia woke up from a stupor and looked around, hoping to see the startled flock of crows. No. It was just one crow with half-open eyes, sitting on the closest pine tree and probably sleeping.

The thick fog that was keeping the lake invisible a few seconds ago had left without a trace. The sun was throwing its brightness across the sky and everything beneath.

"Nessie, get the stick!" The man in the beige jacket was playing with his dog. Chana stood aside, ready for the possible invasion into the game. It was clear to her that any competition with that young and full-of-energy German shepherd would have led straight to failure. All she could do was the imitation of jumping and running, minimized by ten.

"Chana!" It was time to go home, but the "oldy goldie" hadn't had a chance to catch that forbidden stick. She looked at Tia, tilting her head like all dogs do, and glanced back to the action scene. How about it! The very stick was heading in Chana's direction. All she had to do was make a slight jump and catch it. And she did! With a triumph and the trophy in her teeth, Chana stormed out toward the calling girl. A second later, she was disappointed with the realization that nobody was chasing her to take away the catch. The young challenger didn't even notice Chana's victory and was busy playing with his owner.

"Good Chana." Tia patted the dog's head and neck with both hands. "I love you no matter what. Let's go home."

The young woman and her dog slowly walked toward the parking area of the Wild Nature Park. The dog was barely moving its paws, being exhausted with excessive physical exercise. The girl was still under the influence of her dream that sent her away through the centuries, guarded by the mysterious fog. Both needed good closure on the happening in the park.

"Rowena…"

Tia stopped and looked around, trying to find who said that.

"I came here to talk to you. It is very important. Please…"

Tia turned in the same direction she was looking a second ago and eye-bumped with the Beige Jacket. He was standing right behind her and holding his dog on a leash. Deep inside, Tia got scared a little, but momentarily camouflaged the unwanted emotion with a comment.

"I thought your dog's name was Intuitiveness." She forced out a smile.

"Nessie is the nickname." The stranger petted the German shepherd puppy.

Tia's fright turned into curiosity. "Your dog has a nickname as well? It seems like she is very special to you."

"No. Nothing special. Just a good companion." He smiled.

"What about the other name you've just said? Let me guess…" Tia sarcastically put the guessing expression on her face. She looked side up with squinted eyes as if she was trying to find the answer. "Was it your dog's middle name?" She stopped acting and gave a piercing look to the stranger. Right away she heard the man's voice in her head: "Rowena was the little girl's name. She lived in Norway in the seventeenth century."

For some reason, Tia continued the conversation without words or any signs of discomfort as she was doing it all the time. Her stare into the man's eyes became softer. "How do you know all this?" She stepped back and measured him up and down with a curious look. "There is something familiar about you. Do I know you somehow?"

"Of course you do. Everyone on this planet knows each other. All you need to do is remember. If I give you a few names of mine, they won't mean anything until you recall."

"Recall what?"

"Recall all of your other existences in the past centuries."

The man's voice wasn't showing any turbulence or other possible signs of lying. Should Tia believe or leave? "Well, there is a presence of telekinetic communication. What can be weirder than that? I should take this event for my consideration and see where it leads. I gotta sit down...Yes, that will do..." Tia sat on a bench.

"I am Junntie, by the way," the stranger sat beside her.

"Tia. I see, you've already known my name." The conversation took its usual Earthy way. "The reason I am still talking to you, Mr. Junntie, is because I have nothing to do right now, and the environment here in the park seems safe to talk to a stranger." Tia diplomatically paused. "And your way of speaking...how should I put it...amuses me." Her discreet tone of voice reliably hid the growing interest toward this person. Tia threw a sideway glance at him.

Junntie seemed like he didn't even hear Tia's last words. He turned his whole body toward her, put one arm up on the bench, and, looking straight into Tia's eyes, said, "Tia, do you believe in the existence of multidimensional worlds?"

"I believe in science. In everything that has been studied and proven. Multidimensional world existence hasn't been scientifically proven yet. Until it happens, I prefer to remain in a neutral zone." Tia playfully side-tilted her head.

Junntie imperturbably continued the conversation. The personality of the mannered and friendly man who has just played with his dog beside the lake has changed unrecognizably. Cold black eyes penetrated

Tia deeper with each word, increasing her attention. "All I can do right now is give you some information that will keep you safe."

Tia remained quiet.

"You have heard that more people are getting affected by something that makes them act differently. I am speaking about the double personality syndrome. Noah Fjusher…he called you Rasara, Nicole. He begged you for forgiveness and tried to protect you from something upcoming…"

Tia's arrogant smile left her face. All she wished in this moment was to memorize each of Junntie's words. *Why do I feel such a comfort and trust toward this stranger?*

"*Do not trust Noah. Trust your own intuition.* Without intuitiveness, no discoveries exist. Intuitiveness is the very first step toward everything new, especially to something you are not able to prove. You just know it exists. When you have reached this state of mind, you stop caring about the world that is still seeking for a scientific explanation to its existence. You just know the truth, and only this matters. I don't have to tell you anything more because sooner or later you'll figure it out on your own. Trust yourself. Use your intuition. Know."

Tia couldn't believe she was accepting all the information without any doubts. *This man is so familiar to me. I know him very well. But… who is he?*

Junntie stopped talking for a moment.

Tia took advantage over this pause and enquired, "Sir, I have never seen you before, and at the same time, I can't fight the feeling that I know you very well. Even the names Rasara and Nicole don't sound strange to me. Do you know anything about it?"

Tia didn't hide her emotions or her eyes from this stranger. She knew their color was changing at the moment she spoke. On the contrary, she wanted Junntie to see them too.

Junntie looked away. If he only could…time…uncertainty… waiting…

"You'll be fine, Tia." he looked in her eyes. He took her hand, kissed it, held it for a moment beside his lips, and put it back on her knees. "You'll do fine. I know that."

Chana's lazy barking brought Tia back from the trance. She looked at Chana, then around. She smiled. "What a beautiful dream! What an unusual name! Junntie…June…Junnie…Junntie."

Tia walked toward her new car with a smile on her face and a tired dog on a leash. The beautiful dream was still occupying her thoughts. Tia didn't see any people around but the magic of the dream. "The answer is on its way. I just need to remember…"

She knew she would.

PART III

Broken

The annoying peekaboo game of clouds and sunlight through the bedroom window forced Noah to open his eyes.

"It's really bright for early morning." Noah looked at the wall clock and immediately sat up on his bed. "Holy crap, it's noon!" He looked around. Something didn't feel right. He tried to stick his feet into the slippers that were usually placed right beside his bed. He couldn't find them. "That's not right…Where did they go?"

An anxiety attack was about to identify its existence with short, fast breathing and cold sweat. Noah wiped his forehead, touched his hair, and froze for a few seconds.

"It's not right…" He tried to touch his hair with the other hand, just to confirm that unwanted sensation—the sensation of dried hair gel. "When did I do my hair? Have I taken a shower already?" He sniffed his armpits, touched his cheeks and chin. "When did I shave? Why am I wearing a bathrobe over my pajamas?"

He started breathing faster, trying to catch as much air as he could. His whole body was shaking, his eyes rolling up. His soul wanted to storm out of his physical body with great pain. Noah was having a seizure.

In a couple of minutes, the pain started leaving Noah, slowly moving toward his head. Both his feet tried to relax under the restless sensation. The needlelike pinching discomfort all over his body slowly faded away. Only his neck remained stiff. The pain concentrated inside

Noah's head. It seemed like the back of his eyelids reflected with agony from his brain that was filled up with electrical impulses and fired all at once with billions of lightning flashes. Noises of cracking and clinking began to dominate over the painful dance of the metallic storm.

After a few more seconds, the thick white sound irrevocably swallowed them. All pain and clatter were gone. Only a hiss…a loud and steady hiss. "Lis-s-s-sten to me, my dear Noah…" The hiss turned into words.

Noah immediately recognized a voice of the angel from his dream. A pleasant smile imprinted on his face, and weightlessness absorbed into Noah's whole body.

The angel's features were appearing slowly on the back of his eyelids.

"I love you, Noah…I have always loved you…"

Ripples stirred the reflection and turned it into a different vision.

Noah screamed in happiness. "Rasara! I knew…I knew you loved me! I missed you so much…He…he gave me a chance to prove my love to you. Nicole…Tia…" Tears of happiness rolled out of Noah's closed eyes.

The voice became very clear. "Kondrat, if you want me back, you have to listen to each of my words and do everything I say."

"Anything for you, my Rasara…"

"Soon you are going to wake up. Act without mentioning my name or any names you've recalled. I will guide you toward victory. I am yours. Tia will be yours. I am possessing you with the memory of all your lives through the centuries. Say only what I want you to say. From now on, I reside in your mind. Do you accept me?"

"Yes, my Rasara. I accept you completely."

"So it has begun. Wake up now!"

The vision vanished as well as all physical and mental discomfort.

Noah opened his eyes, jumped into the trouble-seeking slippers, and opened a two-door closet. "What garbage." He pulled out a black T-shirt and sweatpants from the closet and left his room.

Two of Noah's roommates and two staff were having lunch at the kitchen table when Noah approached the fridge.

"Good morning, Noah. Did you have a good rest?" Lucie looked at Noah with a friendly smile and continued to assist one of the group-home residents with the lunch ritual. "Violet and Betty want you to sit beside them and try some pizza. Don't you, ladies?"

Two pleasant women in their seventies looked at their new roommate. Violet touched her dandelion hair with the same hand she was holding a spoon and, showing her perfect dentures, said, "I've just had my hair done. Do you like it? You are a handsome young man. Sit beside me. Have some pizza." She paused from eating and gave a chance for Lucie to wipe her mouth with a bib.

"Yes…beside me…hair done…young man…pizza…" Like an echo, Betty repeated her roommate's words. She didn't look at Noah. Probably didn't really care. The piece of pizza she was having was more important right now than the welcoming speech. And why even bother? Anyway, she would have plenty of time to talk with Noah. He lived here now.

Noah made himself a cup of coffee and approached everyone at the kitchen table. "I know you." He looked at Lucie. "I thought you work only at night." Noah leaned back onto the kitchen island, crossed his legs, and put one hand in the pocket of his sweatpants. "This coffee is very good. Is it Arabic?" He sniffed it and took a sip with his eyes closed.

Lucie and Trista looked at each other. Noah acted differently today. How different? More as a person without mental disabilities. They kept observing him.

Noah took a few more enjoyable sips. A blush of a very strong red color spread over his face. It was hard to believe that such a pale-skinned person like Noah could produce even a touch of the hue.

Trista carefully put a napkin on the table, preparing for the possibility of CPR, and freed one leg from under the table. She was ready to fight for Noah's life. Lucie agreeably looked at Trista and touched the key on her wristband for the safe with locked medications.

Noah's face looked like a big strawberry with yellow leaves on top. A pleasant smile on his face, savoring the coffee, correctly identified that he was alright. Trista and Lucie held their position. Suddenly, Noah opened his eyes. The sweet smile disappeared from his face. He looked at Lucie with strong confidence and said, "It's Lucie, right? I would like to go shopping for new clothes today. Can you drive me to the mall after lunch?" Noah's red eyes became even redder on the blushing skin. If it wasn't for the two eye whites around the irises, his entire face would look like a red velvet cake. "I am ready to go now. Hurry up! I'll be in the living room." Noah finished his coffee, put the empty cup in the dishwasher, and left the kitchen.

Lucie and Trista looked at each other in confusion. For a few seconds, they remained speechless, without an ability to process any information.

Violet's vocal interference immediately put everyone back in their places. "I need to go shopping too. My clothes are too old. Can you drive me to the mall?" She looked at her bib and touched it with a spoon, leaving traces of food on it. "And it is dirty. I definitely need a new blouse…a red one please. Betty, do you want to go shopping with me? I'm sure you do."

A spoon full of food in Lucie's hand strategically interrupted Violet's monotonous speech and immediately redirected her attention back to eating.

Lucie got up from the table, giving Violet full control over her food, and left for the living room.

Noah was sorting out his footwear in the front-door closet. Piles of shoes, runners, boots, and sandals were sticking their parts out of three tightened-up garbage bags. He barely noticed Lucie standing beside a couch and observing him.

"All this has to go." Noah straightened up his back, grabbed the bags, and put them outside, leaving the door open. "Are you ready to go? We have to visit lots of stores." He pulled his coat down from a hanger.

"Noah, are you sure that all your footwear is in bad condition? I've seen them. You have very good shoes." Lucie pointed to the bags.

"They might look good, but they're already out of fashion as well as all my clothing." Noah squinted at Lucie. "You can fool the old ladies in the kitchen, not me. So get your car keys. Hurry up!" He was already one foot out of the door.

"Noah, I want to talk to you." Lucie's voice made Noah stop and turn around. "Do you have enough money to renovate all your clothing?"

"I thought it was your responsibility to provide me with anything I need in this group home. Aren't you?" It wasn't hard for Noah to stand tall and look down at the very short Lucie.

Noah's statement did confuse Lucie. She had never worked with such an individual. For a moment, she had a thought that he might be taking advantage of being placed in a group home. *What if Noah doesn't have mental disabilities but is pretending to? What if he looks for the easiest way of living?*

She decided to keep the conversation simple with no emotions attached. "Yes, Noah. I am responsible for your well-being, but it doesn't mean that your wish is my command. Our agency provides basic needs to people and helps them to improve their lives by supporting their health and wellness, social life, and other aspects of their lives. If you want to buy expensive things, you need to work because the provided budget won't cover such a huge spending. If you wish to request a certain amount of money for clothing, please talk to Paulina. She will contact your mom and talk over your requests.

Your mother is your guardian, and she is responsible for all your extra spending. I am just helping you with the knowledge of living here."

Lucie noticed a sign of hesitation in Noah's eyes and his slouching posture. He looked like he was trying to figure out what was going on here. It gave her some confidence. According to the numerous trainings on the proactive approach to the individuals in service, Lucie made a checkmark to herself. *The first step is done. He is doubting his plan. Now I have to alternate the situation and redirect Noah onto a new plan.*

"If you want, we can go to look for new clothing and check the prices. Tomorrow you can talk to Paulina about the exact amount of money you would request. What do you think, Noah?"

Noah remained quiet, eyes down. I'm going for a walk in the neighborhood," he mumbled without looking at Lucie and was about to shut the door behind him when he paused. He turned around. "Where's Tia?"

"She took a couple of weeks off. Until then, Trista and I will be your company, Noah. With your help, we'll do just fine." Lucie smiled. She had identified the breaking point of the behavior escalation. She did it! She was able to prevent Noah from going through the entire five phases of the assault cycle. Still, the trigger of Noah's behavior wasn't clear for her. Lucie knew that the answer would come along later. She has just started getting to know Noah, and it wasn't easy for him either to accept such a big change in his life.

Lucie locked up the front door behind Noah and returned to the kitchen. Trista, Violet, and Betty had just finished lunch and were enjoying coffee over their nice conversation.

"I hope God gives us all the strength we need till Tia is back." Lucie poured coffee in a mug and joined the company.

Violet immediately spoke her mind. "God will help. He loves everyone. He loves you…He loves me…He loves Betty…He loves Noah…"

"God…Help…Love…Betty…Noah…Everyone…" Betty agreed as well.

Four ladies were sitting at the kitchen table. Two of them had a conversation by speaking to each other at the same time. The other two held the same thoughts without speaking or looking at each other. And none of them felt a slight distraction in this perfect chaos of daily life. Get that, universal balance!

An unusually dressed man was walking in the neighborhood. A long black coat was able to hide his short legs and touched the built-in heels of his military boots with each step he made. A black tie flawlessly laid on the collar of his red shirt around his thin neck. Brushed-back straight yellow hair sealed the bald spot on top of his head with a pound of hair gel. Dark sunglasses on a murky day created a mystery of each of his movement.

Almost two weeks had gone since Noah had a conversation with Tia in the kitchen of his new place. The fog of disappointment around residing in a group home started to vanish, showing positive outlines.

Sometimes we have to walk through the long and dark tunnel to finally see the bright light in the end.

Noah knew that this chance had been given to him a long time ago—the chance to fix all his mistakes that kept following him through the centuries. And this time, nobody would put any barricades on the way to his happiness.

Those long walks in the neighborhood helped Noah to realize that the happening was inevitable. Here it is, the only love of all centuries has finally been assigned to him. This life would be the last opportunity for Noah to make a choice: to hold it tight or let go again and die with regrets. The decision has been made—to hold.

With a confident, tall-shoe-walk, stone-cold, never-blink slow motion, Noah was making his daily rounds in the neighborhood. Not a single change could escape out of his cool sunglasses' eagle gaze. Noah was running in his head all possible scenarios on how to seduce Tia. Two more days, and he will see her again. And then what? Probably, he will take her to a movie or park. Okay, which park? Right...After lunch Noah, had to ask Trista to drive him to the best park of Gray Stone. He would make himself prepared for the upcoming date. *Well, Noah...You are a genius!*

A beginning is always seeking for an end. What is in between? A desire. Desire to get what is being wanted the most in that journey. A desire is the perpetually generated energy of all times. It kills or brings back to life. Seduces incredibly organized individuals for paradoxically irrational deeds. Leads losers toward victory. A desire rushes in front of us, time to time looking back with its charming smile that makes us speed up again. A few more steps, and we are there! The long-awaited goal is almost reached. The leading runner stops and turns his face to us. The face of ...despair. When did it happen? What did we miss? Our plan was undeniable. Too late. The end of life.

Trista pulled over to the parking lot. "Here it is. The most beautiful park of Gray Stone. Do you want me to take a walk with you?"

"No thanks. No assistance needed." With a sarcastic smile, Noah got out of the car and turned his face to the sun. "Nothing can be done over right working of the sun but wait it out..." His lips pressed against one another, trying to create a decent smile.

Noah took off his sunglasses while keeping his eyes closed. He inhaled the fresh air and looked around. "It's perfect! We'll come here for a picnic."

He spotted a few picnic tables with attached wooden benches. He walked toward the lake. "Wonderful! My plan works out by itself. We'll take a walk to the lake and stop right here, on the lake deck." He touched the wooden handrails and looked down to the waters. "I can pull out some gibberish about a beauty of the lake. Girls love this stuff. She will give me an admiring look. I'll take her hand and walk her to that bench…" Noah rushed to the bench right beside the water. "We'll take a seat and look into each other's eyes." He put his sunglasses back on and pushed his body forward, visualizing Tia beside him. A sweet smile, this time a real one, spread all over his face. "What a poetic moment…I can see a kiss coming…"

For a few seconds, Noah got swept off his feet and into the fantasy world. He even heard Tia's voice, saying, for some reason, "I have never seen you before and, at the same time, I can't fight the feeling that I knew you very well…"

"Ah…Even in my fantasy, she speaks to me, I can hear her. What a blessing…"

Right after that, he heard another voice, the voice of the angel: "Open your eyes, Noah. This is not a dream. Look!"

Weird electricity ran through his body, leaving goose bumps everywhere. Noah opened his eyes. Fifty meters away, on the bench under the old pine tree, he saw Tia and a man sitting together. Noah could see her face very well, but barely heard their conversation. Tia looked serious. The man beside her was wearing a beige jacket. Noah was able to see only his back and right side of his face. Now the man was talking. What was he doing? He took Tia's hand…lifted it to his mouth…and… *How dare he! He is kissing Tia's hand! Who is this man?*

Now Tia was talking to him. She stopped, and they sit quietly for a minute. The man started to get up. *I can see his face…It's…I know him! Junntie! What is he doing here? Why is he speaking to Tia?*

Outraged, Noah jumped from the bench and made a step forward.

"Stop! Be smart. He is not your target. It is Tia who is in danger because of him…" The voice of the angel became stronger, louder. "The plan you are working on has a good start. The rest of it will be on my command. You are going to tell Tia how dangerous Junntie is. Now, listen and remember…"

A man in a long black jacket and dark glasses was sitting on the bench right beside the lake. He clung to the back of the bench with one hand and pounded his knee with the clenched fist of the other hand. It looked like the man was ready to get up and run or jump or fight or…involve himself in any possible and impossible action. His dark sunglasses were hiding the piercing gaze of his flaming eyes, and the face was red from the blood pumping under his skin. Thank God it wasn't wintertime, otherwise his excessive breathing would form sharp arrows of frozen mist. Why was he so freakishly furious? What was he looking at? It is so nice and quiet in the Wild Nature Park today. Kids are playing with each other…couples are walking beside the lake…a lonely girl is sitting on the bench and looking at ducks…

She is leaving now.

The man turned his head into the same direction, following the girl. That's it! He was spying on her! Where else could you see anything like that? Only in movies and…in one of the best parks of Gray Stone!

The Spread

"An unknown epidemic disease has been detected globally. It is affecting people who have been diagnosed with acquired mental disabilities due to posttraumatic stress and brain or head injuries. All of them have the same pattern in the symptoms' development such as trying to save their family members, close friends, even ex-lovers from some sort of upcoming danger. The affected individuals claim the fact of recalling their previous lives and all the names they have had in the past..."

The news on TV has totally occupied Marsha's attention. She didn't even notice her daughter's arrival.

"They call people by different names, very unusual names, and act very protective and possessive toward them, telling everyone that they have been identified as 'the chosen ones,' and only they would know how to deal with the upcoming danger, so the others have to listen to them and do exactly what they say."

Marsha sensed Tia's presence and, without looking at her, pointed to sit down and watch the news.

"I am pleased to introduce our special guest today, Dr. Ben Flegman, the lead researcher of the International Association of Medics Around the Globe."

"Thank you, Stacy, for inviting me. In our research center, we have one hundred patients diagnosed with Recolla disease. The nature of this illness remains unknown. It isn't a virus, so it is not contagious. As you said, this illness affects people who recently experienced head

injury. It could be a concussion, posttraumatic experience, acquired brain injury...anything that could relate to a mental disorder. Our research shows that Recolla patients can be misdiagnosed with schizophrenia in its early stages of development. In Recolla patients, auditory hallucination dominates over illusory manifestation. They hear voices from the past that dictate them to protect their loved ones by hurting others. These people become socially active, very protective, manipulative..."

"I might know someone with similar symptoms. Mom, do you want some tea?" Tia got up and left for the kitchen.

Marsha turned the TV off and followed her daughter. "What if we have tea in the backyard? Let's enjoy the beauty of the fall. Who knows, it might start snowing tomorrow."

Marsha grabbed a big tray with a tea set. Mother and daughter sat under the only apple tree in the backyard and, in silence, enjoyed their tea with honeycombs. They both had good excuses for avoiding the news on TV. Marsha was savoring the perfection of that quiet evening with the most loving creation of her existence. Why not? This heavenly moment can be destroyed at any second by anything.

Tia's thoughts were with the mystical stranger in the twilight of the centuries, and she didn't want to let them away. And so it was.

Aromas of jasmine tea and honeycombs complimented the reality of nonverbal conversation of two people under an apple tree.

"Welcome back, Tia. I hope you've had a good time off. When's your school starting?"

"Thanks, Paulina. It's been on for a week already. This fall I've decided to contribute more time into my job. Things are working out perfectly. On four wheels I can move faster, so no problems in this case."

A usual morning in the group home promised a usual day. Vocal and electronic communication have turned on a flawless mechanism of the daily routine.

"I see many interesting details in Noah's observation notes. It seems like we're not gonna be bored here anymore." Tia was browsing through the individuals' observation notes on a laptop. "He is skipping the honeymoon period, straight to the action. Do you think we could help him to find a job?" Tia glanced at Paulina.

"Yes, he acts more like a person without mental disabilities. We've all had the provocative thoughts that Noah didn't belong in the agency. Well…he had a seizure a couple of weeks ago."

"Paulina, have you heard about the Recolla illness? It was on TV yesterday. According to the symptoms, warning, calling people by different names, being protective…Noah has already shown all of those in the very first morning of staying with us."

"Agreed." Paulina paused and looked at Tia. "Let's not rush with any conclusion. We'll proceed with the usual routine of a good observation, communication, cooperation…What are your plans with Noah today?" Paulina hid half of her beautiful eyes under a set of huge eyelashes while refocusing on her laptop.

"I am planning to bond with Noah by giving him a couple of options for outings. Would be nice to hear if he has his own suggestions. Just usual stuff that people usually do to know each other. When is he arriving?"

"Right after lunch."

"Perfect."

Video call beeps interrupted the perfect business routine in the residence. Paulina leveled her laptop to take the call and pressed the Answer button. "Hello…"

Big nostrils behind a massive chin splashed over the computer screen. "Good morning, Paulina. How are you doing?"

"Good morning…" Paulina peered into the image, trying to

recognize the caller. "Sorry, I can't see you clearly... Something is wrong with my camera... I guess..." She was trying to be polite.

"Pull the phone back, Mom."

Paulina recognized Noah's voice carried from the other side of the communication device and figured out whose chin-nostrils set was flopping around her computer. With a smile, she continued the conversation. "Nelly, is this you?"

"Yes!" The face features tried to fit into the screen of Nelly's shaking cellphone. "I am going to bring Noah in half an hour. What time are you guys having lunch?"

"Usual time, noon." Static interrupted the video. "Nelly, do you hear me? I've lost the visual as well." Paulina tried to fix it, pressing buttons. Broken words and videos were popping through the static. Paulina recognized Noah's features, but his voice sounded different, more like wheezy weak.

"Tia, meet me in the Wild Nature Park. We will have lunch there. I'll get the food."

The connection broke off right after this message. Suddenly, the power blackout highlighted the screaming disappearance of those unnoticeable noises that have been implemented by technology into humans' lives. Undistinguished-before sounds of refrigerator, radio, air conditioner, and coffeemaker became silently heard.

Both ladies patiently waited, staring into the black screen of the computer. The power went on again. Deep breath...and work continues.

"Well, Noah has chosen an outing without looking at my options. Good for him." Tia checked the time and proceeded with the outlines of the afternoon with Noah.

The sky was about to spread its rainy mood when Tia arrived in the park to meet with Noah. Families with children were still occupying picnic tables beside the lake. Parents from time to time were glancing at the sky and then at the playing children, giving them a good chance to use up all the energy before taking them home. Single couples and teenagers gathered together hurried with tossing lunch leftovers back into containers and ziplock bags. Half of the parking lot was already empty.

Tia walked toward the lake, looking for Noah's table, but couldn't find it. Assuming that Noah had changed his mind and gone to the residence, Tia approached the water deck. She looked down into the waters, remembering the magical day with that stranger. Cold gray splashes were leaving muddy traces on the wooden poles above the water. Tia shivered a bit, sensing the upcoming cold.

"You're freezing."

Something fluffy was laid on her shoulders down to the back and down to her knees. Tia quickly turned around and bumped face-to-face with Noah.

"Come on, you must be hungry. I got hot coffee in a thermos." Noah tried to wrap a blanket around Tia and smiled.

"Noah…what are you doing? Stop! Stop for goodness' sake!" Tia pulled the blanket off and stuck it back into Noah's hands. "No blankets! Hands to yourself, Mr. Fjusher!" She stepped back and tried to handle the situation with a couple of deep breaths and looked a bit surprisingly at Noah. She realized that a couple of seconds needed to be used without vocalizing any words because of her stupid heartbeats. Those few seconds were enough to catch her breath and notice some difference in Noah's appearance.

For half a second, Tia doubted that it was Noah right beside her. The other half of a second, her brain used on processing tons of information that was supposed to fit the situation. *I am a tall girl, but when I turned around, Noah's eyes were on the same level with mine. He is short. He couldn't reach the normal height of a cupboard to get a coffee mug. Am I short? And what the hell is he wearing? Long black coat…military boots? Maybe some adjustments inside those boots made him taller? Okay, that is the only explanation. He wants to impress me. I am alright now.*

Tia stepped back and one more time took a quick look at Noah.

"Good afternoon, Noah. It's very nice to see you again, and thank you for the blanket. It was very thoughtful of you, but unnecessary." Tia kept the conversation on a business level.

"I am sorry, Tia. I scared you. The weather is changing. Looks like a storm is coming. I got everything for lunch in the main gazebo. Are you hungry?" Noah pointed to the partially walled gazebo. "It is pretty safe in there." He turned around and walked toward the gazebo.

Tia followed him, observing Noah from behind. *Definitely, there's something different about him. The way he walks...wider steps, no rubbing sound of x-shaped legs...his posture...tall, straight. Hair... not very yellow, more like with brownish highlights. Ha, he was really working on the appearance for the past two weeks! Well...everyone has the right to express themselves. I should give him a compliment.*

By the time Tia and Noah got into the gazebo, the gigantic forces in the sky began their battle. The blades of lightning illuminated hot spots of numerous clashes. Inevitable thunders a distance away pinpointed the location of the action, creating chaotic tremors on the lake. The nature attentively waited for the big finale of the battle— rain.

French bread sandwiches and bananas were sticking out from a basket covered with cloth and seductively waited for its guests in the middle of the gazebo's picnic table. Not benches but two curvy plastic chairs with cushions looked weirdly cozy under a string of lights on the roof.

"I've never noticed how beautiful this gazebo was. Did you bring the cushions?" Tia looked at all the fancy stuff and suspected that Noah had a plan. *No assumptions but professional cautiousness—that was Tia's plan.* She looked straight into Noah's eyes. "Noah, your idea of lunch out was wonderful. Do you think it is a good time for lunch right now? Those lights are beautiful but not safe. Do you know what happens when electricity gets in contact with water? Short circuit can be extremely dangerous."

Noah moved his chair closer to Tia, and with a confidence of the man who knew exactly what he was doing, he started to serve sandwiches on plastic plates. Keeping himself busy, he started a conversation. "My dear Tia, I doubt that we'll see any rain today. It's Alberta. The weather here is unpredictable. Usually, it works in the opposite way. The action comes from the least expected directions. And as a proof of the world's best accuracy in my weather prediction, I am asking you to have lunch with me regardless of whatever goes on outside of this shelter." Noah turned to Tia with a sandwich and a banana on a plate. He placed it in front of her, touching a chair with an invitation to take a seat. "You are safe here."

Tia moved away a cozy cushion from the chair and sat down.

Noah sat as well. A satisfied smile was on his face. "Shall we start with sandwiches?" He took a bite, twisting the sandwich with his teeth and leaving traces of meat on the table.

For a moment Tia thought that she saw a red spark in Noah's eyes. *Must be another lightning reflection. Everything around him feels very strange today: the way he spoke, moved, sounded, looked...*

Darkness thickened around the lake, erasing its outlines. Only the fire streaks from out of nowhere subconsciously reminded her about the existence of the lake.

"Here is some sauce, Rowena. It goes well with the veal." Olaf unwrapped the last piece of the food his mom packed for Rowena and sat beside her. "You need to eat more. Look how skinny you are."

"I can't." Rowena gave Olaf a dramatic look with fake sadness in her eyes. Then she fixed her face with a smile and showed a strange spark in her eye. "There are no mirrors in this house."

They both started laughing.

"Thank you, Olaf. I am not hungry right now. I'll eat it later." Rowena moved the plate away and looked at Olaf with the softest and sweetest smile. She wasn't sure if she liked this boy, but there was something about him she didn't want to resist.

Eight years had gone since Rowena and Olaf became friends. Every other day or two, he and Hilde visited Rowena. Sometimes Hilde was busy with the other five children and sent Olaf with a basket of food and clean clothes to Rowena.

"Mom made a new dress for you out of the old ones. Can you try it on? Just to make sure it fits alright." Olaf handed over a folded package to Rowena.

She grabbed the package with excitement and disappeared behind a hung sheet. A minute after, she came out wearing a gown. "What do you think?" She slowly turned around, holding her arms up.

Olaf couldn't believe his eyes. One minute was enough to transform a child into a beautiful young woman. Maybe it was the dress? That one was different from Rowena's usual baggy clothes. It didn't have a tight collar, but an opened curve cut that gently touched her shoulders, showing collarbones in front and straight black hair on the back.

Rowena's movements suddenly awakened the sunlight that was sitting on the floor right beside her feet. Accidentally, she stepped on it and became visible. Golden splash of light jumped on her very tight waist and began to climb on the endless row of buttons next to her breasts that just started to form. Another movement, and the light came alive along the length of the gray linen around her hips and legs.

"Do you like it?" Rowena repeated her question and stopped twirling. "Do you think it's a little tight?" She touched one of a million buttons on the waistline and gave them a puzzled look.

"No…" Olaf swallowed the end of his response. "It looks alright." Suddenly, he started putting all the wrapping papers and empty dishes back into the basket and promised Rowena to visit her in a couple of days. Then he left without even glancing at her.

"What did I do?" Rowena, with a sign of confusion, watched Olaf leave. "Hmm…He didn't like the dress? It sits alright." She tried to look at it over her shoulders, feeling it with her hands. "I can't see anything. I need a mirror." She stopped. A brilliant idea brought a smile on her face. "A waterfall!"

Rowena stuck all the food that Olaf brought her into a basket and left the house.

Here it was, the secret path across the wildflower meadows that only Rowena knew. Hurry, hurry! "Move away, grasshoppers and butterflies! I am in a hurry!" Couple of streams over there, in the woods…Tap-tap-tap…jump-jump…from a rock onto another. "Sunlight, are you trying to blind me? It's better if you don't!" Almost there! Crossing the bridge very carefully…It is incredibly old; nobody uses it anymore. And here it is—a waterfall with waters so clear and smooth, just like a glass or perhaps…a mirror.

Rowena put the basket down and made a few steps across the bridge toward the wall of water. She turned her face and body toward it. A tall, slender young woman in a tight dress looked at her from the other side of the living mirror. Long black hair, scattered over her shoulders, reflected the brightness of the sun in the water.

"Is this me?" Rowena tilted her head a little, keeping an eye on the reflection. She still couldn't believe what she was seeing. She moved both her arms up and down. "It *is* me…I am beautiful!"

Rowena stood a few more minutes like that, staring at the reflection. Suddenly, she began to laugh. "He liked the dress! He liked me in the dress! Hahahaha! He was afraid to admit it!"

Rowena crossed the old bridge and emptied the basket. "Here, birds and forest creatures! I brought something for you in return to keep my little secret." She left the food and slowly danced away back home with the decision that tomorrow, she would visit Hilde and give her a huge bouquet of wildflowers, but she will do it right after

Hilde's family dinner. That way, nobody would know that the last meal Rowena had was eight years ago, the day before her mother died.

"Thank you, Noah. The sandwiches look good. You go ahead and eat." Tia graciously refused to participate in this weird feast, doing her best in keeping the dialogue professional.

For a few moments, pitch darkness swept everything around. There were no visible outlines of anything outside of the gazebo but dark space. A strong wind was whipping the roof of the gazebo with hundreds of broken branches, but not even a single piece of them got inside. The storm became stronger.

"What the hell..." Tia looked around. All objects inside the gazebo remained motionless; even the string of light bulbs stretched from corner to corner didn't make a slight swing. All empty paper wrappers and napkins on the table rested in peace. Tia got up and tried to stick her arm through the darkness outside the gazebo to feel the wind.

"No!!" Noah pulled her back inside, and Tia fell in her chair.

She looked at him indignantly.

"Tia, you have to listen to me and do what I tell you to do. Only then, you'll be safe. I've told you that you were in danger. This is only the beginning, but with me you are safe…just like in this gazebo. All you need to do is to accept my protection."

Tia tried to pull her hand out of Noah's. No success. He was holding it very tightly and was staring into her eyes. His usual reddish irises became dark red and spread all over the surface of his eyes.

"What's going on? There should be some explanation…" For a moment, Tia closed her eyes and forced herself to take a few deep breaths. Do not trust Noah. You'll do just fine…Trust your intuition… The broken phrases of the conversation with a stranger in the park were drilling her subconsciousness.

Of course! It is a hypnosis! My head injury hasn't healed yet. Just relax, breathe...I am dreaming. This is a picnic with an individual, a usual workday. After one more breath, she opened her eyes and looked at the usual fall day outside of the gazebo. There was no sign of darkness or the storm, just cheerful birds singing and trees waving.

Noah was almost finished with his sandwich. Napkins and food wrappers were thrown down on the floor by the slight breeze inside the gazebo.

Tia looked up. Strings of dry flowers tightened from corner to corner and made the place vibe more with the fall scenery. There were no traces of the fancy light bulbs or plastic-cushioned chairs. Two wooden benches kept the steady table in the middle.

"I wanna go home." Noah got up from the bench. Crumbs scattered down onto his knees as he got up. "I am too tired, I wanna have a nap." The usual blank expression in Noah's eyes took over the wild look of that unbelievable confidence he had a moment ago. Long sides of his black coat were touching the grass with every step of his heavy slouching walk. Slowly, he headed toward the parking lot.

Tia sat for a minute, keeping an eye on the exhausted departure of Noah, and tried to evaluate the situation.

Pieces of irrelevant hypothesis, multiplied by the work of billion brain cells, ignited the energy flow.

I'll just keep it easy for now. My head injury overstimulated a shift in the balance of normal brain function, which led to hallucinations, or I became a victim of my own hypnosis based on the media news and all the extraordinary events that have occurred in the past three weeks. I hope it's not the early symptoms of psychosis. I need to get more information on the balance of visual bottom-up and top-down processing in the brain. It's better if I stop thinking right now. The answer will come to me later...

Tia looked at the bright sky, inhaled the aromas of the autumn air, and with a smile, she cast away any evil from the gazebo of her thoughts making a brave step into the beautiful reality.

Self-Seeker

Scattered in pieces throughout the centuries, the human soul clutches at any straws on its way, trying to reconnect with the lost halves. In agony of the endless search, it doesn't realize that the rescuing straw could be turned into a deadly blade, split the last piece, and cast it away into oblivion. Thrown around everywhere in nowhere, the human soul can't be involved in the creative process. What are you, human soul? Are you a creator or destroyer? The truth opens up when the soul learns how to accept itself. In order to be able to do so, it has to reconnect all the missing pieces and become a whole one…

Paulina's nose froze in the transition zone between two doors: one, from the basement, which was opened in a casual way, and the other one from Noah's bedroom, which was shut in a meaningful way. Paulina's nose emitted an "achoo!" sound, which was the sign of the successfully accomplished mission of the hallway's airflow.

"Someone is not really happy," she said, entering the kitchen from the basement hallway. "What is going on?" She pinned Tia with an icy gaze.

"Noah's picnic didn't go along with his plans." Tia opened her laptop, pretending to be busy with the residents' observation notes and keeping her eyes out of sight. She knew how to melt the frost of a superior's uncertainty by addressing casually the unpleasant events. It was clear that the detailed report of the outing with Noah could create a confusion for everyone in the agency with the obvious outcome Tia was being transferred to a different group home, which would keep Noah out of the "bad staff" influence. If this happened, she would not be able to investigate the phenomenon of Noah's illness and, who knows, maybe the entire Recolla disease.

According to the recent events, it was obvious that Tia became a part of this phenomenon, and she would not allow the mystery to disappear without a scientific investigation. So Tia decided to report the truth that everyone could handle and keep her consciousness clean.

"Noah didn't have a chance to enjoy his lunch. All the hotdog buns and French fries he nicely placed on the table were smitten by the wind. He was able to catch one bun, so he ate it. As soon as he was done with the lunch, he lost all interest in the picnic, got tired, and requested to go home." Tia talked calmly to Paulina without looking at her and typing the report about her outing with Noah. She was just doing her everyday work while Paulina was doing hers.

"Poor guy...he sounded very upset. I heard how he shut the bedroom door." Paulina released the ice pins that never reached their target and moved closer to Tia. "Do you think Noah is suffering from Recolla?" In a second, the iced suspicion turned into the warmest streams of a "by the way" chat. "Why do you think he calls you Rasara, Nicole?" A pair of huge green eyes craved for some answers. "I mentioned it to his mother. She told me that Noah was in love with a woman once. She didn't remember her name. That time, Nelly couldn't accept this change and tried to protect her son from any kind of mistakes young people usually make when in a relationship. So he listened to her and stopped seeing that girl. Very soon, he became secluded and spent all the time with his mother. Nelly said that it was the happiest time of their life together.

"One day, they went to their family friends' party. Noah got close to Nelly's old classmate's son, and they became good friends. Nelly was very happy for Noah because he started to go out again, socializing with people. He completely forgot about his former girlfriend and spent a lot of time with Patrick. Two months later, Noah invited his mother to a restaurant to meet with Patrick's parents and announced that he and Patrick were engaged. This news hit Nelly badly, and she ended up in the hospital with a heart attack. Noah got scarred with the idea of losing his mother. He stayed with her in the hospital day and night. After Nelly was released, Noah promised to her to break up with his boyfriend and never get involved in any relationship with men or women.

"Later, he found out that Patrick died, hanging himself. Noah became ill because of it. Depression was hard on him. He started hallucinating, talking with invisibles. A month ago, Nelly came home from work and found Noah attempting suicide. When Nelly cut the rope and released Noah, he snatched the knife out of her hands and stabbed her shoulders, screaming, 'It's your fault! Leave me alone! I wanna die!' He ran away.

"Next day, the police found him sleeping on a thrown-out mattress. Nelly didn't report the physical abuse, but only a missing person. Then she decided to put Noah in a group home, giving him all he wanted: independence with twenty-four-seven assistance. She said that this decision would work in favor of both: Noah would start his life as an adult apart from her, and she would get peace of mind knowing that Noah would never be alone."

Paulina stopped talking, closed her eyes, and tipped back her head. She tried to reverse the stubborn tears and save her perfect makeup.

Tia put her laptop away and left for the kitchen to get a glass of water for Paulina, giving her some time to suppress the unwanted emotions. She knew that the residential supervisor didn't want anybody to see her crying because "it wasn't in the job description." Paulina would rather give a shoulder to cry on to anyone in the group home but herself.

Surprise, surprise, but even a very strong person needs to feel weak sometimes. Today was the day when Paulina decided to reveal her love story, which was so similar to Noah's.

Tia listened to her patiently. At first she was bored because the story was so classically pathetic. Ninety percent of all women are victims of their loving hearts. They become neutralized by their "true loves" because the "true loves" were nothing but marionettes in the hands of their own "true loves," whom they obeyed and listened to from the moment they were born.

As the story continued, the more Tia got pulled into the narration. The perfect response in the end was supposed to be Tia's reply according to her heartbroken experience with a man, but she hadn't had one yet. She…didn't…have…it…yet! Not yet! What if she kept it that way? Of course, instead of wasting her valuable time and good health on entertaining some egoistic person and his manipulative mother, she could use it for doing something meaningful for humanity.

I am so lucky…and a little embarrassed of becoming bored in the beginning. This is a good lesson for me: always listen to a storyteller, no matter how boring they are. There will always be a lesson.

Exhausted from being torn in two directions, Noah dropped on his bed, nuzzling into a pillow. "I am a pathetic little guy!" He was crying without making a sound, trying not to attract any witness to his wetness. "There was a perfect chance to impress a girl, and I lost it. What was I thinking when I accepted the angel's help? I don't need any help! I should've listened to my heart instead."

He sat up, looking into nowhere, grabbing the side of his bed with both hands, and swinging his upper body back and forth like on a swing. Suddenly he sat still. "That's enough for today." With a plucky motion, Noah jumped out of the annoying swing into a standing position, made a fist, and bravely wiped his nose. A few minutes after completing the ritual of placing his high-sole military boots and his cool long black coat in the closet, Noah jumped back into his bed and, with a smile of satisfaction, opened his notebook.

Sinking in the sanctuary of his fantasy world, Noah easily recognized the curvy bench in the garden of the palace of the Arbiter, where three people were having a conversation about the power of fate…

Tia: "You can't even place your question that way. I know for sure whom I should fall in love with. I even know when. Obviously, it is not happening right now here at the workplace. And clearly not with you, Noah…"

Haon: "Life is full of surprises. Sometimes your path doesn't go along with your plans. Who do you think oversees those turbulences?"

Noah: "I share Tia's opinion. People themselves are in control of their own lives."

Haon: "My dear friends, you both sound childish to me. You are so young and have no life experience at all. How can you even think about planning your future if you have no knowledge of what might happen tomorrow or the next hour? What if I tell you that in the next ten minutes, a poisonous snake will appear beside your feet, Tia, and bite you? What are your life plans good for then?"

Tia looked around and grabbed Noah's hand with a sign of worry. "There are no snakes around here in your garden. They are all in the woods or beside the waters."

Haon: "There is not a single snake in here. Indeed. They never merely bite anyone unless they notice an upcoming threat out of you. Speaking of you, you don't have to be worried about a snakebite. You will be bitten by your little friend, who is standing right here in front of you. In a couple of years, you will fall in love with him, and as an outcome of every love story, he'll leave you with a broken heart."

Tia: "Hmmm...well, excuse me, sir, but that's highly unlikely. I will not be looking for relationships until my graduation, and then...I'll be preoccupied with building my career and becoming a scientist. It's as clear as the sky above us."

Haon: "No, please excuse me, but that's how it is. By the way, the sky you were talking about isn't clear at all."

Noah and Tia looked up at the sky and replied together, "It is!"

Haon: "Feel the wind? Take a good look at that crow!"

Tia: "Excuse me, there is no wind. And what crow are you talking about?"

Noah: "I got it, Tia, and gladly explain it to you, my dear. The Arbiter of Mazaria feels very exhausted and, perhaps, ill. May I ask you something, sir? Haven't you, by any chance, spent some time in a mental hospital lately?"

Haon: "My dear friend, you should consider some research on schizophrenia. Well, never mind, Noah! A doctor will help you with the understanding of this illness."

Noah: "I haven't introduced myself to you yet. How do you know my name?"

"I know all your names, Kondrat, and it isn't a secret to anyone in Parallels." The Arbiter's voice sounded differently for some reason, different in an anciently familiar way.

Noah looked at Haon with obvious confusion. The scene with the palace garden turned into a scene of Parallels. Instead of the Arbiter of Mazaria, Noah was about to participate in a conversation with Junntie.

"It can't be that..." Noah tried to catch his breath and looked around. "That's it? I am dead now? I haven't even accomplished anything! What was the point of this spin?"

"You tell me, Kondrat." With the soundless waving of his long black coat with glossy white lining, Junntie rose out from the golden chair in

the middle of nowhere, piercing Noah with his all-seeing eyes. "Don't you notice the degradation of your being? The energy spectrum, which dominates in the spirits of humans, is fading away dramatically in you. I am here to warn you, Kondrat. This life-spin might be the last one for you as a human if you don't act quickly and apply certain forces in order to switch the charge back. You repeat the same mistakes in each life and make the same promises to fix them before the next upcoming spin. There is no progress shown but regress, which is not acceptable among Xahrns to be a spirit-guide for humans. I've granted your present life with the chance to fix the biggest mistake of all your existence. It is your call now: to remain with Xahrns or leave into oblivion. You decide!"

Junntie was standing tall, and Noah felt like the High Spirit was expanding in all directions with every sound of his voice. The black coat has spread all over the night sky, hiding the white lining behind its other side. Soon, a pair of silver eyes or, possibly, two bright stars were the only reminder of Junntie's presence in the darkness.

Noah started losing his balance in this uncertainty. He tried to fix his eyes on the rescuing stars. And as usual, some opposite forces immediately took place in this game, or, to Noah, it seemed like they did. Involuntarily, he began seeing something on both sides of his sight...or did he?

"Eye contact, eye contact. That's the only way not to lose myself." The harder he tried to hold the reflection of the stars in his eyes, the more visions became seductively annoying. "I must not...I must not look at them..."

The annoyings became quite insolent with almost leaving Noah's side vision and claiming the central attention right beside the rescuing reflection of the stars. The great anxiety made Noah close his eyes and open them again immediately in order to take a tiny break.

"No! No! No!" The two bright stars disappeared, giving a cosmic freedom to the annoying sidekicks. Noah was seeing them clearly now. They pierced each atom of his structure with myriads of microscopic *eyes, twirling around and through him in the shape of a thousand spirals. With an invisible command, as one, they rushed toward Noah, covered his entire existence, and exploded in all directions with billions of dots, like crows, slicing the darkness with invisible wings and carrying away with them a piece of Noah...*

"Ahh!" Very loud cawing of crows behind the bedroom window woke Noah up. Covered with cold sweat, he turned his head toward the disturbing noise. "It's just a dream..."

He wiped his forehead and looked out the window. A flock of crows cawing loudly circled above the aspen tree. Soaring up and rushing down to the tree, they attempted to attack something. Noah noticed a little kitten between the branches, probably with the stupid idea of hunting around the crow's nest. The poor thing screwed up its mission and tried to escape. He fell on the grass, rolled over a couple of times, and pecked by the chasing monsters, disappeared under the deck of a neighbor's house.

"Oh, buddy, I was in your situation seven minutes ago. You're safe now. Lucky them...They got a number. I would like to see all of this once the tables have turned." Noah redirected his attention to the oval mirror beside the window, looked at his reflection, bending his head up and down, side to side, touching his chin. "No matter how weak or pathetic you are...if you get a number, the victory is yours..."

A sudden idea paralyzed his movements. He stood still in front of the mirror with a hand on his chin. His brain had turned on its magical function of switching the outer and inner perception. Noah was staring at his reflection, but seeing nothing besides the work of his brain.

"A number! I gotta find people like me! In weakness and depression, we'll unite and make others hear our voices!"

Enlightened by the idea, Noah's heart started beating faster, opening a great way for the blood circulation. The brain cells begun their dance in their chaotic impulses, building up hundreds of theories at once.

Noah was smiling. It had been a while since he felt so energetic.

"What should I start with? So many ideas…"

Multiple pictures with different possible results started bumping into each other in his mind, and all of them had a victory in the end.

Overpowered by the thoughts, Noah rushed to his closet to get ready for the promising day and suddenly stood still. His fast breathing got interrupted with the gaps of deep inhales. Cold sweat covered his skin. Disoriented electric storm in the brain created anxiety and a dull headache. Everything around him started to spin, and slowly, Noah slid down to the floor against the back wall. The painful clicking and cracking sounds in his brain started to merge into words.

"Good start, Noah…I've never doubted you…"

This voice…I know this voice…The angel! Rasara! My priceless Rasara!

"You know what to do. Find as many people as you can, Noah. Look into their souls. Let them open their minds to you. The rest is my job. You are a very smart man, Noah. Only you can do it! Show Junntie who is the victor! And as the victor, you will possess the greatest power of the universe, a power of Mighty! And now… begin!"

The Decision Has Been Made

"Fifty-six, fifty-seven…Noah? Are you alright? Fifty-seven seconds."

Noah opened his eyes. Paulina was sitting on the floor beside him, holding a pillow under Noah's head. Lucie knelt from the other side, trying to stick a tablet of lorazepam into Noah's mouth.

"Noah, take the pill please. It will help you to recover after the seizure." Paulina carefully pulled Noah into a sitting position to administer the medication.

Noah accepted the pill.

"Can you stand up? We'll help you to get in bed. Relax now, have a nap."

Paulina and Lucie transferred Noah into his bed and were about to leave the room.

"I don't want to stay in bed. I am alright. Can you help me to take shower and make breakfast please?"

Both ladies turned around and surprisingly looked at Noah. He was sitting on his bed and smiling. Noah's voice and facial expressions were not showing the usual post-seizure disorientation and exhaustion.

Lucie interrogatively glanced at the residential supervisor.

"Are you sure?" Paulina made a step forward, looking into Noah's eyes with a bit of concern.

"Yes, I feel alright. Just a little weakness in my legs." Noah moved his toes and touched his knees. "I don't want to stay alone in my room." The sweetest smile of an innocent child inappropriately distorted a face of that grown man.

"Lucie, please, bring a wheelchair and help Noah with the hygiene and clothing. I have to find extra staff for today." Paulina left the room immediately.

After breakfast, Noah refused the help of a wheelchair and, with Lucie's assistance, walked into the living room where the lady roommates were watching TV.

"How are you, Noah? You feel better?" Violet, with her slightly noticeable hand movement, invited Noah to sit right beside her in the recliner. "I heard, you were ill this morning. You are alright now for sure." The river of Violet's speech flowed around the living room without any obstacles in its way. "Betty and I were worried about you."

"Worried about you…" echoed Betty.

"You are a handsome young man. You are alright now, sitting beside me, smiling…I like your smile. It's pretty," continued Violet.

Lucie sat in a corner and observed the unusual gathering in the living room. *Noah has never accepted the company of these pleasant ladies since the day of residing in here. And look at him now…Right at this moment, he is listening to them with undisguised interest.*

Violet was going on and on for a good half an hour. She was so happy to chat with a new person in the house and could succeed with a few tasks at a time: holding a conversation with Noah and Betty, checking on her perfect manicure, and sometimes, giving a quick peek at the TV. Her monotonous voice worked as a lullaby for Betty, who fell asleep in the first seven minutes of the monologue and kept waking up every time she heard her name.

Lucie asked everyone if they wanted something from the kitchen. Apparently, a dishwasher, which was turned on fifteen minutes ago, had to be checked right away. Everybody in the living room was happy with the way it was. No requests were made. Lucie left.

"Violet, can I ask you something?" Noah turned his whole body toward Violet and tried to look into her eyes.

"Sure, you can ask me something. You can ask me anything. I am happy to tell you as many stories as I can. I know all of them." The river of Violet's voice continued its smooth flow. Of course, she would add something else, but Noah was ready to make a ripple.

"Do you like your home, Violet? Are you satisfied with your life in here?" Noah kept looking into Violet's eyes, trying to find what he was looking for—the connection with her soul.

Violet looked calmly at Noah's eyes as well and, with the same facial expression, waited for her turn to talk. "Sure, I'm satisfied with my life here. I have a lovely home. Look at my nails, they are pretty. Lucie did a good job with the manicure." She redirected her attention to her shiny nails, then looked around the living room. "I am happy here. Betty, are you happy here?"

Betty flinched from the sound of her name and opened her eyelids. "Happy here." She fell asleep again.

"Betty is happy too. It is a good house, good life…"

"Violet, have you ever tried to do something special with your life? Something that only you would like to do. Something that Lucie or Paulina would completely disagree with?" Noah kept throwing stone by stone into that perfectly designed river.

"Lucie and Paulina are good ladies. They care about me and Betty, always helping us to go out, have some fun. We like to go to parks and have picnics, to movies, birthday parties. I play bingo. Do you like to play bingo?" The river swallowed up all the stones without making a splash.

A huge rock was ready to be launched onto the glassy surface of the water. Noah leaned toward Violet, touched her hand, and whispered in her ear, "What about going on a date or falling in love? You are a beautiful woman, Violet. You can have any man you want. All you need to do is to listen to me. Are you listening to me, Violet?"

"Sure, I am listening to you. I would like to go out with you. You are a handsome man. Look how pretty you are. I am pretty too. I love my nails. Do you love my nails?" The rock has been thrown and stuck in the middle of the river. The streams politely embraced the rock, rejoined behind it, and continued the journey.

Lucie came back in the living room carrying three glasses of lemonade on a tray. A serene nap and delightful dialog were complemented with the freshness of the drink. A few minutes of silence allowed the TV to become the center of attention.

"This illness affects only people with recent head injury or posttraumatic stress. The affected individuals possess the ability to spread it with eye contact toward others."

Noah stopped drinking lemonade and focused on the news.

Betty was savoring each sip of the drink with her eyes closed and a smile on her face. Violet emptied her glass pretty fast and thanked Lucie. In a few seconds, by the power of the freshly made lemonade, the old lady turned on her verbal flow on the healthy drink and happy life here in the residence.

Only Noah left his drink untouched and, leaning forward, tried to catch every word on the TV. The news report came to an end, but the lemonade remained in a glass of the person, sinking deeply into his thoughts.

Suddenly, Noah, looked at Lucie and said, "When I came out of the seizure, I heard that you were counting. Why?"

Noah's question shocked Lucie. This was the first time in her twelve-year work experience when a mentally challenged individual showed such a curiosity in his illness. A few seconds were enough to overcome the confusion and come up with some explanation.

"When a person is having a seizure, it is very important to know the exact time because if a seizure lasts longer, your brain can be paralyzed. That's why we have to make sure that there's enough time to call an ambulance to take the person to a hospital for immediate help."

"Ambulance for immediate help," repeated Betty and tried to take a sip from the empty glass in her hands.

Betty's input into the conversation and "fooling" around the empty glass lightened up Noah's face with curious excitement. Oh, how badly he wanted to see the expression of disappointment on her face after realizing that there was no lemonade left in the glass…Bummer!

Betty's face faded away in that wide smile of satisfaction as if she tasted the drink. Unbelievable! The glass was empty!

"You have no idea in what mysterious ways our brain works." Lucie read the wicked idea out of Noah's mind and took the empty glass from Betty's hands.

The next minute, a frustrated pattern took over Noah's face.

Noah didn't say anything back and continued to slowly sink into his thoughts and the recliner. *Obviously, people like Violet and Betty don't fit in my plans. Their brain is being protected by the illness they were born with. It means I have to find people with recent brain injury to get into their souls through the freshly wounded brain, as was said on the TV. Where do I find them though?*

"Are you alright, Noah? You look upset. You don't like your lemonade? Do you want me to call an ambulance? Lucie, you should call an ambulance. Noah doesn't drink his lemonade." Violet redirected her verbal streams onto Noah.

Suddenly, Noah felt like another wave of anxiety was about to accumulate with the power of Violet's endless talking. He stood up really fast and, before leaving the room, said to her, "No, Violet. I don't need an ambulance." He stopped. "Ambulance…" The word made Noah pause and get back in his chair. "Ambulance…hospital… Of course! Wounded people go to hospital!" A weird smile distorted his face. The oncoming cloud of anxiety had disappeared without a trace. *I have to simulate another seizure…a longer one…to get into the hospital! But how? I've had seizures but never seen what they looked like. Or I can suddenly "fall" and "hurt" myself. They will drive me straight into the traumatology department! You are a genius, Noah!*

Lucie was quietly observing the scene of the living room stage from the invisible audience seat somewhere in a corner. She had witnessed that little argument between Violet and Noah. Sensation of the upcoming anxiety with its possible outcome in a form of a seizure made Lucie ready for the counterthrust.

Noah's movement back into his chair looked as if Noah was experiencing the aura prior to his seizure. Just to be sure, she kept watching him from behind. What she couldn't see was Noah's face with an expression of a wicked smile and a side-to-side careful glancing.

What happened next was a matter of seconds. Noah got up fast from his recliner and exclaimed, "I am so tired of all this nonsense!" He made a step toward the kitchen and tripped over something on the floor. Falling, Noah hit his head on the corner of a coffee table and screamed.

In ten minutes, he was picked up by an ambulance. Ten minutes later, he was placed in the Traumatology Department of the Regional Hospital of Gray Stone in the room with four other patients in there.

The first step of the planned mission was accomplished with full success.

Her cell phone ringing interrupted Tia's browsing through the latest news and published research on the Recolla illness. She closed her laptop and left the library to take the call. Lucie called from the hospital regarding the emergency with Noah's fall.

An orange Honda Civic took the last free parking spot beside an emergency entrance of the Regional Hospital. Tia looked around. "What is happening in here?" Three police cars and a fire truck with the lights on cordoned off the entrance. People were getting out of their vehicles and showing sincere interest in the scenes around the hospital's parking area. Windows of the ice cream cafeteria across the road were covered with people's faces instead of colorful advertisements of the kinds of ice cream flavors. Perhaps it was a new ice cream flavor—the flavor of "curry OCD."

Without a second thought, Tia left her vehicle and headed straight to the main entrance of the hospital. Two police officers in bulletproof vests blocked her way. "Ma'am, this is a restricted area. Please leave."

"I've just had a phone call from the hospital regarding the individual I work with." Tia calmly looked at both of them. The situation that's supposed to feel extreme to everyone didn't get Tia uptight, no matter what was going on behind those doors.

"Your name, ma'am?"

"Tia Phrever."

The police officer checked his tablet and let Tia proceed to the entrance, walking along with her. "Please follow me, ma'am."

The police officer pointed to the emergency side door of the building and walked in with Tia.

Lucie, Paulina, and Nelly were already in there, waiting for her. Tia greeted everyone. Escorted by the policeman, the group proceeded to the security room, full of monitors.

Two men in white robes and one in a black jacket with a SECURITY sign on its back were sitting at the desk in front of the computers and discussing something. Interrupted by the visitors, they got up and introduced themselves.

Professor Kidd was a tall athletically built sixty-seven-year-old man with thick silver-blue hair around his face. He looked like Santa Claus. His light blue eyes were surrounded by countless wrinkles and made an illusion of him constantly smiling. Massive white eyebrows were glistering with silver with every movement of his face, creating an image of snowflakes that were stuck in his hair. Baby-pink facial skin didn't go along with all this grayness. He spoke softly in a manner of aristocratic politeness. "Good afternoon, my friends." A perfect smile escaped from his bushy mustache-and-beard set, showing bright red lips. "I am Professor Kidd. This is my colleague, Dr. Kozlov."

There were handshakes all around and the usual pleasantries: "It's nice to have you here," "Pleasure to meet you," "Hi, how are you?" "Pleasure is mine."

"It's so nice to see such good-looking people in here." Santa's charm spread its relaxing effect on everyone in the room.

Nelly jumped toward him and stuck her hand almost into the professor's face. "I am Nelly, Noah's mom. I am so grateful that such a wonderful doctor takes care of my son's health. I bet your family is so blessed to have you around."

The confused professor didn't expect such a response and stepped back speechless, but still smiling politely. All he could do at this moment was to touch Nelly's fingertips and imitate a very light handshake, or, in this case, finger shake. A couple of seconds was needed to build up a huge iceberg of the uncomfortable silence.

"Noah Fjutcher-r-r was admitted in Tr-r-raumatology Depar-r-rtment about one hour-r-r ago." Dr. Kozlov stepped up on the ice of the awkwardness and broke it immediately to hundreds of tiny pieces with his strong Russian accent. "Professor Kidd and I would like to redirect your attention on the security footage that is being recorded since Noah's admission." He made a fast turn toward the monitors, inviting everyone to follow him. His curly black hair contained enough hair gel to keep it in decent order. Bending his skinny torso over the computer keyboard, Dr. Kozlov pressed a button and stepped back, observing everyone's reactions through his deep blue eyes hidden under arrows of black eyebrows.

A security personnel folded the window blinds down. The footage showed Noah being delivered into the room with four beds, divided with hospital curtains in between. He had a bumpy bandage on the right side of his head. A few seconds later, after the nurse was gone,

Noah got up from his bed and pulled back the curtain between his and the other patient's bed. Then he came face-to-face with the other patient and, looking into his eyes, told him something. The patient immediately left his bed and did the same to the person resting beside him and so on. In a few minutes, all four men were walking around the room and started tipping over all the medical equipment. Ruined tables and chairs were thrown outside through the hospital windows. Noah left his busy roommates and walked into the next room. After two minutes of being in there, he moved into the next room and the adjacent rooms as well. In the meanwhile, the whole department started panicking. Possessed by this unusual behaviour, all the patients in the department were crushing everything and everyone in their way.

Dr. Kozlov asked to stop the video and looked at his guests. Paulina, Lucie, and Nelly remained speechless and stood still, which was a completely acceptable reaction in this situation.

Dr. Kozlov looked around, trying to find Tia in that dark office. He spotted her facing the entry door. She wasn't moving at all. The only part of her body that seemed alive was her long straight hair. Scattered over her back and shoulders, they were moving slowly, just like being animated. Cold goose bumps covered his body. The doctor got closer to the girl and looked into her eyes. In the dark room, he couldn't see Tia's eyes but saw two dark spots instead. Dr. Kozlov assumed that Tia's eyes were closed, and he was looking at the very dark makeup on her eyelids. He touched her shoulder. Tia slowly turned her head toward Dr. Kozlov. He numbed. It wasn't the heavy makeup on Tia's eyelids, but her very eyes. They didn't have whites or irises. They were completely black.

"You haven't found Noah yet?" Tia's voice pulled Dr. Kozlov from the stupor.

"No, we haven't." He flinched and figured out that the recent events in the hospital started playing tricks on him as well. There were no "alien eyes," neither slow motion of the girl's hair, but the work of the air conditioner and shadows playing through the window blinds. He didn't have any choice but to accept the only explanation.

"What do you mean you haven't? Did you lose my son? My Noah? What is going on?" Nelly ran toward Dr. Kozlov and then back to Professor Kidd, repeating the same questions. She looked like a mama duck waddling her short wide body on those little x-shaped legs. The excitement of seeing a handsome well-mannered professor had disappeared as well as her fake sophistication.

"He locked himself up in a janitor's storage."

Emotionlessly, Tia turned her face with clear gray eyes toward the monitors and the people beside them who were quietly observing Tia and Dr. Kozlov.

"Excuse me, young lady." Professor Kidd squinted at Tia. "In what name of god did you know that we lost Noah?"

"I didn't. It's simple psychology. You've never mentioned about the department or room number where Noah should have been located by now, in case we wanted to visit him. Besides, I've spotted Noah in the video when he was entering the storage. It's on the second floor."

Only at that moment, everyone noticed that one more monitor was on and kept running the recorded video.

Tia couldn't believe herself. It was a lie, and at the same time, no emotions were shown? What am I? I must be getting very good at keeping my emotional state neutral, but a bit concerned on turning into some kind of emotionless machine. And when did that monitor start to work? No time to think. She made eye contact with Dr. Kozlov and Professor Kidd, for the purpose of showing off her clear gray eyes.

"My dearest child, are you one of my students?" Professor Kidd made a step toward Tia and took her hand. Smiling into her eyes, he kept talking. "I am so glad to see that my knowledge and experience continue to live in my students."

"Thank you, Professor." Tia felt a little uncomfortable and, without being rude, returned the pleasant man from heaven down to earth. "I believe that you can utilize me in the mission to get Noah out of the storage room without any physical or emotional harm." She looked at everyone around and stopped her eyes on Nelly. "Of course, if this is alright with you, Nelly."

Nelly had already found the safest place for herself in the room. And this place was right beside this well-educated, well-mannered, and handsome Professor Kidd, no matter what direction he was moving to or who he was talking with. Nelly kept herself in the center of his attention. She was so glad that everyone's attention was being redirected on her again.

"I am. I am alright with that as long as I go in there as well. My Noah will never say no to his mom. He's been always such a good son. I am sure, sir, if you have children or grandchildren, they love you dearly too."

"It's quite a serious situation in the hallways right now," the security guard interrupted Nelly. "Police and our security team were able to monitor all the rooms with patients as well as operation rooms. So half of the hospital is not functioning right now. We have identified twenty-three patients who were causing the chaos. Three patients are still missing, including Noah. If Noah is in the storage room, it makes them two who are out. There is no guarantee that those two patients stopped making interactions with other people and increasing the infected numbers. Me and two more police officers will accompany Ms. Phrever and you, ma'am, on the way to the storage room." He looked at Nelly and left the room to get in contact with the police.

Dr. Kozlov stepped into the conversation. "Obviously, one of us has to go as well." He looked at his colleague. "And I would be honored to do it myself, Joseph. We can use the security radio to stay in touch. I would like to make a request for the possible sedation use." Dr. Kozlov looked at Nelly and the professor.

"I think the sedation is one of the necessary preparations right now. The situation we are dealing with is quite extraordinary." Professor

Kidd stepped back from Nelly and looked at her, slightly bending his head down. It was important for him to see her face because she was standing very close to him, and all he saw was the top of her head.

Nelly tipped her head back, showing a pair of colorless eyes and a wide smile. The feeling of being noticed by Professor Kidd made Nelly excited. "I am giving my consent on any actions, Joseph." She made a step toward him.

The professor's eyebrows went up. His red lips separated from one other and locked up again. "Hmm…Wonderful!" He looked around as if he wanted to find something in the room but couldn't, and touched his nose for some reason. "Let us proceed! I am staying in here with Paulina and Lucie. Please, contact us, Doctor. We'll be watching you, and God help us all." He rushed toward the two ladies beside the monitor wall.

The hospital hallways sparkled with its usual immaculate cleanliness when Dr. Kozlov, Tia, Nelly and three police officers proceeded toward the elevator. Taking the stairs was considered dangerous at this time. Weird emptiness surrounded those six walking close to each other. No words, just soundless steps, heavy breathing, and ear-splitting heartbeats. White reflection of the floors and walls crossed out with white sound of silence and created an unpleasant feeling of anxiety.

A few more meters till the closest elevator. Now passing the cafeteria where the lights left by the personnel who were evacuating in a hurry exposed unfinished meals on the round tables. A few tipped-over chairs were still lying on the floor. A smashed pacifier stuck out its dead tongue, petrified in the last scream of no use.

In the elevator, police officers proceeded first, leaving their companions behind. One officer listened through the elevator doors and nodded to his partners. He pressed the button. The doors opened, and the group stepped inside the elevator. The same procedure was repeated on the way up to the second floor. So far, so good. The elevator doors opened right in front of the janitor's room.

"I hope he is still in there," Nelly whispered, looking at Dr. Kozlov and Tia.

"Nelly, Doctor"—Tia got closer to those two—"I know what's in Noah's head. I heard a few names from his fantasy and believe that I can play around them. Let me go first."

Nelly and the doctor agreed momentarily, giving Tia a whole stage, and they stepped down into the audience of the hallway. Three guards pressed their backs against the walls on both sides of the janitor's room, keeping hands on guns underneath their vests.

Tia closed her eyes for a moment and exhaled. With a quiet tone of voice, she said, "You can open the door, Kondrat."

"Rasara?!" The sound of someone jumping on the floor, and then a few quick steps toward the door, made everyone hold their breath.

Tia heard Noah's feverous breathing on the other side of the door. She looked at the security guards and mouthed, "Let me in. Do not touch him." She then addressed Noah. "Yes, Kondrat. It's Rasara, and I need your help. Let me in."

The sound of an unlocking door pushed Nelly and Dr. Kozlov a few steps forward. Tia turned to them with her hand stretched out and whispered, "No!" They stood still. The door opened. Tia got in and locked it behind her back.

In a second, the other side of the janitor's room door looked like a patient who was having a problem with his heart, and four people carefully listened to his chest, laying their ears on it.

Fluorescent light tangled in Noah's yellow hair, making them transparent. Inflamed pink whites of his eyes, merging with his natural red irises, created the image of a completely red-eyed face. The pale blue hospital gown hung down to the floor, touching Noah's bare feet.

Feverous breathing jumped in and out of his open mouth, searching for the right words.

"Rasara...I...I...can't believe...you...you are needing my help. I'll do anything for you. You know it." Noah was getting closer and closer to Tia with his widened arms, ready for a hug.

Tia held her ground and stretched one hand toward Noah with the stop gesture, then strategically turned her palm clockwise down, changing the restrictive gesture into a polite invitation to sit. "What if we sit down? You, Noah, please, take this chair, and I will sit across the table."

The tranquility of Tia's voice made Noah sit down right away. Tia sat at the opposite side of a little metal table, the only table in this tiny room. *I've no idea what to talk about with this strange man. Okay. Go with the flow, Tia, as you always do. It's the best way if nothing else comes up. Or...let him talk first!*

And that was the wisest decision in this situation. An unbalancing disturbance of the neural circuit, running by a sensory neuron from an eye receptor straight to the motor neuron of the limbs in possession of Noah's body, identified itself across the table.

Noah couldn't wait to start the conversation with Tia. Spasmatic movements of his body made him look unsettled, exited. Otherwise, it seemed like his dreams were about to come true. The woman he was trying to reach through the centuries begged him to open the door of this tiny room just to be with him in the shadow of a half-functioning fluorescent lamp. One more second of this everlasting silence, and he would explode in millions of pieces of anything that could possibly create an emotional explosion.

"How are you, Kondrat?"

This simple, everyday question brought Noah back to life. The love of his numerous lives was concerned about his well-being. Noah looked at Tia with wide-open eyes and transformed the inhaled air into words.

"My dear Rasara, it is you who is being in charge, not me. Why are you asking for my help? The plan created by you is working!" A victorious smile reigned all over his face.

"Kondrat, consider this conversation as being a next part of the plan." Momentarily, Tia highlighted the steps of her own plan for the "plan of the conversation" with Noah about who knows what. "I have to make sure that you know exactly who you are and who I am. I have to make sure that you are the right person in this plan. Tell me more about Junntie, Nicole, Rowena, Kondrat. Just take it as a test you have to pass to proceed on to the next level."

Tia had no idea what she was talking about, but whatever came out of her mouth was coming with cold confidence, power, equanimity.

Noah's face, along with his body expressions, came to life. He looked like a lucky student who was pulled out a very easy exam ticket, knowing that victory was on its way. Noah got up and started walking back and forth between the wall with a set of vacuum cleaners and the other wall with all kinds of mops, brooms, brushes, sponges, and shapeless buckets. He was walking tall, holding hands locked up in front of his chest. The ridiculous hospital gown flung open with every movement he made, but Noah didn't care because an invisible crown was sitting tight on his head.

"You and I are the guardian spirits of human forms we've been taken through all centuries. We always knew each other during our previous life-spins. The names of our spirits are Kondrat and Rasara." Noah stopped and looked at Tia with sadness. "For some reason, I kept making the same mistake in each of my previous lives by wanting you so bad, and when you were with me, I hurt you…I don't know why I was doing that. In the last life, we had a family. I loved you and our little daughter so much. But my niece needed me more, and I had to leave you and our little Sandra. I couldn't forgive myself till the last day of my life, which ended tragically."

Something very heavy pressed Noah down. Obviously, it wasn't the invisible crown he was wearing a few minutes ago. He started to breathe faster, applying a visible effort to each of his breaths. Noah pulled a chair out from the table and, exhausted, dropped heavily on it. Looking nowhere, he continued.

"Rowena loved me too, but I was afraid of being accused of having relations with a witch, which wasn't true. I knew that she has picked me, Olaf, despite Hendrich's strong feelings toward her."

"Who is Hendrich?" Tia was carried away by Noah's narration and completely forgot about her new role at the moment. In a second, she realized it and, clearing her throat fast, proceeded with the same confidence. "You are doing well, Noah. Keep going."

Barents Sea sometimes gets tired too and wants to go to sleep for a few months. Just a few months, under the secure covers of winter sheets, is enough to be reenergized for the next short summer to serve all the living creatures in Greenland and Norway.

The Barents Sea loved to take care of wildlife by providing them with fresh fish for food and tasty lobsters and shrimp for dessert. It loved to play with millions of seabirds during the winter nap, throwing to them juicy codfish, haddock, halibut…

If only the Barents Sea could speak, it would tell us a single story about each bird of the forty species that has been harvesting around its waters.

The sea has always become amused by playing with dolphins, whales, seals. The heart of the Barents belonged to beluga whales. What fun it was to watch them playing in pairs or in a group of more than one thousand, pushing them up to the very surface of the shiny waters and returning into the deepest expansions.

Barents Sea has never had anything against human nature. People's dream of controlling the nature was considered as an entertainment to the sea in so many ways: swinging their ships in the waves, giving or taking away their fish catch, stealing boats and hiding them under the water, destroying people's habitats on shores…. It was always something up the sleeve of the sea that would remind humans to have respect for the unlimited power of nature.

A few centuries were gone along with the playfulness of seagulls and whales. The Barents became bored and turned its face toward humans. With all its observation, the sea learned a lot about human nature. People always wanted to be powerful. This fact has been known since they were still in the same line with other mammals. Once people have chosen a leader among them—the strongest, wisest, richest one—they started to obey his rules, and at the same time, they didn't want to know what would happen to those who decided to go against those rules. The empowered people would never accept those who happened to be different, who could shake up their authority. Being different has been acceptable for the leading person and the people whose difference was legalized as nonthreatening.

Countless times the sea saw how people, trying to get rid of their enemies, were accusing them for something they had never done. The Barents always sympathized to "the truly different humans" because they kept coming back to the sea and talking to it, asking for advice or help. If the given advice was helpful, the truly different became friends with the sea and nature, but cast away from their kind. Hundreds of those who have been accused in the "potential danger" for no reason rested in peace or pieces under the waters of the Barents Sea in the year of 1662.

"I'll miss the beautiful voice of your waters…"

Rowena was standing on the very edge of a cliff when a huge wave hit the rocks and softly touched her feet by the broken splash. Her long black hair was messed up by the wind and the salty moisture of the sea. Her blue-gray gown stuck to her figure, pressed by the cold March breeze and showed patches of ice on the wet spots. "I'll be visiting you always. When you see a piece of a rainbow in the splash of your waters, it will be me, saying hello to you…"

"Rowena! You silly girl, what are you doing here?" Hendrich took off his coat and wrapped it over Rowena's freezing body. "We have to leave. People are searching for you everywhere." He pulled her hand toward the pathway and down the cliff.

"I am not going anywhere." Rowena's voice was barely heard. She resisted to make a move.

"He is not coming. You have to see the truth. Olaf betrayed you. It was him who testified against you. I don't care if you are a witch. I love you and am ready to run with you anywhere to keep you away from the people of Vardo. Please, trust me. I love you…" His deep blue eyes were full of tears, or maybe the sea touched them as well. The same height with Rowena, Hendrich looked huge beside her because of his strong masculine body. He tried to cover Rowena's numbed skin with his long black coat that was constantly being blown away by the cold wind.

"There she is! On the cliff! Seize her! Hurry, hurry!" A mob of villagers with pitchforks and torches was heading toward the cliff where Rowena and Hendrich were standing.

"I beg you, Rowena, there's still a chance to escape. Jump with me down to the water. I am a good swimmer. Trust me! Please!" He looked into her eyes and stood still.

"Goodbye, Hendrich." Rowena's eyes as well as her whole body became blue, then very pale blue.

Hendrich embraced her, still trying to warm her up and protect from the freezing winds. "I love you…I love you…My Rowena, I love you. If they take your life, I'll die with you."

He hugged her vain body, pressed his face against Rowena's cheek, and closed his eyes, ready to be executed with her together.

The mob stopped right behind him. Strange silence made Hendrich open his eyes. He was still feeling Rowena's body in his arms, but barely seeing her. The pale blue color of her skin became more transparent, and in a couple of seconds, he could see only her eyes and lips saying a silent goodbye. He didn't feel her body anymore. She disappeared. Only the black coat hung on his arms along with Rowena's gown.

A shrill scream, continuously multiplying on hundreds, broke the silence behind his back. The crowd rushed back down, away from the cliff, and screamed in fear. "Witch! Witch!"

"You have to understand me, Rasara. I was really scared that time. You were a witch. What would you do when you saw someone who was able to move objects without even touching them or…or…to hear rolling thunder when they were upset?"

Noah's last comments pulled Tia back from Norway to Canada, ignoring the possible concerns about time and distance.

"What's the point of loving Hendrich? He loved you, but you've never loved him. Your heart always belonged to me." Noah continued passionately. "That's why I am trying to fix life for both of us in order to be happy again…together."

"What are the other names for Hendrich?" Tia finally redirected herself into the conversation of the present time.

"Well, I don't really know. In each of your life, there was a presence of a guy who cared about you, always tried to protect you, but for some reason, there was no emotional involvement from your side. I have an idea who it could be, but…would be better if I just keep it to myself. Only one thing I know for sure that it is the very time to correct all mistakes, once and forever. I will fight till the end."

Tia knew that on the other side of that door, people were listening to this ridiculous conversation. And this conversation didn't sound promising for Tia's professional reputation. The best way to fix this situation was to get Noah out of the room and finish what has been started.

Two forces were fighting inside her head. One was a professionalism, which didn't allow Tia to ignore this interesting phenomenon of the very unknown illness. There was a possibility that Tia, with Professor Kidd's supervision, would be able to discover something revolutionarily important about Recolla. The other force had an opposite charge: was it even possible to make up a story like that? Noah was telling Tia her own dreams and visions. He knew about Junntie. What if Noah's story was not the work of his ill brain? If not, then Tia was getting ill too, showing the same symptoms: hearing voices and seeing people with strange names. From one perception it was scary, but from the other point of view, experiencing the same symptoms might lead to the correct analyzation of the disease progression.

She fully accepted both concepts. But there was a third one as well, which was flowing between those two, getting them closer to each other, and when they become as one, the outcome would be visible. What if...Noah's story was real? What if people were just not ready to peek at this hidden, but possibly existing, reality?

No mystery. Only science. That was her final decision. Tia sat straight and let Noah finish his sentence. "Noah, do you think it would be more comfortable to talk about it at home? I bet you are hungry and tired. And look what you are wearing right now." Tia judgmentally looked up and down at Noah's clothes.

Noah agreed unexpectedly fast. He got up from his chair. "Our plan has just started to come true. I have to continue..." He looked at Tia interrogatively.

"Noah, consider that your work today is done, and you go home to rest for tomorrow. What do you think?" Now Tia was acting as a professional.

"Yeah...I am quite tired. Would be nice to have a good dinner and read something." Noah proceeded to the door with that relaxing smile, probably visualising himself of writing in his notebook.

With a smile, Tia looked at Noah walking toward the door. Exhausted to death, he didn't really care about his clothes. His naked buttocks showed prints from the metal chair he was sitting on a few seconds ago because his hospital gown was able to cover only his front.

Tia heard some noise when Noah's blue buttocks disappeared behind the janitor's room door. She rushed out of the room. Security guards seized Noah from both sides while Dr. Kozlov was administering a sedative into Noah's arm.

Slowly Noah began to lose balance. His eyelids were closing gradually. Noah didn't resist. He even tried to say something with a smile. Tia stooped over down to his face and was able to hear Noah's words.

"Whatever...I don't care what you are doing to me. The only... thing...I...care of now...is...Haon, the Arbiter of Mazaria..."

On Their Own

"Try this tea, Rasara. You'll like it better."

"Mom, I am still sleeping…" Tia attempted to pull a blanket over her head to escape from her mother's creatively painless wake-up call. Stroked by the subconscious alert, Tia opened her eyes. "Rasara?"

Marisha was pouring jasmine tea into a cup and throwing smiles at her most favorite creature in the entire universe. "Welcome back to Zaclear, my darling."

"Already? How did I die?" Rasara looked confused. She sat straight up in her armchair and tried to remember the last day of her life, which didn't want to be unveiled.

There was no bed with a blanket, but a small living room with two armchairs beside an oak coffee table in the old village house. Peaceful flames in the fireplace made chunks of wood crackle and release amber sparks every time they got burned down. Lemony-orange curtains half-covered long skinny windows around the room and allowed the blowing outside snow to take an envious peek into the cozy evening tea ritual. None of the most welcoming places would be completed without the final touch of a little kitten that looked like a ball of ash that was sleeping beside the fireplace and stretching its paws from time to time.

"I am proud of you, Rasara, in the present life-spin." Marisha moved a teacup with the strong aroma of jasmine closer to the still-confused girl and smiled. "Have a sip. It'll help you to wake up."

Marisha sat in the other armchair and picked up a saucer with a cup, giving enough time for Rasara to get adjusted to the sudden change of decorations.

Rasara gave a close look to her hands and arms. Then she got up and walked toward the long mirror on the wall. On the surface of the vintage-style redwood mirror, Rasara recognized the reflection of a tall slim girl with long straight hair and gray eyes who she has been seeing every day for a couple of decades now. "Still Tia…alright." Rasara exhaled with relief and turned around. "So why are we here in Zaclear if our human forms are still alive? Can we leave them unattended?"

"Darling, please sit with me and relax. Have tea. You'll get all the answers soon."

Marisha's welcoming warmth resonated with Rasara's aura and neutralized all negative waves around the room. Slowly, Rasara walked back to the living room and sat across from Marisha. She inhaled the aroma of jasmine and smiled with her eyes closed, slightly tipping her head back. "I'll never get tired of this. Having tea with you has always worked as a cure for me. It releases stress and reenergizes at the same time." Rasara's words were wrapped in the finest fabric of memory fog. Each word was showing its configuration and then disappearing behind a veil of dreaminess. "I remember when Doug left me, all I was waiting for was a weekend. Right after picking up my little girl from kindergarten, we drove out of the city to see you and have endless chats around this coffee table with lots and lots of jasmine tea…"

The unusually loud sound of a teacup touching a saucer interrupted Rasara's trance. She opened her eyes. Marisha held the tea set with both hands and stared at Rasara.

"Mom…what's wrong?" Rasara put her teacup back on the coffee table and anxiously looked at Marisha.

"Tia is a young girl. She's not married yet and definitely has no kids." Marisha focused herself on placing honeycombs on Rasara's plate.

Relaxed, Rasara lay back in the comfortable armchair and tried to catch up on her thoughts. "Hmm…I don't know. Some sort of déjà vu, probably. Maybe I've seen it in a movie or read it in a book." Rasara smiled. "As Tia would say, our brain works in ways we can't even imagine." She put a piece of honeycomb on a wooden teaspoon and looked through the liquid-gold honey onto a peaceful flame.

Marisha got up and started to throw small wood planks into the fireplace. Without looking at Rasara and keeping the conversation as the "by the way" subject, she carefully continued, "Do you think Tia is going to have a family one day?"

"I don't know, Mom. She is very preoccupied with her career. All she thinks about is the possible connection between the unusual changes of her mental state and Recolla illness. As a young researcher, she tries to apply only scientific explanations to anything abnormal. If an explanation hasn't been found yet, she accepts the fact that more research is needed to be done. She has changed tremendously. This journey is the easiest quest for me as a spiritual guide. Tia is capable of finding the right ways without any of my help. Sometimes I think that she is not receiving my signals. The connection between us is so fragile or doesn't exist at all."

Rasara got quiet for a few seconds and let the amber honey to trickle down back into a saucer and gave Marisha a worried glance. "Junntie told me not to control her but observe. Honestly, I have stopped redirecting her since she got accepted to that university. Losing the connection with Tia is the hardest thing for me. I feel incomplete without her…"

Rasara left her chair and got closer to Marisha. She sat on the floor beside her, embraced Marisha's knee, and put her head on them. "Mom, if Tia doesn't need my help anymore, you…please stay with me…like always…in each life spin. Always be my mom…please."

"My dear child." Marisha gently stroked Rasara's hair. "My darling. There is nobody in the universe I love more than you. It doesn't matter who you represent on Earth, Tia or another human in your next spin. You will always be Rasara, the same little spirit who travels with me."

A pair of gray eyes with a green flare looked at Marisha through the magnifying lens of tears, reflecting the amber out of the fireplace. "What if…the spiritual connection gets loose…and Tia won't need me anymore? I can lose you too, Mom."

Rasara sat back on the floor and wistfully looked at the settling down firewood. The green flare in her eyes were displaced by the golden reflection of the flame in the fireplace.

"It seems like Tia is developing a new spirit…on her own. If it's true, then the Parallels will balance out the excessive energy, and I will lose my existence."

"Or receive something you've never thought of." Junntie showed his presence in the room. Earthy casual blue jeans and beige jacket sat on him equally presentable with any "out of the world" garments. The orange-golden reflection of the fire in his pupils brought out his deep black irises. With a soft smile, he looked at Rasara. "Energy readily changes from one form to another. The law of Conservation of Energy states that '*energy cannot be created or destroyed.*' You should know your nature, Rasara."

Junntie got closer to the fireplace and, like all outsiders in winter, let his palms feel the solar energy that had been collected by the firewood millions of years ago and now was releasing its energy in the form of the flame.

Rasara immediately transferred herself from the floor back into the comfy armchair and, leaning back into it, gave Junntie "the look." She didn't feel any urge to participate in the conversation, yet she was angry at the Highest Spirit in those casual clothes for the interruption.

"On Earth, we make phone calls before visiting." Rasara touched her forehead, trying to hide her eyes and, possibly, her thoughts.

Marisha stepped into the conversation. "Hello, Junntie. It is very unusual for Xahrns to be called in during their incomplete life cycle. We still have strong connection with the represented human forms, which pushes us toward expressing ourselves in any humanly possible ways. Please, forgive us."

Marisha and Junntie slightly bowed in agreement.

Rasara continued her protest under the cover of her hand.

Junntie took off his jacket and hung it on the back of a wooden chair beside the fireplace. Then he sat on that chair, slightly bending forward, and rested his elbows and locked hands on his knees. For a moment he looked at them, then lifted his eyes on Rasara and Marisha. "Welcome back to Zaclear. You both have been already aware of the recent events." He spoke softly, with prolonged pausing, which was unusual from his ordinary speeches. "This unexpected meeting with Xahrns causes a great stress in the Parallels. It has never happened before. The extraneous energy is taking over the Earth. Some of the spiritual guides have lost the connections with their human forms." Junntie looked at Rasara. "One spirit didn't come back to Zaclear…"

Rasara quickly looked at Junntie, forgetting about her protest. "Kondrat?"

Junntie slowly nodded. "Rasara, I'd like to hear more about the fact you were saying that Tia was developing the astral self. What made you to come up with this concept?" Junntie's voice remained soft, but his eye contact with Rasara demanded more information.

Rasara left the cozy depth of her armchair and leaned forward, ready to talk. "When the three of us talked in the park about implementing the experiment of releasing control over Tia's decisions…Tia has been managing her life without being controlled for a while now. Any moves I would have redirected her with have been already done on her own. I was just observing her. Tia is a young soul. This life-spin is the first one in the twelve-spin's cycle. Her life is supposed to be fulfilled with mistakes."

Rasara became quiet. The ash-furred ball beside the fireplace stretched its four paws in the same direction and yawned, rolling out his tongue and showing all his teeth. It lifted its head and spotted the source of the last verbal outburst around the coffee table. Catching the young girl's attention, the furball got up and headed toward her, yawning and stretching his back legs, attempting to get onto Rasara's lap.

Rasara enjoyed the view for a few seconds and continued. "Tia keeps changing every day. Now she is capable to adjust herself to any situation. It was quite a shock for her to get used to the eye colors changing. Guess what…she decided that some abnormalities in her appearance were quite acceptable if she looked at them from a biological point of view. People's skin becomes pale if they get scared, Tia's eyes become colorless if she gets scared. Excessive redness on people's faces identifies madness, and red pupils on Tia's eyes identify the same emotional state and so on. Her mind is analytical. It seems that she accepts everything without fear of the unknown. If there is no scientific explanation to something, she gets even more excited because she looks forward to the new studies, new chances to discover something. Sometimes I think that her and me are one, and at the same time, completely separate beings. I have tried to communicate with her. When she heard my name, the other memories started revealing…"

Rasara froze for a second, staring into nothing, digging in her memory. Then she lifted her big eyes at Marisha.

"I know…It wasn't déjà vu. The memory from my…her…our previous lives. I remember now. She made me remember my previous life-spin!" Rasara got up from her chair. "The tables are turning. She doesn't need my help anymore. It is me who needs Tia's help!"

She looked at Junntie then Marisha, hoping to get some answers.

With hands apart and eyes wide open, Rasara begged, "Anyone? Please, say something. I don't know anymore where I am standing… Please…" Rasara put her hands together and, exhausted, dropped herself in the chair.

The fireplace was ready to wrap up the dying flame in silence.

Junntie and Marisha exchanged meaningful glances along with approving smiles. The Highest Spirit stood up and threw a couple of wooden planks into the fireplace. Instantly, the room lit up with amber glitter and started to look like a huge honeycomb in a sunny day. Junntie moved his chair closer to Rasara's recliner and looked into her eyes with a comforting smile.

"It's time for you, my dear angel, to know the truth."

Rasara stared at him blankly.

Junntie continued. "When Bohg created Parallels and sent the spirits to help people with decision-making, civilization on Earth began to gain its momentum. Each spirit had to go through the twelve life-spins, serving their human forms in every life. Working together with people, spirits were pushing them toward new knowledge. Humans call it evolving. Regardless of that, each human being had certain problems in their life-spin. For some reason, they kept repeating the same mistakes again and again in each new life that was slowing down or even destroying the real purpose of their life. Even the spirits were not able to help people because they haven't been created to remember all the previous lives of humans and their repetitive mistakes. The spirits could enjoy the memory of their last human life only during the transition between death and birth in the Parallels' conferences. None of them, spirits or humans, were able to get rid of the mistakes but minimize or accept the consequences and live with them, heading toward completely different goals. How many people are on Earth? Every single person sooner or later repeats the same sentence: 'If I knew this was going to happen, I would have done it differently…'"

Marisha brought a teapot with freshly brewed tea and filled up the empty cups on the table.

Rasara grabbed a cup, inhaled the sweet-scented jasmine aroma, and took a sip. There was nothing more desirable at the moment than the taste of tea.

Junntie continued. "In the moment when a human life is being conceived, the true purpose of life was assigned along. The life journey begins with the very first cell of the existence that contains all information from the previous lives. Basically, the journey continues."

Junntie looked at the flame reflection in Rasara's eyes and turned to the fireplace. Seemed like he was talking to himself, remembering something that was gone forever.

"Blessed is the person who was born free. Free of his parents' decisions for his future. Free from all the rules of existed political system. The person who didn't have any fear or complications. Who knew exactly where he was going, what he was doing. Those individuals became as potential cocreators of their life goals. No enemies, but good friends and acquaintances." Junntie paused, being hypnotized by the relaxing crackling of the wood or, maybe, by the boring perfection of his narration.

"If the life of this human being was so perfect, he wouldn't need a spiritual guide though," Rasara interrupted Junntie's trance. "And… it doesn't sound real. Life is full of adventures, complications, positive and negative emotions…That's what makes people feel alive! That's what the universe needs, the transmitted energy-flow from the Earth! I feel for those unfortunate spirits. They probably, were so bored by just following their human forms. One life-spin, and the goal has been achieved? I don't believe… And where is this spirit now? Was he coming back for another boring spin?" Rasara looked grim and put her teacup back on the table. She got comfortable in her recliner, slightly rocking, and waited for Junntie's response.

Marisha touched Rasara's hand and, with a soft smile, looked at

Junntie. "Junntie, please, try to understand Rasara. It's not like she is trying to be rude to you, absolutely not. Rasara's situation is very delicate. Tia is showing full success without her. Definitely, she is developing her own spirit in the middle of her first life-spin. What will happen to Rasara?"

Marisha was speaking with a smile, like she knew the answer, but was still trying to "interpret" Rasara's concerns to the Highest Spirit.

Junntie's face was serious. He took Rasara's hand and locked it in his palms. "My dear little spirit, you don't have to worry about anything. This is a starry moment of your existence. You are free now."

Rasara pulled out her hand from Junntie's and jumped up from the chair. The poor furball that found a cozy spot beside Rasara's feet jumped on its paws and, with a frightened *ME-E-OW!*, left the scene immediately.

Rasara's eyes were releasing green sparks; her hair moved in slow motion. Tall and skinny, with her back bent toward the unwanted messenger, she looked like a puma preparing to jump on her prey. "What do you mean 'free'? I can't be a spiritual guide anymore? I have Tia. She is still alive. I nee—*she* needs me. So what am I now, stuck in the Parallels, doing nothing? If it's yes, I don't want to be free! I want to go back on Earth. Please!"

The aggressive puma suddenly turned into an exhausted cat that missed her catch and had to go home with nothing in her teeth. She stopped talking and sat on the arm of her recliner.

"I am sorry, Junntie," she said with an apathetic voice. The green flame sank into the silver emptiness of her eyes. Her chin almost touched her chest. "There will not be any interruptions anymore." Rasara looked at Junntie with clear gray eyes and proudly lifted her chin. "Please, continue."

"That's exactly what I meant," Junntie said solemnly. "You are able to fix all the arising problems in a moment. Bravo, Rasara! Spoken like the Highest Spirit!"

With satisfaction, Junntie leaned back in his chair and continued.

"To be free, it doesn't mean to be 'stuck' in the Parallels. You can choose whenever you want to come back to Earth and take any shape you want. You can live a human life and at the same time be a spirit. If you choose to be born again, you have to find human parents and possess their newborn child. Growing in the child's body, you will always know who you are. You can help people with decision-making, coming out from nowhere in any shape in their path. Or you can stay in the Parallels with me and Marisha and continue to work on the problem we are trying to solve in this moment."

"Marisha? Wait a minute…" Rasara gave a surprising look to her mom and then Junntie. "Mo-o-m?" Rasara became speechless and started moving her index finger from Marisha toward Junntie.

Marisha smiled and nodded.

Junntie continued. "I was the first free Spirit who was released after only one life-spin. My human-form life was perfect, just like in the movies or books. The person I was serving has developed his own astral self, marching toward his life's goals without any deviations. I have chosen to possess a newborn and lived with them among people since, time to time meeting with the Creator, discussing the human evolution."

"What about you, Mom?" Rasara's eyes showed its usual green spark of curiosity.

"For me it took almost two centuries to accomplish my goal." Marisha was expecting this question and gladly shared the story. "I have decided to stay with my little Rasara and be her mom in each of her life. God is the witness to my greatest sadness when I observed how much you were suffering from the same mistake in all your lives. And look at you now…Tia is ignoring all the people in her path who would become as a potential barrier on the way to her life goal. Her intelligence and spirituality are on the same level, completing each other."

"But she has not accomplished anything yet. Her life and career are in the very beginning stage," Rasara interrupted Marisha.

"Yes, my darling," Marisha agreed. "When a human being starts to develop their own astral self, it means they are on the right path. You have no idea how proud I am. My little Rasara grew up and became the Highest Spirit." Marisha came closer to the girl who was still pretty surprised and kissed her on the forehead, leaving a tear of happiness on Rasara's cheek. Then she wiped it off and stroked her hair, looking with love into Rasara's eyes. "I wish that Tia will find a decent man who would share with her the same philosophy of life."

"Okay, what about the Great Balance? If a human form develops its new spiritual guide, and the old one doesn't disappear...it means somewhere, somehow, some spirit has to...you know...become nonactive." Rasara tried to find a soft synonym to the word *die*. "And what happens to those human forms who succeeded with their purpose in life? Do they become something special?"

"Yes, they do." Junntie took his turn. "They become the main driving force of the civilization. The new spirits who have been developed by those people have a connection to us, the Highest Spirits. The Highest Spirits have access to all wonders of the universe. We decide when and how much knowledge should be unveiled to mankind through those special individuals. For instance, in a few years from now, Tia will discover a cure for almost all mental diseases, but her work will be hidden from regular people by the government. Tia will be secretly practicing the cure among her family. Only a century after, another special one will accidently run into her discovery and start using it, and so on. Nobody would know the scientist to whom this breakthrough belonged in the first place, but everyone will have access to it." Junntie looked at Rasara and smiled. "I wish to say that I am sorry for Tia...but I am not. She will bring to the end all she has started. What a fulfilling life it will be. And you, Rasara, will lead her to the victory, just like Marisha is being here for you. Now you tell me, are the Highest Spirits disturbing the Great Balance?"

"Absolutely not. They are keepers of the balance." Rasara was eagerly absorbing each word of Junntie. Later on, she would realize that all he said has been already known by her for a very long time.

Suddenly, all objects in the cozy living room began to lose their forms, turning into shapeless blurry spots. An orange shade of the flame in the fireplace overlapped other shades of amber walls and reddish furniture in the room.

Rasara looked at her hands. They were disappearing as well, turning into some beige substance. Everything around kept expanding down to their molecular structure, then subatomic, including Rasara. She became a particle of the entire universe, and the universe fit its infinity in her. They became as one. All the existing and nonexisting revealed itself to Rasara. There was no knowledge she didn't have access to.

The Great Law of Universe has unveiled itself to her.

"Everything is so simple! Why didn't I see it before?!" Her voice resonated throughout the Universe, piercing all the galaxies and coming back to its source.

Another voice took its place somewhere very close. "Unfortunately, we can't apply the Great Law of the Universe to humans. Their primitive ways of thinking make complications in all aspects of their lives."

Rasara came back to herself, looked around, and recognized the room and two other beings beside the coffee table. "I've just got a revelation," she said quietly.

"We know." Marisha touched Rasara's hand. "Welcome to the Spherus, Parallels for the Highest Spirits."

Rasara looked around. "Are we in the Spherus now?"

"Yes. I know it doesn't look different from Zaclear," Marisha continued with a smile, "because you didn't choose it to be different. The Spherus is all about your choice. A free spirit has a free choice. As the Highest Spirit, you will never make a harmful choice, that's why you possess free will forever."

Rasara gave a waggish look to her interlocutors. In a moment, the cozy room with a fireplace disappeared, and the company of three appeared to be sitting on some crushed rocks of space dust and constantly tried to block away some space objects that were crossing their path.

"Very funny!" Marisha sent a sarcastic look to Rasara and punched another rock approaching her.

"Sorry!" Rasara "relocated" her companions back into the cozy room. "I got carried away a little." A smile didn't want to leave her face.

"I am glad that you like your new role." Junntie kept looking at Rasara, enjoying her playfulness. Then he pulled his emotions together and, with a serious expression, continued, "Let us return from heaven to Earth. As we speak, all Xahrns are receiving my approval for not controlling their human forms. We have to escalate the energy flow from the Earth. No matter if the energy is positive or negative, it will be generated by the people of Earth, which is a natural factor in this process. All spirits will stand by the people, just in case if they ask for our help." Junntie focused on Rasara. "May I ask you, Rasara? What will be your action on Earth as a free spirit?"

"I will stay with Tia until her astral self gets strong enough. I am still too attached to her. This transition from spiritual guide into the Highest Spirit will take some time for me to adjust."

Rasara spoke in a very quiet voice, thinking out loud. The way she spoke or sat in her chair, even a slight movement of her hands and facial expressions, all began its change. A baby spirit transformed into the fully grown, independent Spirit.

Parallels

"Whatever, I don't care what you are doing to me. The only… thing…I…care of now…is… Haon."

Noah didn't resist the sedative shot and let Dr. Kozlov proceed with his plan. Exhausted, Noah looked for any excuse to run away from the awful reality into a sanctuary of the enchanting garden of the Arbiter of Mazaria. With a smile, he was falling in trance. There it was—a forever blooming garden and his child-angel standing beside the acacia bush, waiting for Noah with open arms.

"I am coming, my dear Rasara. Only in your arms I find peace."

Noah was falling through the clouds, watching the birds fly around him, and he tried to reach them. He was getting closer to his desired destination. His heart was beating faster, tuning up with the angel's breathing. Noah saw the angel's big welcoming eyes and swaying long hair. He smelled the aroma of blooming trees all at once. One more moment, and their hands will freeze in touch.

What happened next was unexpected. When Noah touched the ground, he felt like he was falling through the air, while his feet went down through the grass and all the beautiful flowers of the garden. He tried to catch the angel's hands to stop falling but couldn't. Her hands were made of the air. Falling, Noah kept grabbing everything around in hopes to remain on the surface. Terrified, he screamed, "Rasara! Help me!"

The angel was still standing with open arms, looking up, smiling, not even noticing Noah's descent.

Absolute darkness…Zero gravity…Dumb perplexity…

"What now?" Noah looked around and saw nothing. He started making swimming movements to escape from this stupid hover. Nothing worked. Desperate, he gave up. "I am nothing in the middle of nowhere…"

Suddenly, Noah felt heaviness in his lower stomach, hips, and thighs. A sensation of liquid metal injections through his whole body made Noah touch his arms. Odd, but the rule of vacuum didn't work in the hip area. The strange weight was pressing in one direction, leaving the upper back and extremities loose in the opposite. The heavy bottom led his whole body to swing back and forth, from side to side. Finally, it became squeezed by an invisible giant hand and, with a great force, pulled Noah out of this cosmic suspense into another darkness.

Noah found himself standing on his feet in a very small room. He could see a wide bed covered with fresh but wrinkled sheets and pillows. In front of the bed was a table made of granite with one squared leg in the middle. On top of the table was a candelabrum with sockets shaped like lilies. Thick wax candles were burning in the four golden lilies. The room smelled of eucalyptus and mint. The shadows from the candelabrum crisscrossed over the floor.

Noah immediately recognized the bedroom he had previously described in his notebook. It was the place where he was supposed to meet the Arbiter of Mazaria and have a conversation about eternity. *So much for the wishful paradise in the Arbiter's garden*, he thought.

A naked mistress, Anna, was sitting on the rug by the bed, stirring something in a pan that gave off healing aromas. She was the only view in this depressing hellhole that Noah could rest his eyes on. Moonlight running through the curved iron bars of a tiny window made Noah read between its lines a spell of the ancient desire for all men—the spell of physical intimacy. Spilt over Anna's straight back from the neck to her bottom, the silver tan was disappearing in the shade between her buttocks. The backs of her lucky feet held her perfect porcelain hips. With each stirring movement, Anna slightly wiggled her back and buttocks, allowing crossed candelabrum and moonlight to dance on her skin.

"Lucky shadows…" Noah almost fell into the sensual hypnosis and started talking to the playful lights. The sweet trance was interrupted by a wheezy cough of someone on the bed.

Noah's gaze was drawn to the bed with the one whom curious Tia, in the blooming garden of the Arbiter, had tried to convince of the humans' willpower over anything else. This "anything else" being was, in fact, sitting on that bed.

"Who am I in this scene? Tia?" Noah dug in his memory and found the answer pretty fast. He looked at his hands and body. The attention got focused on the unusually obtrusive pants around his groin area. "Definitely not as Tia." He intently looked into the darkness over the bed. As his book said, "Two eyes bore into Noah's face." (Well… Here I am.) The right eye had a golden spark deep in its center and could pierce anyone's soul to its depths; the left eye…there wasn't any of it left for the left eye. Even the place where the eye should be attached to was missing. The upper left quarter of his face somehow vanished in the darkness of the bedroom.

"Moullar!" Noah couldn't hold the scream.

Naked mistress turned her magnificent body in Noah's direction and granted him with the most welcoming smile.

Noah screamed even louder. "Rasara!"

A highly charged voltage passed through his body. Shivering, Noah made a step toward Anna, smiling so wide, as if it were possible to describe in any existing languages. Looking closer, Noah's smile began to straighten up. He noticed that the beauty in front of him had a double existence or…maybe…Noah had a double vision caused by the shock. Anna was still sitting on her knees while keeping her perfectly sculptured buttocks on the back of her feet and stirring something in a pot.

As a hologram, Rasara's body separated out of Anna's and stood up straight before Noah.

"They can't hear or see us. This is your book level. Everything goes according to the narration. All the extra stuff, like you and me, is unnoticeable to them. You do exist in this book, but not in this scene. So at this moment, you are invisible."

Anna-Rasara was standing right in front of Noah, not even trying to cover her perfections, but ignoring the fact of being that much opened to him.

Noah understood that it wasn't nice to stare at the lady's parts while she was participating in the conversation with him, but he couldn't help himself. He has never seen such perfection in his entire life. And besides, it was right there, the distance of his stretched hand, but he didn't even allow the idea of lifting his hand on the forbidden fruit. It was enough for Noah to be just a witness of this miracle vision. Every inch of her body wasn't created to be touched. It was designed to inspire, meditate, pray, and cleansing of consciousness. He was looking at her like at a masterpiece, holding in his breathing and being afraid if he breathed, she would disappear...

"Kondrat..." Anna-Rasara made a step toward Noah.

Noah moved his gaze up to her eye level. "I am here. I am yours." Anna-Rasara took Noah's hand and put it on her breast. Then she got very close to Noah and whispered in his ear, "Are you ready to take over the world?" She pressed Noah's hand onto her breast, embraced him, and sealed his lips with hers in an obvious agreement.

Everything started spinning around Noah. He felt how the real woman's body was leaning on him. The perfection, by itself, has invited Noah into the ritual of love. Was he dreaming? Who cares? The most beautiful woman in the entire universe was melting in Noah's arms. He squeezed her breast with one hand, making rotating movements, and slid the other hand down to her back, feeling those perfect buttocks. Screw the philosophical conversation with the Arbiter of Mazaria in his ever-blooming garden…all the mysterious narration of his book. Screw all this! He had almost reached his destination. One more moment, and their bodies, like their lips, would ally forever.

Anna-Rasara pierced Noah's entire body with her silver eyes through his eyes and, without breaking the kiss, said, "One word… just one short word. Are you ready to be with me forever? Are you ready to give me the power over your body and spirit?"

Spinning darkness ripped off the small stinky bedroom out of the scene and glued the two bodies together in the vacuum of cosmic space.

The most intoxicating voice and possession of the dream made Noah lose control over his ability to think and speak. His physical being had dominated over his spirituality. The energy from every corner of his body headed to its point of concentration. It wasn't necessary to understand the meaning of words, but only the sweet sound of them was enough to proceed with his journey.

"Pants…need to get rid of the pants…" This was Noah's biggest enemy right now. If he didn't own the inner destiny in a couple of seconds, it would be considered as death.

"The word, Kondrat. Give me your word!" Anna-Rasara unzipped his pants.

"Yes!"

Noah's whole body screamed in ecstasy and immediately shrank to the size of the dominated organ. Falling through a spiral tunnel and hitting its curves, Noah sped up in darkness. His eyes were looking for any visible marks around to identify how fast he was moving. There was nothing visible but air resistance and constant throwing from side to side. "So much for capturing the dream…or is it supposed to be this way? Did I do? If I did, I should feel the pleasure." His ability to think was coming back to him.

Anyway, what else are you going to do when your physical appearance becomes invisible? Only one thing—to grow your brain.

Mixed feelings of disappointment and uncertainty landed Noah back into the tiny bedroom. Nothing has changed in this place since Noah lost himself in the fantasy world. There was no need to adjust his vision for darkness from out of darkness.

Moullar lay sprawled on the bed, wearing a long nightshirt that looked so fresh that Noah could catch the scent of dry lavender from between its layers. One of his arms was stuck out of a blanket. Anna had applied the stirring mixture on it. The pain must be gone, and Moullar sat up on the bed, picked up a crystal ball from the night table, shook it, and looked carefully into it.

Forgetting his disappointment, Noah focused on Moullar's actions with a degree of curiosity. Momentarily, he began to mumble the exact words from his book's part where he described the work of the magical crystal ball: "Moullar penetrated his gaze into the inner reflection of the crystal ball in his hands. The lights and shadows shaped up and became alive."

Noah got closer. The crystal ball became as a miniature model of the Earth and showed North America. He recognized Canada with lots of pointy mountains and the green carpet of pine trees. The more he focused on a certain spot of the crystal ball, the wider the views of landscape started to unfold to him in that spot. Alberta captured his eye by its rectangular shape and a sliced lower left corner by the harbour of mountains.

"Hmm…I thought that Alberta was popular with its lakes. Perhaps I was mistaken. I can see only constant prairies and a little stripe of mountains on the border with British Columbia. Oh, there it is, Lake Claire, the largest one in Alberta…Wood National Park…It must be Gray Stone City over here…Yep, it is. Hah! It looks like a kitten, jumping for a ball of yarn!"

Under invisible-looking glass, Noah was surveying an unfolding view of the city of Gray Stone. His eyes were wide open and sparkled with curiosity.

"God must feel all the time what I am feeling right now. God or…"

Noah looked at the one who was sitting on the bed and right away focused his attention back onto the crystal ball. Magnifying the city deeper and deeper, Noah noticed lots of red sparks on the streets of downtown.

"What can it be?" He looked carefully.

The entire street of downtown was covered with chunks of ruined bricks and broken benches. Lots of trees were damaged by furniture thrown from windows, and sidewalks were covered with broken glass. Power lines created sparks in contact with water from crushed water pipes, creating sparks and led to a fire. Pine trees on sides of the street were passing the flame one to another. People were running in and out of buildings, trying to figure out what was going on. The entire second floor of a jewellery store was on fire. Tongues of flames were bursting out of the windows and crushing them in hundreds of tiny pieces. Traffic was in disorder. Almost all police of Gray Stone cordoned off the whole downtown area, creating lots of detours and barricades.

Observing this chaos, Noah spotted a few people wearing hospital gowns. They were ruining everything that crossed their way. Any objects in the hands of those people were utilized as weapons. One was holding a computer chair and used it as a window crusher. Another one, armed with a huge radio or CD player, was holding its cord and throwing it on the parked vehicles. Another young man was having fun using his feet and legs by kicking everyone and everything in his way: people, dogs, even a statue of the founder of Gray Stone. Was he hurting himself by kicking the statue? That was a very good question.

Somehow, through all this disorder, Noah's attention was focused on the orange Honda that was slowly driving through that disaster.

"It seems familiar to me. Where have I seen this vehicle? Tia! It looks exactly like Tia's Honda!"

Noah's heart began beating faster. He focused on the driver. Yes! The gray-eyed blondie! Where is she going in this terrible time of a day? She is on the phone, but I can't hear her. Damn! Too bad…

For some reason, Tia's car wasn't following the detour signs, but proceeding straight in the middle of the cordoned-off area.

"No! It's dangerous! Tia, stop!"

A tree dropped down right in front of Tia's car. Noah saw how the vehicle stopped, and Tia came out. A teenager with a huge CD player or perhaps a radio ran toward her…

"Tia, drive away! Run!" Noah tried to touch the crystal ball with the intention to stop the potentially threatening young man, but his hand went through the ball like through the air.

"You can only observe the book level, not interfere with it. It's like reading a book. Even a writer can't change his creation. If he corrects the narration, it will be a completely new book, which will exists in a new book level." Anna-Rasara touched Noah's shoulder and granted him with an insincerely sad smile. "And besides, why do you still care about her? You've got me forever now…" She walked around him, sliding her hand over his shoulder, chest, completing the circle on the other shoulder. "It is me who is giving you the best pleasure of your life. Not her. You have made the right choice, Kondrat. You are mine now." Anna-Rasara kissed Noah's lips and, getting down on her knees, became as one body with the Anna of the book.

Noah woke up in a cold sweat. He looked around. A big room with glass walls surrounded him. There were no windows, no extra furniture, just a hospital bed screwed down to the floor. He sat on the bed, rewinding his dream, and suddenly jumped in a standing position.

"Tia!"

He ran to the glass wall and started screaming for a nurse. No one was around; only a couple of cameras on the ceiling turned their all-seeing eyes on Noah.

"I know you see me! Somebody, please help! Tia's in danger! Call the police! Somebody!" He ran from side to side of the room, touching the glass walls and, in agony, looking for a sign of life in those cameras. No result was found. Noah became agitated. He began to hit his head and fists on the glass.

A nurse came and in a calm voice asked if Noah needed something. Noah lost self-control, trying to scream away his concerns and expressing them with ripping off his hospital gown and pulling his hair. "I have to help her! Let me out! Please, let me out!"

Dr. Kozlov was called immediately. He entered the secluded area. Noah ran toward him and collapsed in convulsions one step away from the doctor. A seizure had begun. Dr. Kozlov administered a sedative, a two-milligram injection, to ease the seizure. With nurses' help, Noah was transferred back on his bed.

The Turning Point

"There are lots of barricades and detours on the streets of Gray Stone right now. According to RCMP updates, a few people are responsible for creating the chaos by damaging vehicles, breaking windows, and looting in downtown area. There haven't been any casualties yet, but we insist you to remain at home if there is no urge to go outside."

Marsha went through a few channels and turned the TV off.

"Morning, Mom." Tia sat on the couch beside her mother, holding a silver tray with a teacup and toast with coco-butter and fruits on it. "Want some tea?" She looked so cute and cozy wearing puffy white slippers on her bare feet and a gray cotton robe over a long silky nightgown. Her long straight hair was tangled in a braid.

"No, darling, thank you. I've had breakfast already." Marsha put the TV remote control on the coffee table and relaxed her back. "Do you work today?"

Tia enjoyed her drink with a smile and didn't rush into the conversation. She nodded and took a bite of the crispy toast.

After all, who would agree to ruin such a peaceful morning in a quiet neighborhood? November was doing its work according to the early Canadian fall. The mornings were still cheery with the sun shining through the clear blue sky. The first morning frost powdered up the last brown spots on leaves of the apple tree outside of the living room window. All grass had almost silvered overnight and looked forward to the sun to do its magic by melting the frost away. Unfortunately, when time calls, a big fight for irretrievably lost freshness is not effective anymore. And the only action that would be appropriate in this situation is the act of accepting the change, steam it in a teapot with a pinch of jasmine, and nourish your heart and soul with that drink. It will always make you feel better, especially on a day like this.

A crow cawing on the apple tree from the other side of the window foretold of a cellphone ring, which has manifested the beginning of another busy day in the very peaceful neighborhood. Right away the relaxed heart and soul sent back a signal for the positive brain work. The cerebellum immediately connected with cerebrum and coordinated the muscle movements of the neck and hand, which made Tia to turn her head and pick up that phone. A couple of short words only. No emotions during the phone call. To be precise, no emotions were shown on Tia's face, but Marsha's eye caught something that no one else would pay attention to. Instead of the perfect gray eyes that were resting under the dark-blond eyelashes a few seconds ago, a mirror of the silver tray on the coffee table reflected an orange-amber hue that spread over her daughter's eyes.

Tia put the phone down and looked at Marsha. "I gotta go to work. There is some emergency with a client."

"What about your evening shift, honey?" Marsha got up from the couch and was about to take Tia's plates away.

"You're right, Mom. I'll finish it. A couple of minutes won't change anything." Tia picked up a cup of tea and, sip by sip, slowly, with her eyes closed, brought to an end the sacred morning ritual.

Marsha threw a worried look outside where the big crow was still sitting on the apple tree.

"I'm ready now." A pair of the clearest gray eyes with a darling smile touched Marsha's face. "Love you, Mom." Tia kissed her mother, fluttered from the couch, and disappeared somewhere in the stairway area.

Tia's orange Honda Civic was heading toward the downtown hospital when a few signs with DETOUR warnings began to get the drivers' attention. Soon, the traffic became busier, and beside the DETOUR signs, orange rectangles with equally important signs of BARICADES AHEAD started showing up.

"A little too late for the road construction season. It's almost wintertime..." This quick thought was jumping from one driver to another when they got closer to downtown. "Must be some serious car accident." That was the exact second thought, one and for all. The traffic became slow and soon ended with a complete stop after all.

Tia checked the time. She had already exceeded all possible excuses for a delay. "Well...it's not my shift, and there are definitely some problems ahead. So I am alright." Keeping cool and calm, she turned on the local radio station.

Listening to the news about the downtown disruptions, Tia sank deep into her thoughts, trying to find a connection between the past month's events and the news. There were no movements on the road but lots inside her head. She was sitting and analysing the situation for a good fifteen minutes. The radio helped her to draw a better picture of what was happening.

Some noise on the back window got Tia's attention. She glanced into the rearview mirror and saw a huge crow walking on the trunk of her car. "Hah! Even birds confuse vehicles with sidewalks. What exactly is going on over there?"

By the quick look at the side passenger window, Tia noticed that a child was looking at her from the other car on her right. Poor kid had distorted horror on his face. Tia quickly realized that the deep thinking turned her eyes into "the alien's black flats." In a few seconds, sunglasses were strategically placed on Tia's face, giving enough time to relax from the annoying thoughts. When she turned her face back toward the scared child, and she took off the shades, the whole family of three were staring at her from out of their vehicle. Tia looked at them with a cute smile. The father of the family immediately returned to his driving duty of the nonmoving car by holding tight the steering wheel. The disappointed mother began to teach her child with outstanding imagination to some manners. The confused kid tried to defend his previous observation by saying something and pointing on Tia. Obviously, it wasn't his lucky day.

Tia couldn't hold her smile and burst out with quiet laughter. At the same time, she deeply sympathized to that child because his feelings got hurt. The closest people in his life didn't believe him. What could he expect from the rest of the world?

The relaxing laughter cleared up her mind a little. The knocking on the back window switched Tia's attention to the previous subject. The crow on the trunk flew away toward the park entrance on the right side of the road. Tia held her gaze on the bird for a few seconds and came up with a new plan of creating her own detour. Her new idea didn't take much time for the proper analysis and granted Tia with the consent to make a turn into the park zone. A car behind immediately filled an empty spot. There was no way back.

The orange Honda drove into the park, crossed the parking lot, and made a clean exit up to the bridge. It was illegal, but nobody was around, and anyway, desperate circumstances called for desperate measures.

This time of day, the bridge wasn't that busy as it used to be on weekends, when people tried to get into parks together with their families and family pets.

"I should start to use this detour to go to work. It's a bit longer but not so busy." Tia was proud of her new discovery and headed straight toward downtown.

There were no signs of detours or barricades on her way. It meant that she didn't violate any driving rules. Satisfied, Tia entered the back alley of downtown and then the central street. What she saw next was shocking. First levels of apartment buildings on the sides of the street were breathing with fire. Upper-floor windows exploded from the high temperature and rained on sidewalks with broken glass. A few people wearing hospital gowns were running around and destroying everything in their way.

Tia became terrified and stopped the car. Observing this for a minute, she felt sorry for the spot she left on the trafficked street. After considering all the pros and cons, she decided to proceed ahead. Slowly but surely, Tia stepped on the gas, bypassing the broken furniture and burned branches of pine trees on both sides of the main street.

A tree fell down a few inches apart from Tia's vehicle. She had to stop. There was no other way to pass the fallen tree, only to remove it manually.

Tia looked around and got out of the vehicle. A young man in a hospital gown appeared from nowhere right in front of her. He was holding a huge stereo set and intending to drop it on Tia's car. There was no intelligence detected in his eyes; cruelty, evil, and emptiness were sealed behind their silver tincture.

Tia's first impression was that this human being was possessed with something unnatural, demonic. She recognized him immediately. It was a patient from the hospital whose behavior had changed after Noah's visit in his room.

Tia looked petrified. It was difficult to describe the exact feeling in that situation because a deep fright paralyzed her ability to move, feel, or think.

She was glued to the ground, staring into his eyes. The person stopped doing any frightening movements and maintained an eye contact with Tia as well. It seemed like all the forces that made Tia petrified were leaving her body through her eyes and transferring into that young man.

Noticing that there was no potential threat from the man anymore,

Tia forced herself to move slowly toward him, still maintaining eye contact.

The young man was standing still. Then after a few seconds of staring, his face color began to change from gray into his usual golden brown. He tried to lift his hand with the odd weapon, the cord of a radio set, but his movements turned into convulsions.

Step by step, Tia got closer to him without releasing the invisible string between their eyes. Suddenly, the stranger's whole body started to shake, and he dropped down on the sidewalk. Tia didn't rush to administer first aid or CPR as a Good Samaritan, which would have happened if she were at her workplace or in some other normal circumstances. Observing the casualty was the best choice at the moment. One more choice rushed through Tia's head—to run! But it was immediately replaced by the young scientist's curiosity—to stand by and study the unknown phenomenon.

She looked at that young man, almost a boy in his teens. A hospital gown barely covered his fit body with lots of cuts and burns as a result of his aggressive behaviour. His feet were bleeding from all the big and small pieces of broken glass in them. His fingernails were mostly damaged or missing. He lay unconsciously beside Tia's feet.

"He doesn't seem dangerous now. I should assess him for broken bones..." She made a step forward and backed up right away in uncertainty.

Police Patrol arrived and called for emergency. The young man opened his eyes and looked at Tia. Those eyes were full of tears and didn't require any words. Like two dark leaves in the late fall, they were fighting against early frost of disappearing silver tincture, which was all over his dead eyes a minute ago. Pale emptiness of the winter had melted under the warmth of still active November sun. And that sun was standing and looking at him.

When the emergency team arrived and transferred the boy inside the vehicle, he got all his energy together and said two words, looking into Tia's eyes: "Thank you." Then he passed out again.

Tia was successfully escorted to the Gray Stone Regional Hospital after leaving the emergency vehicle and endless explanations to police about her business downtown.

Besides a few police cars around the hospital and lots of security personnel inside, the hospital functioned normally. As always, people were arriving, getting the needed medical attention, and leaving the building. The less fortunate stayed inside for further treatment.

Tia was escorted into the office where two doctors and Paulina were waiting for her.

"Sorry for being late. There was so much traffic everywhere." Tia glanced at the policeman who still looked at her with suspicion. "I took a shortcut and got in trouble. Thank you so much, Officer, for making my arrival faster."

With sudden confidentiality the policeman replied to Tia, "No problem, ma'am, happy to help. Right now, downtown is a very unsafe place for driving. Please avoid the area if you can."

"Will do. Thank you."

Tia and all the company politely waited until the brave cop left the room.

A pager beep sliced the silence. Dr. Kozlov checked it and turned toward the monitor in the admitting department. "One more Recolla patient is being admitted."

A photo and information of the new arriving patient began to run underneath the screen.

"That's Josh Cobbler." Paulina pointed on the photo ID.

"Do you know him?" queried Professor Kidd.

"Yes. His father is the executive director of our agency."

"And he is on his way," added Dr. Kozlov, checking the emergency messages on his cell phone.

Tia recognized that young man as well and felt like she had to let everyone know what happened half an hour ago. "I've seen this boy. He wanted to damage my car. Then something happened, and he stopped, then fell in convulsions. He is severely injured." She tried to look closely at the monitor where Josh, secured with sheets and belts on the stretcher and with an oxygen mask on, was rolling into the elevator.

Professor Kidd asked Dr. Kozlov to step out of the room. "I know Josh's father very well. Serge is my patient for more than forty years. The confidentiality of his illness has never left the walls of this hospital." He paused and meaningfully peered over his glasses into Dr. Kozlov's eyes. "Serge Cobbler was diagnosed with schizophrenia and epilepsy when he was a teenager. Apparently, the medical plan I came up with successfully keeps his seizures under control. No one has any idea of how ill this man is. And now, his son is about to be diagnosed with the same illness. Recolla patients don't have mental diseases."

Dr. Kozlov, catching his colleague's drift, impatiently continued the reasoning. "According to Tia, Josh wanted to damage her car and suddenly stopped, then he had convulsions. You think in that very moment, Josh started developing his father's illness? When he was healthy, he's got Recolla. After the seizure, Josh became aware of his previous violent behaviour!"

"Exactly!" Professor Kidd's face lit up with a smile, sensing the possible breakthrough in Recolla study. "We need to be sure that our hypothesis has all the supporting evidence. Doctor, please, complete Josh's assessment immediately and get the report ready. I will stay with our friends in the office." The professor returned to the room.

"Professor, how is Noah doing?" Tia came closer to the monitors on the wall, trying to find Noah's room.

"Noah had one more episode an hour ago." Professor Kidd pressed a button of preadjusted recording and ran the video. "Apparently, what we used to call seizures that Noah had history with were not seizures. Computed tomographic scans and magnetic resonance imaging didn't show any brain atrophy or damage. In addition to this, we ran electroencephalogram to confirm any presence of seizures. All the results came back negative. Noah has never had mental disabilities. Placing him in a group home was a mistake. We don't know his real problem yet. If this is the fancy new illness, Recolla, then let it be. We can't even give a correct diagnosis because of lack of studies."

"Is there any suggestion regarding Noah's treatment? If he doesn't belong in a group home, then what will his living situation be?" Paulina stepped into the conversation.

Professor Kidd continued, "I am afraid that Noah will be transferred to the new department in this hospital where we keep the potential Recolla patients. We will assess Noah, run necessary tests, do some studies. His mother has already signed all consents."

Dr. Kozlov entered the room.

"I am sorry to interrupt." Tia expressed her concern. "If Noah doesn't have mental disabilities, he can't have a guardian. His mom would no longer be in control of his life. He is an adult and responsible for his own decisions. We can't keep Noah in the facility against his will. What about the rest of the Recolla patients? How did you proceed with them according to the treatment administration protocol, Professor?"

Confusion was seen on the professor's face. He glanced at his colleague, seeking for some help.

Dr. Kozlov replied with pleasure, "Yes, this is a very delicate subject. Certainly, we have no rights to force patients with any treatment, unless they show violent behavior, which is not safe to the public. Some of them agreed to receive medical help. The others made a wise choice of the treatment instead of being detained by the police and spending some time in jail. All our patients are responsible for their own actions. Almost all of them are seeking help. I am sure that Noah will make up his mind as well. We just need to find the right way to help him make a good decision." Dr. Kozlov and everyone in the room gave Tia a meaningful look.

Tia's confused glance disorderly jumped over all the faces back and forth, and after a few seconds' pause, she made a conclusion. "You…want…me to do it."

"My dear child"—Professor Kidd took Tia's hand—"you and Noah have an invisible bond that could be understood only by the two of you. I've seen how you mastered the most difficult situations with Noah. You, my dear, have found the right path for your career. Speaking of your career, as one of my best and gifted students, would you, Tia Phrever, accept my invitation to participate in the studies of Recolla illness?"

Tia couldn't take her eyes away from that sweet pink face and snow-white smile of Professor Kidd. She felt flattered and at the same time sensed that this old and experienced scientist was asking Tia for help. Somewhere deep down, Tia knew that this brilliant mind has gotten stuck with his research and looked for some fresh blood, nontraditional thinking, something completely out of this world, and his old-age intuition pointed to Tia.

"I would be honored."

Those words became a turning point in Tia's life and career.

"What do you say, Tia?" Santa Claus was about to close the deal.

Tia wasn't sure what had just happened. Forgetting about any precautions of her mood change, she was looking at the old man through her widely opened eyes, and pouring silver-green light through the amber touch-ups around the pupils, she replied, "I say…sure…"

PART IV
While We Were Dancing

- *2* -

Noah stood still at the very top of an extensive staircase. His cool boots with built-in heels sank in the very thick orange carpet. His long black coat was unbuttoned on his chest and spoke of self-determination. His liberating, out-of-the-way gaze reflected devotion to his dream. His entire look was screaming of a great hero. Were there any mirrors around? Noah was dying to see his awesome reflection, but at the moment, he decided to remain hard-shelled. And by the way, if this coolness were given for some reason, it would have been better to accept it without any emotions. "What is down there? Looks like a ballroom." Noah tried to figure out the place he was relocated to at this time.

Yes. It was a ballroom. The descending staircase, where Noah was standing, led into the huge cave. Thousands of candles and flaming torches were adjusted in every dent and protrusion of the cut stone walls. The enormous candelabra, made of thousands of candles, hung in the middle of the ceiling and observed the dancing crowd beneath. Regardless of myriads of candles, the light in the ballroom had a hue of dying ember. Some visitors were still arriving through the strange gate that looked like a gigantic fireplace in a wall. As a matter of fact, it was a fireplace in the wall. Guests were entering the ballroom from out of its flame, which was bursting away with each new arriving couple. New guests were slowly proceeding up to the staircase to greet the hostess of the ball. Others were carried away in the melody of a polonaise.

All men were wearing black frock coats and white tights. Their significant others had nothing on but sparkly strings with diamonds in their hair and enormous heels on their feet.

Ah...Noah couldn't take away his eyes from that scene. He even forgot about his cool look. Escorted by a very strong heartbeat, his eyes began to study every single body in the ballroom. The last thing that Noah cared about right now was their faces, even the prettiest ones. What, the graceful movements...alluring sway of flesh... unquenchable thirst to possess a couple of those forever...to reign over and subjugate them...

"Isn't it something that exactly defines the meaning of being a man?" A female's voice interrupted Noah's sweet thoughts. "A very powerful man." Anna-Rasara was standing beside Noah and observing the dancing crowd. "Can you imagine your entire existence as an endless party, slow and intimate in the beginning, rising desire toward conceiving of something super sweet and forbidden, in the middle, uncurbed frenzy of passion in any possible and impossible ways, forever..."

She was standing on his left with eyes closed, slightly swaying with her whole body from side to side, feeling the melody with each diamond in her hair, each finger on her hands, each pore on her skin.

(My dear friends, have you ever experienced dreaming in your dream? Yes?! Great! You are not a stranger to Noah's state of mind in this very minute.)

Anna-Rasara's languorous smile with half-opened lips was hoping to find a connection between the playfulness of her fingertips' thrilling strokes over her neck, shoulders, breasts, belly button...

For a moment, Noah forgot about all the naked dancers in the ballroom. He even stopped thinking about his cool look. All his energy was focused on those fingertips. He wanted to see the magic of their final touch…

The diva of seductive perfection began to speak to Noah. With a barely heard voice trembling in the rising excitement, Anna-Rasara breathed, "I am inviting you, Kondrat, to conduct the ball of every living creature on Earth through the dance with everybody in this room. Your passion will be your guiding star. Fulfillment of all your desires will be the only goal in this solemnity. Lead this ball to the victorious end. Become the Lord of the universe And so…begin!"

———————————

"There is nothing we can do right now but wait." Dr. Kozlov placed the stethoscope back on his neck after examining Noah. "Coma is unpredictable in length. It can last a few hours or few years."

"I guess we are done for the day." Professor Kidd looked at everyone in the room. "I want to thank you all for arriving in such a short notice. We'll keep in touch. And you, young lady, are welcome to hang around in the Recolla Department. There is a nurse at the front desk. Her name is Avery. She will take you to the Human Resources Department for signing up your practicum papers." He gave such a warm smile to Tia and walked her to the desk to meet with Avery.

Tia left the hospital after all the paperwork was completed and all Recolla patients' files were read. She lost track of time, jumping onto the path toward her dream career. So many things to do…so much information to receive…piles of studies to check…

Her slight dizziness reminded her about her skipped lunch and almost missing dinner. She checked the time and rushed to her car. "Why's the human body dependent on food? It's just a waste of time. I can't imagine where the human race would be by now if we didn't spend our time on sleeping and eating. Well, maybe it's the very time to solve the problem! I am so ambitious. One step at a time, Tia. Time…time…time…

With a huge smile and millions of thoughts about how to improve life of humanity, Tia got into her vehicle. Ignition…side mirror…rear mirror…"eye con" check…stop!

A new routine on controlling eye color before driving, named eye con by Tia, wiped the smile from her face and made her pull back on the transmission. Apparently, led by unrestrained excitement with the career proposal, Tia forgot about any precautions on her eye color change. Dark surface of the rear mirror reflected golden-green light running out of her eyes.

Tia turned off the ignition and tried to put herself into the professor's shoes when he proposed to Tia to work along with his team on the Recolla research. *Where was I standing? Face-to-face with the professor, looking into his eyes. Alright…he was wearing glasses. It means poor sight. The office had natural light. Bright sunny day plus a few monitors on the wall and one on a desk. It could play in my favor as a refraction of rays with the lens of my eye, creating a spectre of light…different color…Okay, in this case, I am safe. What about the others? Before the professor spoke to me, I was standing beside the monitor wall apart from everyone, trying to find Noah on the screens. I am good. They saw only my back.*

Tia sighed with relief and put the lost smile back on her face. Ignition…side mirror…rear mirror…eye con check…go!

-2-

"My desire has always been to dance with you, Rasara. That's the point of all." Noah kneeled in front of Anna-Rasara and kissed her hand. "I'd rather be with you than become the Lord of the universe."

"And I…" She paused and gave Noah a meaningful look, which showed how his bottomless love started to launch annoying fireworks into her direction. "I am accepting you only as the Lord of the universe. Go now and become!" Anna-Rasara pulled her hand out of Noah's, accidently (or not) slapping his face and finalizing her decision. With the inaccessibility of a statue, she fixed her cold empty eyes on the dancers.

Right away, Noah felt like someone invisible sliced his head across, opened it like a watermelon, and, filling it up with large hail from head to toe, turned his passionate heart into a piece of ice. Sudden alienation of the most desirable creature screwed him up in confusion. He wanted to throw up on his cool boots, but was afraid that by passing up, the internal frozen flesh might turn him inside out.

A tender touch on his shoulder made Noah turn his head left and right. A blue-eyed young man with curly blond hair and full red lips was standing behind Noah. He wasn't wearing white tights and a black crock jacket like all males in the ballroom. His brown tights and red muscle shirt outlined the absolute curvature of his legs, firm buttocks, and all the magnificent parts on the upper body that have been adored by bodybuilders over centuries.

Something hot penetrated Noah's frozen chest and stuck in his heart. The heart-icicle gave a crack...became flexible...started flapping and pulsing blood in all directions, bringing Noah back to life. Suffocated with emotional outburst, he pushed out only one word: "Patrick..."

Forgetting Anna-Rasara's coldness that wounded Noah so bad, he got up to his feet and greeted his dearest friend with open arms. "Patrick! How's it even impossible? You're alive!"

Two young men whose love was destroyed in a bud a few years ago froze in each other's arms.

"I missed you so much..." Noah released his grip long enough to be able to touch Patrick's face and, gently holding his head, covered it with kisses. The last long kiss on his friend's lips fulfilled the thirst of true feelings. "I have so much to tell you. How've you been, sweetheart? I want to know everything..." Noah embraced his lover again, inhaling his hair and neck.

Patrick silently survived the fire of Noah's emotions. Very soon the flame subsided a little, and the friends were able to keep a few inches apart from each other. Patrick kept smiling and, holding Noah's hands, faced him to his right.

A young girl with yellow orchids in her long black hair patiently waited for Noah's attention. Perfectly trimmed bangs covered half of her slanting brown eyes. Her bow-shaped puffy lips, round cheeks, and cute button nose outlined the portrait of an exotic beauty usually seen in vacation commercials. She shyly smiled at Noah.

For some reason, Noah sensed that this girl didn't belong in here. Why? He couldn't explain. He looked around, searching for the answers. Everyone in the ballroom had the same look in their eyes (cold and lifeless), the same body structure (skinny, perfectly proportioned), the same movements (as being programmed to dance, walk, flirt), and the same diamonds in hair and clothes or no clothes at all...

Everything screamed in opposite with this young woman. Uncertainty was written all over her. Noah could tell how difficult it was for her to fit in. She didn't have any clothes on, but long thick hair covered her back and front. Nervously playing with her locks, wrapping and unwrapping them around her tiny fingers, she was constantly checking if her breasts and belly areas were safely curtained by the strands of her hair.

"Ofelia?" Noah released Patrick's hands and turned all his attention toward the girl. He began to figure out what was going on around here and what exactly this place was. Surprised, he approached his first failed love. "Why are you here? Please, don't tell me that you're..." He didn't want to say the scary *dead* word. "You...don't feel well?" He quickly cast an up-and-down look on her body.

"Hi, Noah." Poor girl didn't know how to behave. Seemed like she was happy that Noah noticed her. She made a timid step toward him and, glancing quickly around, replied in a whisper, "I don't really know why I am here. What is this place? Why am I naked? Why are all the women here naked? I am scared..." Ofelia locked her little hands together to her chest like she was praying and, with begging eyes, waited for an answer. She looked lost and frightened.

Noah turned his face to Patrick and said quickly, "Don't go anywhere, please. Okay?"

Patrick slightly bowed, keeping the same smile on his face.

Noah got very close to Ofelia and looked seriously into her eyes. "Where were you before coming in here?"

Ofelia's whole body began to shake. "I was in a hospital with a head injury. Then I heard some voices. They ordered me to do everything you would ask me to do, to obey you, no matter how weird your requests might be. Then I found myself here, completely naked. It is so embarrassing. Are we dreaming?"

Ofelia's short story cleared up Noah's thoughts and shuffled them to the places they belonged. He wanted to tell Ofelia about the fantasy of the book he was writing, the book level and this ball, hosted by the Satan himself for all the dead in sin. He wanted to tell her about Rasara and the fight against the whole universe. About his spiritual-self, Kondrat. And the sudden realisation that he has made an unrecoverable mistake of being selfish and, because of that, now he is in deep regrets. All this was just a trap for his good soul. Rasara is not Rasara, and all around was just a demonic mythology that wanted to screw up his brain...

––––––––––––

Singing along with the radio, Tia was heading home. In a few hundred meters before the DETOUR signs began to take over downtown, Tia, beyond a shadow of a doubt, decided to drive through the restricted area. Proudly considering herself as part of the research team, she wanted to see if Josh's change of behavior was a coincidence at the time when she interacted with him this morning. There were still some individuals out there who hadn't been identified yet. And now, somehow, Tia needed to find a way to get through all the restrictions unnoticed to push her scientific plan forward. What was the worst that could happen? To be detained by police and then released? Exciting, isn't it?!

Her mind was set. Turning down the radio, Tia made an exit into the residential apartment area of downtown. Driving between the buildings and looking for police vehicles, Tia slowly approached toward the restricted area. The police cars' convoy didn't keep her waiting for long. White-blue police cars and SUVs parked a few meters apart from each other and blocked the unsafe area from a peaceful chain of downtown apartment buildings when Tia arrived. There was no chance to get through them unnoticed.

Tia parked on the apartment buildings' back alley. It was a perfect observation point. She could see everything that was happening around the police patrol and analyze the situation.

The November day got tired of watching the fading nature and began to close its eyes. What will it dream? For sure, the vision of the upcoming spring with lots of hot days would be preferable to the endless fires in every second building of downtown Central Square. Or kids playing hide-and-seek in parks instead of that police officer who has just left his watch point and proceeded into the restricted area to search for his partner. Or that girl who was about to get out of her car and cross over the forbidden line, using the unsecured gap in the cordoned-off chain between police vehicles…

It was Tia's luck that she chose the right parking at the right time. Without thinking twice, she quickly left her car and dived under the yellow tape. Trying to be unnoticeable, Tia carefully proceeded toward the disturbing explosions and those unpleasant sounds that indicated abnormalities in town.

She moved slowly, using the back alleys of buildings. A shrill cry from across the street made her stop. It was a man's voice. In a second, forgetting of the conspiracy, Tia ran to the other side of the street, passing the damaged vehicles parked under the joined roof between two buildings. A bunch of crows hiding inside that parking lot got spooked by Tia's run. With very loud cawing, the birds flew out of their shelter and sat on the half-railed balcony across the park stalls, curiously observing illogical behaviour of the foolish girl.

A terrifying view opened before Tia's eyes. She was standing on the same spot of the same street where she met Josh this morning. Barely recognizing the surface, Tia's feet were planted into the sidewalk—or whatever was left of it. Her eyes changed from slanting to big and round. She was shocked to see the place destroyed so much in such a short time. The second floors of business places on sides of the street were completely roofless and downed to the lower levels. The crushed walls and broken cubicles she saw four hours ago were transformed into dust with black embers of burnt trees in between.

Tia was standing in the middle of Central Square that used to be stuffed with big and small buildings with almost no space in between. Now she could see a huge flat surface. The only bumps in this emptiness was the army of disorganized green-yellow fire hydrants that waited for a command from their marshal, the headless statue of the founder of the city of Gray Stone.

A dozen men and women were "working hard" on smashing objects till the size of gravel a couple of blocks away inside the buildings that still had walls. A few people dressed in uniforms, police officers, security guards, and firemen were included in the destroying process, using their guns, shields, and batons as the crushing objects.

A high-pitched scream made Tia turn around. An old man on a wheelchair tried to detach his foot prosthesis, slashing it with a metal wire. It was hard to say what exactly made this man agitated: physical pain and suffering or the task failure. Disappointed with his tool, he threw the wire away and, in despair howled at the sky. In the next moment, the man bent over his knees and began to disconnect a foot holder from his wheelchair. He probably wanted to use it as a replacement for the thrown wire. He lost his balance and fell out from the chair, hit the sidewalk with his knees and forehead, and got stuck in this position with his buttocks in the air.

Tia couldn't observe him any longer and ran toward the man. Without any words, she grabbed the wheelchair, engaged its breaks, and angled the chair behind the man. Supporting the wheelchair with her body, she bent above its back and the person under it. Then she fastened the wheelchair belt under the man's belly and pulled it in the standing position together with the man.

Feeling himself strapped down, the old man grabbed the chair's arms and started shaking and hitting them, shouting in all directions. Suddenly, he noticed Tia and grinned at her like a Halloween pumpkin, showing broken dentures and bleeding gums. After a few seconds of piercing her with emptiness in his white eyes, the man started to shake in convulsions. Soon, he relaxed his hands and looked at Tia with exhaustion and the sign of intelligence in his blue eyes.

"That's better. Sir, please, try to relax. I'll take care of you." Tia grabbed the wheelchair holders and rolled the man back to the alley where she came from.

Tia's state of mind slowly began changing from shocked into analytical. Obviously, the illness has affected more people since she was back from the hospital. And it was just here in Gray Stone. What about globally? There must be something that could stop this madness…

–5–

"Ladies, invite gentlemen!" The voice of the ball hostess brought the party to life. Boring polonaise turned into a romantic waltz. Naked females left their usual partners and, armed with playful giggling, began roaming around, seeking for new dance companions.

Noah glanced at Anna-Rasara and understood that he was being watched. He decided to play along to avoid a conflict.

"Let's dance." He was about to touch Ofelia's hand with an invitation to dance. Ofelia replied with a smile and took a waltz pose. They made a step toward each other and stood still for a moment to adjust themselves in this forbidden situation.

Once Noah's hand slid down Ofelia's lower back and his chest pressed against her breasts, the worries about being watched disappeared at once. Tremulous breathing into each other's necks recalled their forgotten feelings, and verbal communication was no longer needed.

Ofelia rested her head on Noah's shoulder and wrapped both arms around his neck. She didn't want to move faster, but to swing just enough to hear their heartbeats. Noah's cool look and unbelievable circumstances made her sink into this beautiful fantasy. "I don't mind being naked in this dream. It makes the dream more exciting." She smiled at the thoughts and decided to fully enjoy the magic of dreaming.

The silky long hair and relaxed body of the young woman in his arms spread pheromones all over the place and slowly began to knock on the door of Noah's human nature. Soon those two couldn't see clearly what was happening around. They didn't care anymore about everybody's foolish looks, but physical attraction nourished by desired intimacy.

Mesmerizing music mantled the cave walls with sweet languor and melted candle wax. They were filling up all the dents and minimizing all the protrusions. The huge chandelier began to drip hot wax with sparkly flames. As the rhythm of music increased, random lights began to flicker in the ballroom. Moaning sounds of waltz, merging in unison with the crackles of flickering candlelight, flew the melody above its perfection.

> Once the sound has itself found,
> Merging in unison, launched a unique song.
> Reaching the sky with no measure of height,
> Beats flew around and restless hit the ground.
> With no break they got up and stayed awake…

The excess of musical oxygen has resulted its toxicity on every dancing body in a guess.

Dusk was about to light up the streets of Gray Stone with the best invention of mankind. Unfortunately, nothing is permanent without good maintenance. This "best invention" in the downtown area had been destroyed by its creators thirty hours ago. All sources of electricity were returned to their starting point—dust.

Despite the upcoming darkness, it was easy to make shortcuts, pushing the wheelchair with the passed-out man on it through the sidewalks. Tia moved as fast as she could, trying to find the safest path toward the parking lot in between the two buildings where she could take a break and continue to safety.

Crossing a street and leaving Central Square behind, Tia reached the under-roof parking.

Tuned into constant disruption, the crow family agreed not to leave their shelter this time but show some vocal protest toward the outraged behaviour of the strange girl with the unconscious man in a wheelchair. After a few more outbursts, the birds calmed down, folded their necks into fluffed-up feathers, and fell into the rapid eye movement sleep.

Not all the crows were sleeping. The ancient predators' genes of their flying ancestors dictated them to have a couple of watch birds in each flock. Such two crows were observing and sitting apart from the others. They probably didn't care about the messed-up hair and scratched dusty shoes of the young girl, who, regardless of her skinny fragile complexion, was managing the chair with a pretty heavy man on it. And of course, they had no idea why that still fledgling human chick was taking care of a stranger by putting her own life at risk.

Tia left the danger area and stopped for a break. She looked around the under-roof parking lot. It seemed like there was no potential threat in here. Any harm that could be done here was already done. All the vehicles were severely damaged. Some of them still had suitcases and bags inside. Some car doors were opened or broken off and lying on the concrete. It looked like people were rushing out and left their belongings behind. The sound of broken glass was heard with each step Tia made. Even a pathetic garbage can, the most uninteresting thing in the world, was tipped over, showing its contents.

For a second, Tia's attention was captured by the black van parked in the corner of the lot. With clean tinted windows untouched by the rebels, this van didn't fit into the scene. Or maybe, it was just Tia's imagination, and she could be easily mistaken by admitting that she didn't notice the van when she was passing by. Alright. No problems with that. She leveled out her breathing with one deep inhale and lifted her eyes to the two birds that remained awake. A split-second thought hit her. *If those two are watch birds, why are they sitting beside each other?* Tia looked at the opposite corner of the under-roof parking where one of those two birds was supposed to sit. It was empty. A cold shiver ran all over her body. Something was wrong. She decided not to pay attention to the weird feeling and proceeded to the residential area.

Fighting with the disturbing sensation, Tia checked on the wheelchair man. He was still unconscious but breathing. "Okay, buddy, let's do it fast." Aiming the wheelchair toward the exit, Tia grabbed its handles the same way as if she would prepare to make a jump over a speed bump on a bike.

At the moment when she was ready to take off, something very strong grasped her waist, tightly covered her mouth, and pulled her away from the person in the wheelchair.

There wasn't enough time for Tia to figure out what just happened. While being dragged by somebody toward the black van, she saw a man in a police uniform taking over Tia's responsibility. He checked the pulse and eyes of the unconscious person and, calling an emergency vehicle, ran, pushing the wheelchair fast across the street.

So fast...so quiet...Probably the good guys. Why is that crow staring at me? Crows don't have silver eyes...

A very bright light inside the van made Tia close her eyes for a moment. The seat is too comfortable for a prisoner. No violence at all. Should I worry about my eye color? Always... She used the time to adjust her mood and then opened her eyes.

The van was fully equipped. A long wall on the window side was installed with KPIs (key performance indicators), two cameras, and small monitors viewing inside and outside of the parking area. Along the driver and passenger seats all the way to the glove compartment, lots of digital monitors and communication devices were beeping, crackling, diagramming. The windshield of the van looked like a huge cell phone screen with lots of dots, squares, and circles. Its bright neon light happened to be the only source of light inside the van.

Two men in black jackets with silver RCMP signs on their backs were operating the electronic system. They were wearing big black glasses with microphones adjusted across their dark-gray baseball hats. They looked more like federal agents than city policemen.

The police officer who dragged Tia in the van took off his helmet with a plastic visor and sat across Tia. "I am sorry for being rough on you, ma'am." For a few seconds, his eyes wandered around her face with curiosity. "We had to remove you from this dangerous situation. This was a necessary precaution."

Regardless of speaking tough, there was something unsettling about him. It was amusing for Tia to watch those masculine hands constantly playing with his helmet, randomly touching and shifting it from hand to hand. The tough guy was under some kind of anxiety. It was noticeable for Tia how carefully he tried to choose the right words.

"It was amazing how you dealt with the situation." His dark blue eyes looked wide, round, and bulged. They matched up perfectly with a big potato nose and couple of thick ears of a wrestler. All those features were sitting on his bald hilly head. The bottom line was that this hard-shell police officer obviously tried to hide certain insecurity. "How did you do that?" The muscle man began to loosen up and moved closer to Tia with the curious smile of a child.

Tia was expecting this question and, demonstratively looking around and pretending to be very interested in the fancy van equipment, replied to the police officer with the vacant glance of a naïve girl, "Did what?"

Potato Nose backed up a little. Tia's trick worked. They wouldn't ask any serious questions anymore. She kept pretending to be a rebellious teen and cast a compromising look at the man.

One of the operators turned around and, without looking at Tia, unceremoniously dropped big tinted glasses on her lap, the same as they were wearing. Potato Nose grabbed the spare ones as well.

"We have to check your ID. Put the glasses on, please." The operator immediately redirected himself back to the monitors with the assumption that the "naïve girl" would immediately follow his request.

Tia, for a moment, conceived hatred toward the role she chose to play. Obviously they were "good guys," but didn't want to waste manners on this "cute and probably stupid girl." She took the glasses, looked at them with an indulgent smile, angled her head to the side, pursed her lips, and put the glasses back on her knees.

Potato Nose observed Tia's actions with an explicit interest and a bit of a smile. After a few seconds of staring at empty monitors, both operators at the same time turned their attention onto Tia.

"Miss…Glasses, please." The operators patiently waited for Tia's response.

With a mix of defiant equanimity and mocking expression, Tia looked at the confused cops. A couple of long uncomfortable seconds of misunderstanding were imprinted on their faces.

The one operator who looked quite young started losing his patience and began to pronounce each word very slowly with a stop in between, supporting his verbal communication with gestures. "Miss. Could you…please…put…those glasses…on…"

Another silent gap reigned for a few seconds. The boy-cop shrugged with exhaustion and looked at his partner.

A man in his fifties took off his dark glasses and a microphone, turned his chair 180 degrees toward Tia, and with a smile through his gray beard and mustache, said, "Our apologies, ma'am. Being preoccupied with this work, we forgot a few simple things. One of them is to introduce ourselves…"

Listening to his partner's "insanity," the boy-cop turned toward Potato Nose and with exhaustion sighed.

Beard kept talking. "And the other one is to explain to you what we were doing here."

Tia stopped smiling and, getting what she wanted without any words, let the man know that there was a possibility that she might accept the invitation to speak.

The boy-cop took off his goggles, rolled his eyes, and turned toward the monitors.

Potato Nose got himself comfortable in his seat and, with growing curiosity, observed what would come next. It seemed he started to like this girl's attitude. *There must be something else besides the rebellious spirit. Her eyes reflect intelligence.*

Beard slightly leaned toward Tia and began to introduce everyone in the van. "I am Officer Laroche. This is my partner, Tony Kraphic."

The boy-cop still had his back toward Tia but "check marked" the obliged hand greeting that looked like a "talk to my hand."

"We are monitoring any abnormalities in the restricted area and gathering information on the prospective Recolla patients. The guy who nonstrategically captured you is Officer Savarex."

Potato Nose saluted to Tia with two fingers and a friendly smile.

Beard continued, "The reason we asked you to put on the goggles was for the precise identification—"

"I am Tia Phrever." Tia interrupted the officer, who wasn't expecting such a quick response.

The boy-cop immediately put his goggles on and typed Tia's name. Next second, with a long whistle of surprise, he turned around and squinted at her. "Undergraduate in neurobiology and an assistant of the Recolla illness research team. Girl! You are in the right place at the right time! Hah! Apparently, cute chicks can be smart too!" He measured Tia with his curious look and a half-faced smirk.

Potato Nose didn't rush himself into the conversation. His attention was focused on the girl. Will she ignore Tony's comment or swing it back to him? He saw Tia's facial profile perfectly lit by all the monitors' glare. No muscle movement on her face, no nerves twitching at all, and besides, she even lowered her eyes with the intention of picking up the goggles from her knees. His curiosity reached its highest peak. Is she unbelievably simple or impeccably strategic? What's Tony's next move?

The sarcastic smile gradually faded from Tony's face. He extended a pause after the last comment in order to leave enough room for Tia's predictable verbal stings. None of the pretty girls have escaped from Tony's jibs without nasty feedback. With a big disappointment on the upside-down smile, he put his shades back on. What a perfect shield for hiding unwanted emotions…

Potato Nose's eye caught a bright reflection in Tia's glasses when she brought them to her face. He didn't want to miss any information on this girl and quickly threw his shades on his face as well. All he saw was bright-red static with golden dots.

"What the hell is going on?" Tony and his superior tried to press buttons on all keyboards to fix the data.

Tia took off the glasses and closed her eyes. The police officers got rid of their visors as well.

"Sorry, Tia." Officer Laroche took Tia's goggles and placed them inside a titanium chamber and launched the recovery program. "They need a good reboot. It will take a couple of minutes." He started talking to Tony, analyzing the received signals.

Tia opened her eyes and looked at Potato Nose. The man was quietly looking back at her.

"Can you please check on the wheelchair person?" Tia nodded toward the officer's shoulder radio. It was a good idea for her to start talking because suspicions were written all over the officer's face. Lots of questions cried out for a release. The inevitable subject of an upcoming conversation had to be changed without being started, and "fixed" goggles had to be kept away from Tia's eyes. Tia tried to look relaxed and even smiled a little. "Sir, if I asked you about the protocol on the rescued individuals or Recolla patients, would it be classified to discuss?" She crossed her legs, wrapped her arms around her knees, and shrugged.

"What would you like to know, ma'am?" Potato Nose couldn't believe that this laconic person had initiated a conversation. He straightened up his back and slightly leaned toward Tia with his elbows on his knees and hands locked together in between, ready to communicate.

"Is the unconscious man alright? I would like to make a phone call to Professor Kidd. He is in charge of the Recolla illness research team." Tia spoke seriously in a quiet tone of voice. "Where is the police officer who walked away with the man? Shouldn't he be back already?"

Potato Nose pulled back, still looking at Tia but digging in the memory file of his brain.

Officer Laroche for a second got quiet and immediately turned his worried face toward Savarex. Potato Nose grabbed the radio out of his shoulder and pressed a button.

In the same moment, something heavy hit the van roof. Neonic diagrams on the windshield went off, dramatically deteriorating in visibility. Emergency light dimmed up the interior.

"Number two and three visuals are gone." Tony full-screened all the outside cameras. The police officers gathered in front of the monitors.

"It's Toufer! He's been affected!" Tony checked the other cameras around the closest residential area. "Looks like they got him on the way back here. Look…" Cameras were running the video of the emergency vehicle personnel who were transferring the wheelchair person inside the rescue van and locking its doors. Tony rewound the recording on Toufer's portable camera. "See the kid? Half an hour ago he was detected beside the downtown statue, and here he is, proceeding toward Toufer. Here he is again…eye contact…"

A heavy bang from outside made a spiderweb crack on the windshield.

"Tony, get ready to evacuate! You go south. Savarex, give the girl a vest! You two go north. We'll meet in the T-yield." Officer Laroche grabbed a backpack stuffed with weapons and began to unlock the emergency exit in the van's floor.

Savarex pulled out a bulletproof vest from under the seat and gave it to Tia. Tia was quietly sitting on the same seat and wasn't responding to what was happening. Her face was hidden under her long hair. Her head was tilting; arms were twitching and clutched tightly to the seat.

"It's okay, Tia. I'll take care of you. Put this vest on. We gotta go." Assuming that the girl was scared, Savarex squatted in front of her and touched Tia's shoulder. Tia stopped shivering and lifted her eyes up to the officer. Next second, Officer Laroche and Tony saw Savarex recoiling in dismay, crashing the computer on the opposite wall across Tia.

—4—

A mix of melted candle wax and love fragrance hung upon the dancing pairs, forming a foggy cloud. The longer the party went on, the thicker the fog became. Soon, it was impossible to see the ballroom's stone-cut walls, enormous chandelier, deformed candles. Swinging with music, pairs had to stay very close to each other because it was the only way not to lose a partner in that haze.

Sweet waltz gave a way to sexy kizomba, but the rules remained the same—couples had to change partners occasionally. Even if they didn't, the fog would.

Orgasmic sounds of bodies merging in movements were carried around the ballroom.

An endless dream of intimacy enshrouded two lost souls in the middle of nowhere. Ofelia slowly lifted up her head from Noah's shoulder and deepened her brown eyes in the clearness of his eyes. "Why didn't it work in the first place?"

Noah didn't want to talk but keep this moment the same: sweet and dreamy. He knew that the happening was not real. And if it were, it would not last for long. He slowly slid his hands from Ofelia's waist up to her back and shoulders, keeping eye contact and trying to remember each hue in her eyes. "It can work in this place," he whispered passionately and touched Ofelia's face. "It's up to us to make the dream come true."

How many times had Noah visualized exactly the same situation when he was sad and lonely? Firm, fresh skin of a young girl…bow lips so red and inviting…outspoken look of deep brown eyes…mutual love…

It was difficult to say whose lips lay on whose first. If you have tasted the morning dew on the wild rose petals or heard a song of blooming meadows, you would understand the tune between those two.

Sensual kizomba set the mood in the ballroom. From time to time, the dancing pairs were reminding of their existence by pushing around the smoky fog with their squirming movements. Only one pair remained motionless, keeping the smoky cocoon undisturbed and enjoying the magical elixir named a kiss.

With great willpower, Noah pulled himself from Ofelia. Breathing heavily, he squeezed her upper arms and whispered, "Do you wish this dream to come true?"

Ofelia didn't let him finish the phrase and screamed out in ecstasy, "Yes! I love you! I want to be with you forever!" She grabbed Noah's forearms and squeezed them as well. A dreamy smile and rolling up eyes talked of the sweet pleasure.

Noah shook Ofelia really hard, as if he wanted to wake her up. "Ofelia, listen to me carefully. I love you too…so much. Promise me something…can you?" Noah tried to make eye contact with the straying in a wonderland Ofelia.

"Yes. Anything…" she moaned.

Noah looked around cautiously and began to speak very fast. "It's not a dream, honey. This party is in our minds. In the reality we are unconscious. It's up to us if we wake up or not. Look around, Ofelia. They're all dead. Only us who are alive. If you want to continue this dance in real life, we have to get out of here…"

Ofelia's smile began to vanish. The veil of reverie was abruptly pulled off. Consciousness peeked through her eyes. "But how? Who will wake us up?"

"We will." Noah embraced Ofelia very tightly as they were dancing and faced her toward the fireplace gate. "This is the escape portal. All guests arrive through that gate. We have to dance away toward the fireplace and jump into it."

Ofelia's eyes went big and round. She pushed Noah away. "Are you crazy?! It's suicide to jump into that flame! You're sick…Stay away from me! You want to finish with me that way! I hate you!" Ofelia tried to get rid of Noah's grip, thumping her tiny fists on his chest and crying.

Noah forced her resisting body into a hug and covered her face with kisses. "Ofelia…I love you more than anything. You have to trust me…please…It's the only way to get out of here…Please…"

Ofelia stopped resisting and looked at Noah with hope in her eyes, sobbing, "Are there any other options?"

"I'm afraid not," Noah replied seriously. "Are you ready to listen to me now?"

Ofelia wiped her eyes and uttered aloofly, "I'm listening."

Noah exhaled and began to explain to Ofelia the escape plan. "Sooner or later, we have to change partners. If it happens, you'll dance away toward the fireplace and find me there, or I find you. Once we are together again, we'll jump into the gate. Do you understand me?" He gave a good shake to Ofelia again.

Ofelia, trembling in anxiety, tried to put the next few words together. "And…what's…next?" She was shivering increasingly.

Noah pressed her tightly against him, kissed her, and whispered in her ear, "Next…We wake up…and find each other again. And when I find you, I won't let you go." He gently kissed her hair, eyes, and lips. "When we are together again, I'll never let these tears possess your beautiful eyes. The only wetness allowed on your face is the warm rain in summertime and melting snowflakes in winter. I love you so much, Ofelia…"

The strong grips of their arms weakened up and got separated for a second to reunite in a dance position. At the same moment, the sexy kizomba let a fast and happy polka take the turn...

Officer Laroche and Tony looked in the same direction where Savarex pointed, choking in words. He was staring at Tia.

Tia turned her head onto the wall behind her as well, pretending that the danger everyone was looking at was coming from somewhere in the back. Those two seconds were enough for her to readjust the disturbing eye color that caused the turmoil. In a query, she turned her face back onto the police officers. "What?" she uttered quietly, tuning up with the alerting mood in the van.

Savarex's look was intently fixed on Tia's face. His partners were throwing perplexed glances from Tia to Savarex and back. In a few seconds, Savarex pushed the fear down to his throat and said to Tia in uncertainty, "Your eyes...They were..." He was looking for the right word. "Different..."

Officer Laroche threw a suspiciously worried glance at Savarex, took the bulletproof vest out of his hands, and passed it to Tia. "Hurry. We don't have much time." He roughly touched Savarex's shoulder and, opening the emergency exit on the floor, said, "You both go first...Savarex! Get in there! Tia, you're next."

Savarex grabbed the emergency bag and moved toward the exit, shaking his head as if he tried to wake up or get rid of annoying thoughts. Tia followed him.

The emergency exit on the vehicle floor was located right above the opened sewer hole. Tia watched Savarex throwing his bag into the hole and climbing down the ladder. In a few seconds she heard his muffled voice. "Okay! You're good to go!"

Tia sat on the floor and hung her legs down into the hole. "So good I am not wearing my fancy heels today." With this random thought, step by step, she reached the last crossbar of the ladder and looked down. There was a few feet left till the ground.

Potato Nose was ready to catch Tia in case she fell. "Jump now! I'll get you!"

Noises of something heavy crushing, pressing, and thumping began to carry from above. The heavy lid of the sewer hole dropped and covered half of the opening. Then gunshots crossed with a sharp scream of Officer Laroche. Tia looked up and down with fear.

"Jump, Tia! Jump!" Savarex rushed the girl.

The heavy lid above moved a little, and Officer Laroche's face peeked down the hole. Tia was happy to see him and waved to the officer to come down.

"I am jumping!" she shouted down to Savarex and let the ladder go.

Potato Nose caught Tia and held her for a second in his arms, looking in her eyes.

"I am alright." Suddenly, Tia felt some tension and, seeking an excuse to cut off this awkwardness, looked up. "Oh my god..." She met eye to eye with Officer Laroche. "Run! He is affected!" Tia touched the ground and covered Savarex's eyes with her hand. She tried to turn him away from the opened lid and kept pushing the confused officer in his back to make him run.

"Are you sure?" Savarex kept turning at Tia and moving ahead at the same time.

"Yes, I saw his eyes. Go, go!"

Savarex grabbed Tia's hand, nodded with a sign of upcoming action, and ran fast, dragging her behind.

Echoes of thousands of steps in a sewer surrounded the two runaways. It sounded like there was a presence of a few more people in the sewer running toward those two.

Tia didn't have to worry about looking forward or watching where to step. She had someone who led her, someone whom she trusted at the moment, who held her hand so tight that she didn't have to make any effort for her strong grip. Tia felt safe despite of hearing the different set of steps behind, the steps that were carrying danger of the unknown illness and life-threatening possibility.

She wasn't sure if her feet were touching the ground when being pulled by Savarex in that run. She heard some of her steps, soft and muted. Regardless of the fast run, Tia was able to take a good look around. *My shoes are so good for a run. The heels are high but sturdy. I should consider wearing them every day. Hah! There is no stinky water on the ground, and the walls are very high.*

The sewer appeared to be more like an underground tunnel with lots of junctions. It was wide enough to fit three people walking side by side. The walls arched toward the ceiling and held long neon lights built into their bending corners. Tia noticed black letters DT and number 1 printed on the gray walls. They were repeated every one hundred meters.

Savarex's voice interrupted her thoughts. "Can you see who's following us? How far are they?"

Tia looked back. "I don't see anyone," she replied, catching her breath.

Savarex glanced back at Tia and kept running. "How are you? Can you run for a couple more minutes?"

"I'll...do my best." Tia was breathing hard. She had to admit that long-distance running wasn't her virtue, and it would be awesome if she started to exercise.

The tunnel turned left, showing a different set of letters and numbers on the walls. DT1-Rs began to catch Tia's eye. Soon, she felt that Savarex slowed down a bit, and still holding Tia's hand, he stopped in front of a metal door in the wall. Breathing fast and looking back, he opened a squared barely noticeable metal plate on the door. A digital keypad appeared in front of him. Savarex pressed five numbers. The door clicked and slid to the right. He stepped into the room, pulling in Tia as well. The door slid back and clicked, locking up.

Dark silence of the very small room fenced off Tia from the annoying echo behind the heavy door. In a few seconds, sensory lights disturbed the silence with its soft buzzing.

"Oh, good. I thought I lost my hearing." Tia looked around the room.

"Yeah, the sound in here's quite different." Savarex touched a few buttons on the wall and signaled for Tia to sit down.

Tia sat on a metal stool in the middle of the room and quietly observed Savarex working around the information desk.

The buzzing lights went off, and all the screens lit the room with blue neon. The room interior reminded Tia of that police van with heavy equipment inside. Lots of monitors started to track any motion outside of the room. A huge screen on a wall appeared from nowhere in front of Tia. Some graphs and diagrams with lots of mathematical formulas started pumping around the screen, calibrating for something. Soon, silver-blue waves swept up and down, unveiling the view on the other side of the wall.

Tia touched the screen, feeling its surface. "It doesn't feel like glass or any computer screens..." She looked at Savarex inquiringly.

Savarex kneeled on the floor and started to unpack the emergency bag. Keeping himself busy, he replied in short sentences. "No, it's not. THM."

Tia spun the stool toward Potato Nose and, with undisguised curiosity, repeated, "THM?"

Savarex stopped unpacking and, without lifting his eyes on Tia, as if being caught on releasing too much information, slowly said, "Transparent Hard Matter—the new technology." Realizing that he was talking to a girl trapped in an extraordinary situation and holding up pretty well, Savarex softened his voice a bit and added, "That's all I can tell you. Sorry. Some information is classified."

Tia smiled, noticing some change on the serious face of the preoccupied police officer, and said, "Tia."

Savarex looked at her inquiringly. "Hmm?"

"Tia. That's my name."

Potato Nose paused and said in an official tone of voice, "Officer Savarex." Then he got up and began to test the radio on the wall.

Tia didn't have anything to do right now but bug the man. "I bet you have a name, Officer." She spun on her stool again, holding its seat firmly. "I'm not flirting with you. It's just weird to call another human being by his title and last name. It eats away the personality." Tia paused, slightly tilted her head, squinted, and said, "You're a human being...aren't you?"

Savarex smirked but continued to work. "Sure. You bet I am. What about you?" He stopped his work and faced Tia. "Are you a human being?"

"Yes, sir. One hundred percent human." Tia was glad that she pulled a few sentences out of this tough man. A smile of satisfaction printed on her face.

Potato Nose finished his work and sat on the other stool beside Tia. "You looked scared up there, in the van. I am sorry that you got involved in this." The officer turned his back for a second and checked the monitors. "It's safe in here." He paused. "Can I ask you something, Tia?"

"Sure." Tia sensed a tricky question but acted casual.

"When you jumped down to the sewer, you said that you saw Officer Laroche's eyes. Then you tried to prevent me from looking at him. How could he become affected, but nothing happened to you? And in what universe does the crazy wheelchair man become healed instantly when you interacted with him? I've seen the difference in his eyes before and after he met with you..." Savarex pierced Tia's eyes, trying to catch any muscle movement noticeable only to him.

Tia smirked, shook her head a little, and shortly replied with a smile, "Sorry. Some information is classified."

Potato Nose smirked back at her, looked down, then looked again at Tia, and showing unbelievably white teeth of his wide smile, he said, "Well played, miss. Well played."

"I guess I've just discovered an attractive person inside that boringly organized police officer." Tia smiled as well. "It's amazing how much a smile can change people's appearance. Still, I didn't get your name. Is it classified as well?"

Cautious smirks and silent smiles of the two people grew into one frank and wide smile.

Tia couldn't take her eyes off the officer's face. What had just happened? That smile…it suddenly gave that charming personality to the one ridiculously looking face. She has never seen such a dramatic transformation in a person in no time. A set of lumpy nose-ears-cheeks on his bald head gave a nonnegotiable support to that reviling smile. Even the deep dark blue eyes that were constantly possessed with professional promptness looked somehow rarefied with all the neon reflections of lively hues.

"It's not classified. My name is…" Savarex paused. The neon reflection in his eyes became silver. The charming smile faded behind his tightly pressed lips.

A cold breeze snapped past Tia. She jumped out of her chair and pressed her back against the transparent wall.

"Kondrat. Rasara, you have to listen to me. This is the last time when I ask you to have my way. I am the only solution to all problems. All you have to do right now is to open this door. It's a portal to the great power, immortality, apocalypse…"

Tia was standing against the wall and couldn't move a muscle. It was like a terrifying nightmare when she was scared to death and could not make a sound. The only substance that moved with the speed of light in Tia was her thoughts. And they were sending signal after signal to her limbs and vocal cords. *I am so sick and tired of this guy chasing me everywhere. This has to end...right now!* She focused so much on any movements in her body. Nothing seemed to be working. *If I had a little push...any push...* She wasn't even sure that the happening took place in the reality. Tia decided to unleash the main weapon that could benefit in this situation. Her eye contact with the target has been placed immediately. A little effort—that was all she needed. An effort.

Tia tried to find one in order to redirect it toward the stranger. "It's not gonna work this time, Rasara. I am taking over the universe, and the universe holds everything, including your power."

Kondrat in Savarex's body moved closer to Tia and whispered, "Don't you think you should show more affection toward me? Act smart and make a wise choice: to be my slave...or my queen. This is your chance. How many lives have gone? And in all of them, I kept dumping you. This life is your pearl. The sacred wish of the existing centuries will come true. I am here now, your true love of all times, and I...am asking you to be with me forever."

Kondrat pressed Savarex's hands against the wall, locking Tia's head in between, and smelled her face and hair with moaning pleasure.

"Hmmm...It feels so good in the real man's body. I think I will possess this one. Don't you like your new little friend? That's what I thought." Kondrat-Savarex was breathing into Tia's face, aiming into her lips.

Tia wished so much for any possible moves. Even vomiting would make her so happy right now. Any disgusting distractions would be considered favorably compared to the upcoming kiss from this weirdo.

God, please...do something, please. Keep him away from me. I don't know what this is all about. I'm sure Your plan is wonderful like everything made by You, but please, don't make me be part of his plan...

At the present moment, Tia craved for a good prayer. She even promised God to learn one or two real prayers if she gets out of this nasty situation.

Rasara, I've no idea who you are, but somehow we're related. Help... Those were the last words of Tia's inner prayer.

Kondrat's breath touched Tia's lips at the same time when his eyes penetrated her soul. She held her last breath, resisting to accept the next one out of Kondrat's mouth.

Noise from the other side of the transparent wall got Tia's attention. Her eyes were frozen in contact with Kondrat's eyes, but it wasn't hard for Tia to refocus her sight onto the monitors right behind him. The camera captured a huge crow flying back and forth behind the wall...

—5—

The whirl of polka scattered the dancing pairs apart and, with the exciting screams of ladies, began a new spin.

In a blink of an eye, Noah lost Ofelia in the crazy polka beats. With another blink, he was paired up with Patrick. Only a few seconds and no words were needed to forget all global and personal issues when in the arms of a loved one.

Movements of the large dancing circle sucked in Noah and Patrick. Along with the fired-up talk of violins and flutes, dancing couples were mastering the feet alteration with each three steps: right-left-right-hop…left-right-left-hop…One foot is chasing the other… Moving around the ring…Jump! Kick! Move around again…

The bottomless depths of Patrick's blue eyes made Noah forget everything and everyone. He didn't even remember about his new cool look because it didn't matter anymore. The only thing that mattered to Noah in the whole universe was Patrick's lovely blue eyes, soft golden curls, firm muscles under his tight clothes, and his strong hands that were touching Noah's body in the polka dance. All these made sense to exist. How to exist? In the reality or dream? It was not important when your love was in your hands forever.

More couples joined the dancing circle, expanding it in all directions.

Soon, it barely fit in the ballroom. A smaller ring was formed inside the big ring and another one inside the small one. Soon, only couples knew which ring they belonged to in that randomly organized mixer. The law of dance reigned in the ballroom.

"My dear friend, if you could only speak or feel…" Noah squeezed Patrick's hand, enjoying the swim in his eyes. "Like in the old times. Please, say something… I miss you so much, buddy…" Noah stepped aside from the moving dance circle and hugged his dear friend, crying and touching his face. "I love you, Patrick. What do I have to do to wake you up…to get your feelings back?"

"Choose."

Noah pushed his friend away and, holding his breath, stared in Patrick's eyes with hope. "Did…did you just say something?"

Patrick's beautiful blue eyes, full of intelligence, were looking back at Noah.

"Say it again!" Noah looked at his friend as if he was a miracle. Slouching, he pushed his upper body forward with his neck stretched toward Patrick. His wide-open arms were ready for the obvious action.

Patrick crossed his arms on his masculine chest and simply said, "You gotta make a choice, man…Why do you think you are here? Huh?"

Noah was still recovering from the fact that his beloved one, who had died a while ago, came back not only with his perfect appearance, but with the same wickedly cool personality. With tears of joy, Noah looked at Patrick up and down and pulled back his arms, ready for a hug. For a second, he possessed a thought that even a slightest touch could make this "real Patrick" disappear.

Noah was standing face-to-face with that miracle, holding his breath, his palms in front of him in a basketball position.

Patrick's voice reassured his real appearance. "Why do you think you are here?"

Noah put his hands down and exhaled. No doubts, Patrick was real. With half a step toward Patrick, Noah said doubtingly, "To win over the universe?" Noah pulled his neck into his shoulders and cast an angled look of uncertainty at Patrick.

Patrick shook his head and, with an indulgent smile, touched his friend's shoulder. "The happening in here is relevant to your illness. Since death got us apart, you've been trying to understand why happiness kept passing you by. Throughout the centuries, your heart was opened to any love, and you have always been receiving your desired love. Only one problem remained: it didn't matter how big your heart was, too much love couldn't fit into one heart. What happens to a balloon when we pour too much water in it? It breaks. So did your heart. Facing a dilemma between love to yourself, to your girlfriends, boyfriends, your mother, you suddenly came to conclusion that it's impossible to make everyone happy at the same time. People become ill when they get rejected. And you didn't want to hurt anyone, especially those who have been in love with you. So instead, you became sick. Your overwhelmed brain couldn't fight with those thoughts anymore. You started experiencing seizures and hallucinations. Unfortunately, mentally ill people are very protective of the strange voices of their hallucinations and accept them as their good friends. And your 'good friend' from the book of your fantasy, Anna, suddenly wanted to help you, offering the entire universe to your command. Perfect! All your dilemmas are about to be solved! Isn't it wonderful?!" Patrick sarcastically smiled into Noah's face and patted his head.

Noah's confusing gaze was wandering around Patrick's face. "How do you know all this? I've never told you about it. All we had was pure happiness without a single touch of sadness in our previous love experiences."

Patrick put both hands upon Noah's shoulders and, keeping eye contact, said, "You tell me."

Noah's eyes became wet. He turned his face away from Patrick and stooped in misery. Then, on the spur of the moment, Noah straightened his back and forthrightly looked into Patrick's eyes. "My consciousness…in a form of the one who's been having the best understanding of me…" Noah grabbed Patrick's forearms and, with a smile, passionately continued. "You are me. The reason of my failure in all relationships was the uncertainty. I was lost between the love for my mother and my partner. The idea of loving myself has never possessed my mind. I have never asked myself what I wanted out of any relationship. The questions were always 'Will my mother agree?' or 'Will Ofelia or Patrick be happy with me?' Constant stress of trying to be approved has poisoned my life.

"One day I have chosen my mom's happiness over mine because I thought it was the right way to do so. The sense of a big mistake has followed me everywhere since. I couldn't understand what went wrong. The closest person in my life became happy. I should have been happy as well for her. Why wasn't I? This question drove me crazy until now, when I had a chance to listen to my inner voice coming from you. Your affection was everything I've ever needed to feel loved. You, my friend, have helped me to learn to love myself. I've just realized what you were trying to say by 'I had to make a choice.' And by choosing you, I choose myself, my own happiness. I know what I have to do now, and you will help me with this."

Once Kondrat-Savarex became distracted by the flying crow and turned his eyes away from Tia's face, a hot wave of energy ran through Tia's body. She quickly closed her eyes and inhaled. The next action happened fast. She raised her arms and, with a clenched fist, hit Kondrat-Savarex's elbow bends. Kondrat, losing his balance, flung down on his head and immediately got kneed in the face by Tia. Screaming, he fell on the floor, covering his nose with both hands. He was bleeding badly.

Tia ran to the darkest corner of the room, pressed her back tightly against the wall, and, trembling, slid down to the floor.

Kondrat-Savarex stopped moving and screaming. His body began to shake, rolling over the floor. Very soon, the convulsions stopped. Savarex remained motionless in a puddle of his own blood.

Tia tried to even her heartbeats and reduce involuntarily trembling. Focusing on her breathing, she continued to observe Savarex.

Savarex's body was lying on the floor. His face was covered with both hands. From two meters away, Tia could see the man's closed eyes through the gaps between his fingers covered with blood. She waited for a bit, just to make sure that there was no trap around, and stood up. Looking for something that could be useful for self-defense, she grabbed a massive flashlight out of Savarex's emergency bag. Holding her breath, she slowly approached the man lying on the floor. Standing beside his feet, she kicked them a little. Waited. No response. Moving toward his head, Tia poked his hands with a flashlight. Noticing a blood mark on the flashlight, she grabbed a piece of cleaning tissue and wiped the flashlight. Using the same paper, she carefully grasped the officer's finger and moved his hand out of his face. Savarex was bleeding severely. Tia pinched his nose with one hand, trying to stop the bleeding. With the other hand, she held the flashlight ready, just in case of any action.

Savarex's shoulders twitched a couple of times. Then he opened his mouth and eyes. Tia jumped aside, pointing the flashlight toward Savarex.

The officer sat up and cast around a confused look. Noticing Tia in a defense position, he quietly said, "What?"

Tia sighed in relief and put the flashlight on the floor. "Thank God, it's you…" Tia grabbed an emergency bag and squatted beside the officer. "Let me clean you up. You're bleeding."

She put on vinyl gloves and, with sterile gauze and alcohol, began to pad Savarex's face. Then she asked him to elevate his head and hold his nose pinched. "Can you slide toward the wall? I have to clean the floor." She wanted to help the officer to move, bending toward him.

Savarex signed that he was alright to do it by himself. "Can you please tell me what just happened?" he asked quietly.

"I punched you. You were possessed…I had no choice. You were about to kill me."

Tia talked without looking at Savarex. She kept busy with unrolling paper towels and dumping them in the puddle of blood. Soon, two good rolls of paper towels soaked with the sticky red mess ended up in a garbage bag.

Savarex was sitting in the same corner where, a few minutes ago, Tia found her shelter. He observed her quietly. Her long hair was carelessly squeezed into a knot, leaving a few strands out. Fast but precise movements drew a picture of the person who knew her business very well. It was unusual for him to watch this young and beautiful girl cleaning the mess, performing first aid, and, at the same time, remaining tidy in her white blouse and khaki pants. After meeting with lots of good-looking girls in the police department or other unsafe public places during his duties, Savarex promised himself that if someday he had a girlfriend, she would be ugly to average-looking or no girlfriends at all because according to his observations, a good look doesn't go along with good personality. *Must be something wrong with this one. Tall, skinny, beautiful, intelligent…Doesn't talk much, not afraid to get her hands dirty…almost unreal…Lack of self-esteem? Most likely…*

Savarex removed his fingers from his sticky nose and inhaled. A strong smell of the disinfecting substance hit his sensitive nose.

Tia poured the entire bottle of the rubbing alcohol on the floor and took off her gloves. Her attention was turned to the officer. "How are you doing? Can you sit on a chair?" She moved the chair closer to Savarex.

Savarex got up and, with Tia's help, sat on the chair. "Any

leftovers?" He pointed to the wet floor. "For the cleaning purposes. My sniffer's still plugged..." Savarex smiled and continued the conversation. "I'm Jim, by the way..."

"Oh, good! I almost accepted the fact that you didn't have a first name." Tia found a second bottle of rubbing alcohol in the emergency bag and got closer to the officer with a wet pad in her hand. "Try not to move." She cleaned the rest of the dried blood out of his face and, throwing a quick glance at Savarex, giggled.

Jim, half smiling, queried, "What? It's my nose...right?"

"I'm sorry, Jim." Tia, tipping her head back, burst with laughter. "Can't help myself, sorry."

"Fine...just tell me! I wanna laugh too." Jim couldn't take his eyes off Tia's laughing face. *What a sincere laughter.*

Tia stopped laughing and, with a smile, said, "I gave you a nickname when I saw you the first time." She pressed her lips tightly together to lock an upcoming outburst. But she couldn't hide her eyes, throwing away multicolored sparks. "Potato Nose. And now... you became Red Potato Nose..." Tia couldn't hold it anymore and laughed her head off.

"Guess what, missy...I had a nickname for you too!" Obviously, Jim didn't have anything in mind. He paused through the laugh and said the first word he came up with: "Missy!"

"Oh...it's awesome! You're such a boring cop!" Laughing, Tia tapped Jim's shoulder, leaving her hand on it.

Jim became quiet and, with a smile, feasted his eyes on Tia's glowing face.

Tia stopped laughing when she noticed Jim's eyes looking far behind her face. She quickly turned toward the transparent wall and saw Officer Laroche, Tony, and the other policeman who was transferring the wheelchair person to the safe area a while ago. All three men stopped beside the wall and started touching it, as if they were trying to find something on its surface.

Jim whispered into Tia's ear, "You're a scientist…right?"

Tia half turned toward the whisperer, but kept an eye on the outsiders. "A research assistant."

"Right…research assistant." Jim corrected himself. "Do you think they're possessed? I can't see their eye color."

"Absolutely." Tia stood up and slowly proceeded toward the wall. Without looking back, she said in a monotone voice, "Jim, I want you to do me a favor."

Jim, keeping the same tone of voice, replied, "Okay."

"Do only what I tell you to do. Here comes the 'classified' part of the research. Do you understand?" Tia held the ground with her feet apart and hands down her side. She stood right in front of the wall, looking straight at the outsiders.

"No problem." Savarex touched the gun on his vest. It was the only move he made…

—6—

Five circles of breathtaking polka, one inside another, filled up the ballroom. The rings, moving in opposite directions, carried loud laughter, exciting screams, along with the striking music. The candlelight smoke that enshrouded the dancers in the bliss of sensual kizomba a moment ago got swirled up to the ceiling by a hurricane of polka rings and, at a loss, watched the downspin through its azoic silver eye. What was this eye seeing? Honestly, I don't know, and…I don't want to know. But as a writer, I have certain obligations. And one of them is to give you the best description of any place in this book, even the ones that don't interest me anymore. So here I am…

A SONG OF THE UNDERGROUND CHANDELIER

Dreams and Future…imperishable match…
somewhere, beyond the horizon.
Who gave them life? Who started light?
And always kept their eyes on?

What's light? Somebody else's soul,
a consequence of urge…
The urge to sing, to shine, to call
great beauty on the verge.

When it reveals itself from dark
and yenned to be adored,

half-life already melted mark-
for Autumn corridor.

The other half of life—in crave
to see what's in beneath
of cold-lake lily dancing wave.
That's all. The life's complete.

Have you had time to shine in bright
or hear the rustle of stars?
Have you had chance to give your warmth
to reason of your scars?

Have you been melting wax of steel
in healing flame of Love?
Have you forgiven dirty deal,
and sent it free with dove?

So, you can see—it's up to you—
which candle you become:
one for the underground fume
or sparkling on the sun.

All candles burn some days,
that's what they made for.
Their scent forever stays
beneath or beyond the floor.

Creator's work—to light them up.
That's all, no questions asked.
You have to choose which scent you are.
It's not Creator's task.

The chandelier's burning-out candles have created the image of a gigantic spider in the middle of the ceiling, who's hairy legs were disappearing in the silver of a smoky cloud. The spider was looking down at the ballroom with thousands of flickering candles, making sure that nothing was getting away from its all-seeing eyes. Soon, the underground monster fell asleep, giving the chance to the phosphorous veins in the walls to light up the ballroom. They didn't create much of illumination but were bright enough as a background behind the dancing shadows. Time to time, the portal fireplace was spitting out new arrivals and nourishing the phosphorous wall marbles with its light.

The jumping flame of the fireplace flashed all dancers, and two silhouettes that were standing still in the middle of two dancing rings, rotating in polka.

"Dance with me…" Noah grabbed Patrick's hands and pulled him in the jumping twirl of polka. Two young men lost themselves among hundreds of pairs.

If the spider chandelier wasn't sleeping, it would have noticed some unusual mood swing in the ballroom coming out from the oppositely rotating dance rings.

Naked dancers carried on the party, guffawing with each jump and kick. Noah and Patrick entered the smallest dancing ring and, looking at each pair, tried to find Ofelia. One foot chasing the other… moving around the ring… Jump! Kick! Into the next ring…

"I know what you are doing." Patrick squeezed Noah's hands and, with a distorted smile, looked into his eyes. "You are trying to escape." He grabbed Noah's buttocks and pulled him toward himself. "What do you say, darling?"

Noah wanted to stop the dance and tried to get out of Patrick's arms. He didn't understand why Patrick suddenly started acting out. Noah's movements became stiff and uncertain. "Patrick…Why are you…?" Noah couldn't find the right word. A million thoughts in his head started bumping against each other, creating anxiety. Noah began to catch air. His sweaty palms slipped out from Patrick's deadly grips.

"Wow, wow…the little Noah found a way out!" Patrick tried to grab Noah's hand, but messed with the air instead. Noah's hand was made of air! Looking surprisingly at Noah, Patrick stopped the trash talk and said, "You don't have much time for your plan to come true, Noah. You are dispersing. Aren't you supposed to dance with all the guests to gain the power? With each contact you gain, with each deny, you lose. So…be a good boy and start increasing your f——n' power!"

Something clicked in Noah's head and released him from the upcoming seizure. He made a half step back from Patrick and, staring in his eyes, as if he has never seen him before, quietly said, "Who… are you? You are not Patrick." Noah tilted his head, maintaining eye contact. "Patrick would never say any of that nonsense." Noah's serious face stretched with a sarcastic smile, and his eyebrows went up, drawing a few lines on his forehead. "Kondrat…You are Kondrat! If I am vanishing, so are you!" He touched Kondrat's shoulder and didn't feel anything. His touch sliced the air.

Noah stood tall and pointed his finger to Kondrat's face.

"You are blaming me with all your problems. You want me to fight against myself. Guess what?! I don't depend on you anymore! You go to hell and leave Patrick alone!"

A light breeze stroked Noah's hair on the back of his head. He felt a feathery touch upon his shoulder. He turned back. Ofelia inclined her head in reverence and, with a beautiful smile, invited Noah to dance.

Noah reached for Ofelia's hand with the fear of losing his feel of touch. His fingers lay on the silky skin of both of Ofelia's hands. He took a deep breath with eyes closed and exhaled freely. Feeling her skin, Noah slowly moved his hands up to Ofelia's elbows, memorizing them with each finger...up to her shoulders...neck...face. Stroking her heavy but soft hair from underneath the neckline, Noah tried to remember the sensation of the long strands sliding through his fingers and leaving an unforgettable aroma of orchids. He watched the black lustrous streams running through his hands and, squeezing them in the end, carefully placed them upon Ofelia's chest. Then, gently holding her head from both sides, he kissed her lips. One long kiss. It sealed the feelings that have been giving and receiving through the centuries. This innocent, sincere kiss didn't call for a physical desire, but the last memory of a simple human happiness. The last...is always the sweetest one...

"I know..." Noah opened his eyes and looked at Ofelia's. Their lips were still sealed in that kiss, but they could hear each other's thoughts.

"What do you know?" Echoing, Ofelia replied.

"I know everything...and this everything is so simple. Why couldn't I figure it out before?"

Noah's astral self began falling and levitating at the same time. It was impossible to describe the sensation because at that minute, Noah didn't want to describe anything. He was enjoying the wisdom of absolute happiness, love, eternity.

Looking around, Noah felt like a newborn child. His pathetic boring life revealed itself as the miracle he had never noticed before. Everyday problems became so small and ridiculous. The essence of life had come to the fore.

"I know the meaning of love." Noah's consciousness took over his speaking abilities. "It's a freedom to express your uniqueness and be accepted wholly. Love is forceless. It doesn't require any effort to prove itself. It just...exists...in the air...in the soul...like everything around. When you are enjoying the sunny weather, you don't try to assure yourself of how happy the sun makes you feel. You just enjoy it. And the sun doesn't care if you're happy when it shines. It just shines anyway. So as love. People exist for each other without realizing that they don't do anything extraordinary to be in love. They are simply happy with the fact that they found each other, and the rest doesn't mean a thing. We've been put on this world for the purpose of love. It solves all problems and makes everything and everyone better. Unfortunately, not all people possess this gift, and that is the only reason of the existing turbulences on Earth. Those who are missing love have hollow souls. They try to fulfill them with money, power, crime, obesity, meaningless sex…They rise above the Earth and teach mankind the meaning of a fake love, which is nothing but camouflaging their disability. The disability to love. The sad thing is that people listen to those unfortunates and get misled. You and I are blessed. Love has found us…"

Two souls were soaring in a beautiful dream when the rest of the audience went insane in polka's jumps. Tight embraces held steady those two in the center of a small dancing circle because their physical beings gave up all the energy to their souls. If souls could be seen, there would be only one soul for those two people. One song…one happiness…forever…

"I feel it. It's in me too." The vibration of Ofelia's lips sent the flowing energy back into their bodies. "Do you feel my love?"

"It's in every cell of mine." Noah slowly kissed Ofelia and threw his gaze at the fireplace gate. "It's time."

-7-

"Jim, grab the flashlight. Stay in the dark."

Armed with a flashlight, gun, and curiosity, Savarex focused on the outsiders and the girl facing them through the wall. He saw Tia lowering her head and clenching her fist. Her other hand was in the pocket of her jacket. What he didn't see was Tia's eyes. They were closed.

Tony and two officers were touching the wall's surface on the other side without even looking at it. Dead expressions in their eyes showed no intelligence, but it looked like, subconsciously, they were still aware of the emergency room behind that wall. Accidently, Tony's hand pressed the invisible keypad lid. It opened up with a click. Tony jumped back, staring at it with his empty eyes. The other two stopped moving as well. Officer Laroche stepped toward the keypad and carefully touched it. Nothing changed. He randomly pressed all the digits at once in hope to get some result. Outraged, he began to hit the pad with a handheld radio. Tony and his partner, pushing each other, got closer to the target. Soon, the keypad was wrecked, but the door remained closed. Wild bawls of despair mixed with kicking and scratching the wall.

Jim and Tia were quietly observing them. By the corner of his eye, Jim caught some movements on the monitors. A police squad armed with black plastic shields and face covers was entering the tunnel.

A few blinks on the communication device indicated an upcoming transmission.

Jim pressed the receiving button.

"TD1, do you copy? TD1, over."

Savarex grabbed the radio. "TD1, roger." Looking over the monitors, he identified the person talking on the radio and maintained the visual communication.

"TD1, any casualties? What's your 20? Over."

"Roger, TD1-R. Two people inside, no casualties. Three affected police officers are behind THM. The code panel's been broken. We're stuck inside. Over."

"TD1, do you want the door opened? Over."

Savarex paused. He required a few seconds to decide. "If we don't open the door, there is gonna be more of them." He looked at Tia's back.

Tia lifted her head. Without changing her standing position, she said quietly, "Open when I tell you."

"Are you sure? How do you know? They will affect us." Savarex tried to stand up, pressing the corner walls and shooting the words at Tia's back.

Tia quietly turned around.

Savarex shut his mouth and, with horror, slid back in his corner. Two black "alien" eyes stared at him.

"Trust me." Tia turned back and froze in the previous position.

A million thoughts pierced Savarex's brain at once. *So it's true... It wasn't a figment of my imagination...there in the van...I've seen it. She's doing it again. Who is she? An alien?*

The radio has interrupted Savarex's nightmare. "TD1, roger. Do you want me to open the door? Over."

Savarex looked at the monitors. A couple hundreds of meters, and the police squad would be here. He looked at Tia's back. She remained still.

The radio went nuts. "TD1...Roger...TD1...Are you alright? Respond. TD1?"

Fifty...Thirty meters...and the rescue team would be here. Will they replenish the Recolla army or succeed with the mission? There was no definition of success in this case. How to neutralize the affected people without harming them? There was no cure found yet.

"Now!"

Savarex heard the word and saw Tia pulling out a flashlight from her pocket. He picked up the other flashlight left on the floor, and pressed the button on the radio. "Roger, open the door! Out!" He dropped the radio and had his gun ready.

"Roger...Wilco," said the radio on the floor.

The last reply was followed by several clicks from the transparent wall. Three affected people on the other side became quiet and stood still. The wall was slowly sliding to the right, clearing the entrance.

Savarex saw Officer Laroche's mate-white eyes and distorted smile when the door unveiled him and Tia standing face-to-face.

Tia remained motionless. The only move she made was opening her eyes. What happened next was very fast. Savarex wasn't sure if it actually went in the order he has seen. A reflection of silver-blue-green light filled up Laroche's eyes for a couple of seconds. The weird smile washed away from his face. The broken radio and a gun he was using for wrecking the keypad dropped on the floor. The officer was standing still in front of Tia with his arms hanging limp, but he was still keeping eye contact with her.

The moving wall unveiled Tony's presence next to Officer Laroche. Realizing that Tia was standing close to him, Tony swung for a punch, aiming into her face.

Still keeping eye contact with Officer Laroche, Tia pressed the "ON" button of the flashlight and redirected it right into Tony's face, blinding him.

Tony's hand dropped down. He remained still, keeping his eyes on the light.

Toufer pushed Tony aside, trying to get into the room. Tony lost his balance and fell on Officer Laroche. Toufer hit the top of that body pile and completed it with wild screaming, stretching both hands toward Savarex, trying to reach him.

Tia turned off her flashlight. For some reason, she didn't rush to help Officer Savarex, who was stuck in that corner of horror.

The police squad arrived shortly, hiding behind their shields and pointing their guns toward the emergency room. At last they entered, blocking the room from both sides. The police team quietly observed Officer Laroche and Tony, who were convulsing on the floor.

Officer Savarex was sitting on the floor and screaming very loud in the corner of the emergency room. He was pointing a flashlight into Officer Toufer's eyes.

Tia approached Savarex and touched his shoulder. "Jim...It's over..."

Savarex recoiled and stopped screaming, still pointing the flashlight on his target.

Tia gently pressed down Savarex's hand with the flashlight in it and sat on the floor beside him, holding his hand. They were sitting quietly in the corner and observing how the newly arrived police squad were taking care of the people who were recovering from Recolla.

Savarex turned his head and looked at Tia. "What the hell? Again...they're gray!"

Tia snorted silently. Green sparks began to dance in her smiling eyes. "It's classified."

A square-shaped man in his forties dressed as a superior entered the room. Dr. Kozlov followed him. Noticing Tia sitting in the corner, he rushed toward her and gave a hand to get up. "Tia! Are you alright? Let me help you." He glanced at the superior, who was bending over Savarex and furtively said, "We received the videos of your action.

Before they capture you"—the doctor pointed to the squad—"I'd like to have a few words with both of you alone, please."

Tia stood up with the doctor's help and replied, "Sir, do you remember the conversation about the possible causes of seizures? That was the reason for getting myself involved in this situation. I've had some experience with a few affected people, including Joshua. It has given me positive results. What you saw a few minutes ago was an experiment in order to assure that my method was not coincidental. I tried to trigger a seizure by using a bright light or"—she looked at Savarex with a smile—"a very loud noise in the form of a terrifying scream. Those signals have petrified the affected people and then caused them a seizure-like response. We know that mentally ill people can't be affected by Recolla. When the visual or audio signals simulated the seizure-like response, the brain got mixed up by the fake response and started to act as if being involved in the real seizure. The self-healing process has begun. When the seizure was ended, as you see it now…voila!" Tia pointed to the recovered officers.

"People became completely cured." Dr. Kozlov finished Tia's sentence. "So simple!" He couldn't take off his popped-out eyes from Tia's face. "I have to call Professor Kidd…It's so simple…incredibly simple!" Dr. Kozlov left the room to make a phone call.

"You are Tia Phrever?" The superior police officer touched Tia's shoulder. "My pleasure to meet you, Tia. I am Officer Flock." He shook her hand. "Do you mind if I have a few words with you?"

Tia looked at Savarex. "He lost too much blood."

"Please, Tia, you don't have to worry about Officer Savarex. He'll be alright." Officer Flock adjusted his voice pad and was ready to record an interview with Tia.

Tia looked at him and said politely but with a tone of confidence, "I am very tired. This is my calling card. I would be happy to talk to you tomorrow…" She paused. "In the afternoon. Will you please excuse me? I am going home right now."

With the expression of independence on her face, Tia walked around the massive and confused superior officer, left the emergency room, and headed toward the world above the ground.

A whirlwind of polka raged in earnest. Yellow-green phosphorous glows on the walls absorbed bloody-red color from the flashing fireplace and turned the friendly and innocent dance into insanity.

Dancing couples began to attract others and fell on the floor, moaning in enjoyment of physical pleasure. Piles of randomly congregated bodies wiggle-waggled in ecstasy.

Noah and Ofelia looked around. The unimpeachably vertical in the previous dance crowd showed more and more horizontal rearrangement.

A few more minutes, and it would be impossible to get lost among the standing dancers. Still dancing couples gradually became tripled, quadrupled, and so on until they couldn't remain in the standing position and got landed in conjoint playfulness.

Noah squeezed Ofelia's hand when he noticed that two naked women and a man in between were heading toward them. Aghast, Noah backed off, lugging away Ofelia. Losing balance, they both tripped over a few bodies on the floor behind them and fell. The walking trio accelerated their pace toward the fallen couple. In a few seconds, all five would be entangled.

Noah and Ofelia were flapping their legs and arms when they tried to find a steady surface to get out of the moving huddle. Convulsive touches of strangers scattered all over their bodies. Suddenly, the stirring pile opened up in between Noah and Ofelia, and two strong hands pushed them out. Rolling down to the opposite sides of the body pile, Noah and Ofelia looked back. In the same moment when they got pushed out, the approaching aroused trio fell right into the spot where Noah and Ofelia struggled and landed into Patrick's open hands. Smiling, Patrick quickly nodded toward the fireplace, urging Noah and Ofelia to step over their confusion and immediately proceed with the escape plan.

Noah quickly stood up and gave Ofelia his hand. Dancing in a run, they reached the portal. Now, they had to wait for the next arrivals and jump into the flame together.

Prankish polka turned into the random sounds of all the instruments in the orchestra. The perfect music got swallowed up by the increased howling, moaning, screaming. Detached tunes, sneaking away from the crowd's insanity, high-pitched, their existence with the hope to survive.

Soon, the entire floor became covered with wiggling bodies. Only two people remained standing. Safely locked up in each other's hands, they barely swung in dance. No words said…no emotions shown… just quiet coexistence of two souls.

A voice in Noah's head made him stop the dance. *Pathetic piddling little soul. You must be proud of yourself. A brilliant idea of escaping from hell.*

He looked around. The green-yellow fog in the ballroom had taken away the last hope from surviving music sounds and honed the groaning in beneath. Peering through the fog, Noah made out the outlines of Patrick, standing in the middle of the ballroom among the fallen bodies. Right behind him, Noah noticed a woman in a red cape and a huge black diamond in her hair.

Anna-Rasara was standing at the top of the ascending stairway and looked at him. "You think you are special? Look around, Noah. All this describes your filthy nature. You humans are nothing but followers of your animal instincts. Reproduction and survival are your priority. Where would you be without your astral selves? On the same line with the rest of animality. You might escape from here, but you can't escape from your degradation. Kondrat has been banished from the astral world. He is not allowed to be up there with you anymore.

Without him, you are nothing but a crawling worm. Good luck with your last life-spin…as a brainless being!"

Anna-Rasara turned around and flapped her cape, unbarring a pair of perfect long legs. She vanished in the fog. At the same time, the flame burst out of the fireplace, spitting out new arrivals.

Noah grabbed Ofelia's forearms, squeezed them hard, and with tears in his eyes screamed, "Promise me something!"

Ofelia looked at him blankly.

Noah began to shake her tiny body as if trying to wake her up. "Ofelia, promise me, you'll find happiness…despite of anything. Promise to me!"

The poor girl looked confused and said, "I…I promise."

Noah hugged Ofelia tight and, crying out, pushed her into the flame behind her. "I love you, Ofelia!"

Ofelia's big astonished eyes and reaching-out hands disappeared in the flame.

Noah lost his balance and fainted into Patrick's arms, who was standing behind him.

PART V

Awakened

Sunlight peeked through the morning clouds and took a walk down the Earth. West Canada…Alberta…Gray Stone…Tia's room. Wake up, sleepyhead! Another wonderful day is waiting for you!

Glancing through the window curtains, the sunlight reached the wall thermostat. Click. Let's make this room warmer. That girl in bed deserved to sleep a little bit longer.

The warm air began to wander around the room, inviting curtains to join the tour. It touched the crystal ball between curtains and made it twirl. Catching the movement in a window, sunlight hit through the hung jewel and scattered around the walls and ceiling with silver-gold dots. The dance of a new day has begun.

Clicking sound of the thermostat woke up Tia. She felt a pillow with her cheek and smiled. Then, remembering something, she quickly pulled a blanket onto her face, leaving her eyes and forehead uncovered. Holding her breath, she looked around the room. For a moment, Tia was confused with the location. She was still living in her yesterday adventure. Then she focused on the dancing dots around the walls and exhaled in relief.

Keeping her morning routine unbroken, Tia grabbed a little mirror from the side table. A pair of perfectly gray eyes with amber rings around the pupils looked back at her. "I was scared a little, but the color didn't change." She sat up on her bed and looked in the mirror again. "Hah…the same color."

Knocking on the bedroom door interrupted Tia's little experiment. She put the mirror down.

"Are you awake?" Marsha's smiling face peeked in the door opening. Was it going to be a very sunny day, or just a presence of the dearest person in the world who suddenly lit up the room with coziness, love, comfort?

"I brought you something." Marsha put the tray with pancakes and honeycombs on Tia's bed. "The tea is steeping and will be ready in a minute." She sat on the bed beside her daughter, brightening the morning with sky-blue eyes.

"Mo-o-m…I thought we've agreed that breakfast in bed was for lazy people only." Tia gave a surprising look to her mother.

"For lazy and special ones." Marsha put both palms on Tia's cheeks and looked deeply into her eyes. "And you are that very special person." She kissed her forehead. "You deserved that, honey. I've heard about your adventure last night…My little girl…" She kissed her again and left Tia in charge of the breakfast.

While Tia was diligently stuffing her cheeks with pancakes, Marsha moved the curtains and let the sunlight in the bedroom. Then she left to the kitchen to check on the tea.

Tia didn't realize how hungry she was this morning until she took a first bite. All this stress and excitement of the other night worked on her appetite very well.

Aroma of steeped jasmine tea sneaked into the bedroom, bringing Marsha along. Ah, what a perfect November morning. Freezing sky preserved a brightness of sunlight inside its solid crystal dome. There was not a slight movement in nature this morning. Silence. If you listen carefully, you can hear the dreamy wind, hidden under each prickle of the pine trees and each feather of fluffing birds, in between snowflakes on the ground… It's so sad that the realisation of possessing the most valuable treasures in life takes a very long journey until it is fully understood. Simple dark blue, almost black, knee-length skirt; gray front-buttoned cardigan with dark-blue stripes on its front pockets and collar; nylon stockings and neat tight slippers. And the face…that dear face with kindly smiling eyes and prankish buttoned nose. Why doesn't it stay forever, just like that? Mama… she forgives everything and loves forever no matter what. She turns very boring things into something special, unforgettable…just like this cold but cozy November morning. It doesn't take a lot for her to make it memorable. The magic of jasmine tea and honeycomb pancakes steeped with the energy of mother's love. That's all you need to feel special…loved.

Quenching hunger by the great work of chewing by both sides of her mouth happily increased Tia's ability to think. "How do you know about my 'little adventure'? When I came home, you and Dad were already sleeping. I didn't want to make any noise in the kitchen and went straight to bed. Did Professor Kidd or Dr. Kozlov call this morning?" Tia tried to figure out the source of information.

Marsha kept smiling and stroked Tia's hair, tucking one stubborn strand behind her ear. Then she looked very seriously into her daughter's eyes and quietly said, "The birds can tweet, you know… especially the big ones…"

Tia immediately stopped chewing and fearfully looked at her mother.

For a few long moments, they stared at each other.

Suddenly, Marsha burst in laughter. "Oh, honey! You should see your face right now! Hahaha, I'm just messing with you. Your name's all over the news this morning! You're famous!"

Tia pushed the chewed pancakes down her throat and grabbed her little mirror. "Same…the color didn't change."

Marsha suppressed the final laughter and said, "What's that, darling?"

Tia turned her face to the light from the bedroom window and looked in the mirror again. "It's the second time in the morning

I've got scared, but my eyes remained the same color. Usually, they become pale, almost white, when I feel scared."

"Did you really get scared or…sure you got scared?" Marsha fought with an upcoming smile, trying to hide it.

Tia paused and tried to live through the "scary" moments of the morning again. "Yes, I was scared for a moment. Well…it wasn't like real fright, but still…It was some unpleasant feeling, I guess." She shrugged and pursed her lips.

"You probably had those mixed feelings for a few seconds, but deep down you already knew that the worst has long gone. Am I right?" Marsha put her hand over Tia's, digging into her inner voice.

Tia remained quiet for a while, absorbing her thoughts and looking nowhere. "Mom, you're right. I've peace of mind now. For the first time I feel so confident, not afraid of anything, because something tells me that the only fear that exists is fear of death. And death…is nothing but a transition into another life. Basically, it's a very necessary thing for each of us. Why do we have to be afraid of something that makes us smarter, stronger, gives us the opportunity to fix our mistakes made in the previous life? The bottom line is that there is nothing in the world that I could feel unhappy with. It's all about life and acceptance."

Marsha pulled her hand out of Tia's and said very carefully, "Honey, how do you know that there is another life?"

Tia was still swimming in her thoughts. Then she said, "I don't know, I just…know. Rowena…Nicole…Rasara…me…Life is endless. Blessed those who still have guts to march fearlessly through the centuries toward their dreams, ambitions, inspiring others for seizing new opportunities. Life is the constant movement ahead. When you stop once, you stop forever."

Dogs barking from outside interrupted the strange conversation.

Tia shook her head and quickly looked around. Noticing empty plates on the tray, she said, "How can I say no to this! You're spoiling me! Thanks for the breakfast, Mom." She glanced at the clock. "I better hurry up. It's gonna be a very exciting day at the hospital."

Tia kissed her mom, who, for some reason, remained sitting on Tia's bed and speechlessly looking at her daughter.

In fifteen minutes, the orange Honda was heading toward Gray Stone Regional Hospital.

Recoil

Lots of people admit that Saturday mornings on Earth have unusually strong gravitation, especially during falls and winters. It works in favor of those who are enjoying long-awaited weekends in order to sleep in. What about the others who had to fight through the gravity to wake up early and get ready for work? They must feel pretty miserable. Let's run a quick experiment on some people who work this Saturday morning. For instance, that girl in the orange Honda heading toward downtown.

Leaving the residential area with its boring playground zones behind, Tia, rebelliously challenged still-sleeping wind to race. Saturday morning. No traffic at all.

Tia checked the mirrors for any police cars, cranked up the radio volume to full, and stepped on the gas. Getting in vibes with the speed and freedom, she opened the driver's window to feel the wind. "Woo-hoo-o-o!" Randomly sliding from one lane to another, driving on the double yellow line, crossing it, and daring toward the upcoming traffic lane, the fearless gal smashed to ashes the gravity's peaceful mood of the early Saturday morning.

Spotting an approaching vehicle, Tia immediately switched onto the right-lane traffic flow and glanced into the left-side window. The upcoming car passed by carrying away its driver's face, frozen in bewilderment.

"I guess it's time to be normal again." Tia threw her smiling mood away into the rearview mirror. Bright green eyes shot back at her. "Yep, time to hold the horses."

The traffic became busier by the time she was getting closer to downtown. All the DETOUR signs were taken down. Passing by the exit into the National Park zone, Tia recalled her yesterday's "emergency detouring." Not needed today. She smiled at the bunch of crows that were still napping on a pine tree.

Entering the downtown area, Tia decided to take a tour around before getting into the underground hospital parking.

It was unusual to see construction work downtown during weekends. The majority of central streets and avenues were opened for traffic, and the rest of damaged business properties were being cleaned and maintained with countless skid steers, street sweepers, and excavators. A couple of large backhoes were making horribly loud but full of hope noises in the opposite parts of the ravaged City Square.

Tia turned into a parking lot beside the apartment building where she left her car yesterday evening. She pulled in, got out of the vehicle, and stood for a moment, looking across the street at the under-roof parking where her underground adventures began.

A familiar voice behind her interfered with Tia's thoughts. "Came back for more, missy?!"

Tia turned around. Savarex was standing beside a police car, leaning back with legs and arms crossed. His dark-gray uniform with crackling radio on his shoulder outlined the seriousness of a policeman on duty. Black toque with stitched RCMP logo was pulled down to his forehead, almost touching a pair of dark aviators. His previously red nose has changed color to purple and spread around his face. The upper lip was stitched, and a couple of small bandages covered something on the officer's right temple. Regardless of this inconvenience, Savarex gave Tia a big smile and made a step toward her.

"Jim?" Tia peered into his face. "How are you? Aren't you supposed to have a few days off?"

They approached each other slowly.

"I know, I look my best today. But you…" Jim made a step back and, looking up and down at Tia, completed his sentence. "You look terrible! How's it even possible to get out of a freaky fight in the dirty sewerage without a scratch and in perfectly clean clothes? As I remember, you, missy, dealt with some serious mess down there."

Smiling, Tia tilted her head to the side and, in unison with Savarex, said, "It's classified."

One unarmed sincere laughter was shared between two strangers.

Tia stopped laughing when she noticed a drop of blood coming out from Jim's lip after he cracked a smile.

"Jim, you're bleeding. Your lip…" She unintentionally got closer and touched his chin, inspecting the damaged skin. "You should clean it up and apply some antibiotic cream before it gets infected."

Jim didn't move a muscle but quietly enjoyed Tia being this close to him—her voice, touch, glance, breath… All these created something that he would never interrupt. For a moment, he wished to bleed to death if it was the only way to keep her around. Soon he realized that he was supposed to say something despite the pain. "Yeah…I broke myself in laughter." He lowered his eyes and touched the bleeding lip.

Tia shifted her feet and locked both palms together as in a conclusion of something. "Umm…it was awesome to see you again, Jim… Don't work hard, and…get well soon." She patted his shoulder. "I gotta go to the hospital."

Ignoring the shooting pain on his bleeding lip, Jim endeavored to prolong the conversation and, with a bit of hope, threw toward the leaving girl, "Did you find the cure? Just curious!"

"Sure…*I spare*…" Tia waved to Jim and got in her car.

Professor Kidd, Dr. Kozlov, a few more doctors from the Recolla department, and four reporters were waiting for Tia in the head office of the Gray Stone Regional Hospital. When she entered the room, everyone started to clap and congratulate Tia with the breakthrough results of the research. Two reporters and two camera personnel from local Gray Stone television channels started recording the event.

Tia got confused with the surprising development and lowered her eyes for a second because she didn't know in what nuance she has been dragged this time. Then remembering that every awkward situation has a way out, she stood tall and gave the crowd an open look. It was the very time to recall Marsha's words: *Green it out, girl!"*

Professor Kidd and Dr. Kozlov approached Tia right away.

"Well done, Ms. Phrever!" Dr. Kozlov shook Tia's hand. "How did you get the idea to use a flashlight on the affected?"

The cameras got closer from the opposite sides of the room, trying not to miss the conversation.

Tia tried to ignore them and, glancing at both direction with a trace of distrust, replied, "Actually, Doctor, it wasn't my idea, and this wasn't a new technique."

Two hands with microphones almost got stuck in Tia's mouth. Unexpected silence reigned in the room.

Tia continued, "I hope, you remember the conversation that day when I was invited to participate in the research group. You and Professor Kidd talked about a new patient. Professor said that Recolla patients don't have mental abnormalities. And the seizures they are experiencing through the recovery process are not seizures. Why? Because they don't have the illness that usually targets seizures."

Tia paused, glanced around, and suppressed the unwanted emotions. All people in the room were looking at her. She pushed the discomfort down to her throat and continued.

"So this comment made me think of the nature of seizure-like activity. If this 'fake seizure' is nothing but the last stage of the Recolla illness, then what was the target? In medically approved seizures, any routine that overstimulates brain cells could become a target for seizures. It could be exhaustion, seasonal change or change of routine, loud sound, bright light…It could be anything. All this creates anxiety, which leads toward seizures. When I was passing through downtown and accidently got involved in a very unpleasant situation with one affected person, I tried to use my flashlight to stimulate the retinas of his eyes. Noticing that epithelium in his corneas was pretty abused by the outside world, I tried to increase brightness of a flashlight and made the ray pulse through his eyes. So the light was received and transformed into the electrical impulses. By the time when the optic nerve has delivered the signal to the brain, the brain was not ready to accept such a quick shift and tried to readjust its function from being affected by the illness into its normal work. Here comes the seizure-like activity as the transition to recovery."

Tia paused. That was all she had planned to say today to her colleagues, not to the city press. Obviously, she had to come up with any scientific explanations to avoid the real cause of people's recovery. And this hypothesis was the most realistic one.

The absolute silence turned into random whispering around the room.

A lady reporter stepped into the video frame right next to Tia and, looking into the cameras, said, "Hmm…quite a detailed response we've got here. Hi, I am Cindy Look, GS1-Channel. Tia, you were saying that the breakthrough idea didn't belong to you. What did you mean by that?" After the phrase, she turned her face from the camera onto Tia, expecting for a reply.

Tia ping-ponged her confused gaze to the reporter, then to the cameras and again back to the reporter. She did the same with her finger and, giving up, said, "Are you talking to me? I'm sorry, I thought you were talking to the cameras."

Everyone in the room took it as one of the "mannered jokes" and proceeded with polite laughter.

The slightly embarrassed reporter partially participated in laughter as well, and then factitiously turned her whole body toward Tia, remaining in defiant silence.

Tia tried to recall the reporter's question. Of course, she could politely ask Cindy to repeat it, but the invisible game of egos between the two professionals was on.

"Right...to whom the idea belongs..." Tia gave one more chance to the reporter to repeat the question and, after a split-second pause, proceeded with the possible reply. "Cindy, are you sure that the question even deserves a consideration? This breakthrough idea hasn't had any approval yet. Even if it becomes scientifically approved, all the credits will be given to the whole team of researchers. This idea is based on the fundamental knowledge of the millions of dedicated scientists of all centuries and can't be possessed by a single person. The idea behind each discovery is and will always be working toward improving people's well-being. It doesn't even matter to whom it belongs. What you've heard in here was just a rough sketch of an undergrad. Today, it should be discussed with the research team, not going viral. Thank you."

Tia stepped outside of the video frame, leaving speechless Cindy Look to look for a professional way to end her report.

Heading toward a water cooler, Tia gave away a mix of confused smiles and polite glances to the people around. *I gotta get gray contacts for such events.* The worry made her thirsty. Passing the emergency eyewash station, she glanced in the little mirror behind the eye water pump. "Glossy silver with purple dots. It's pretty damn bright. Oh well, now I know the hue of worry and unexpected events." Finally, she reached the water cooler and grabbed a plastic cup from the shelf behind it.

"You're quite a fighter, Ms. Phrever." The voice of Dr. Kozlov made Tia roll her eyes. The water cooler released excessive air bubbles, communicating its approval for the girl's rude facial expression.

Tia didn't rush to turn around toward the voice and took all the time she needed for placing a plastic cup on the water platform of the cooler, pressing the "ON" button, and waiting for the cold water to fill up the cup. Then slowly, with hundreds of sips, she quenched the thirst. Only after that Tia turned around and faced Dr. Kozlov.

"No, I'm not. This is supposed to be my first day as a research assistant. And instead of discussing yesterday's events and making plans for the next step, I've got a reporter sticking two microphones in my face and making my life miserable in front of everyone."

Tia threw the cup in a garbage can and glanced in the wall mirror again. Purple spots disappeared, leaving the glossy silver in place. *Close enough. Work of cold water? I guess carrying an icy water bottle will be my next habit!*

Tia gave Dr. Kozlov the "I dunno smile" and shrugged. The rest of the interview performances they both spent quietly in the corner, beside the water cooler: Dr. Kozlov guarding his young associate from any possible and impossible interruptions, and Tia thinking of how the morning happy energy has been transformed into the energy of this rebellious event.

Another morning in town. The same as the rest of them and different like all of them. Well, to be honest, mornings…days… nights…seasons…They are and will always be nothing more than decorations on the stage of human lives. Only people's emotional state could add some difference to those decorations, for instance, just like the morning we have witnessed a few minutes ago. Supressed with "Saturday gravitation," the morning energy jumped out from its asylum and, carried by that irrepressible human being, transformed into something bigger and stronger. That was just one example. How many other people in the same morning have given the boost to the lazy energy of Saturday? You tell me.

On the Right Path

"And it's too early to come up with a conclusion or to promise anything right now. We are still a work in progress. Lots of tests have to be done." Professor Kidd was trying to end the press conference, paraphrasing everything that has been said, but the reporters kept attacking him with upcoming questions. Soon he was just standing and rubbing his beard.

With overt sympathy, Dr. Kozlov and Tia looked at their colleague struggling in the spotlight.

"We should help him somehow." Dr. Kozlov constantly played with his fingers and had no idea why this plastic cup was in his hands. The doctor's restless glance was jumping from that empty cup onto each person in the room and, using the same trajectory on the way back, disappeared in the same cup in his hands.

The girl beside Dr. Kozlov looked pretty relaxed, most likely bored. From time to time she was sipping ice-cold water and observing the blues of the dancing bubbles in the water cooler.

The conference room door opened up, and a nurse's face peeked through. Spotting Dr. Kozlov, she approached him immediately. "Doctor, we need you in the Intensive Care Unit right now. A patient came out of a coma with some unusual behavior." She left the room right away.

Dr. Kozlov stopped playing with that annoying cup and looked at Tia with a great deal of excitement. "Bingo!" Theatrically bending his knees and curving his whole body, he threw the cup in the garbage. Armed with the weapon of a perfect excuse to end this press conference of the suppressed confidence, he marched unceremoniously toward the "ruthless" reporters to rescue his dear friend.

"How many Recolla patients are being admitted right now, and how long does it take—?"

The phrase broke up and flew away from microphones toward the third person who has intruded into the dialog. It took one professional moment for Cindy to bring the dying interview back to life. She approached the cameras and turned her face halfway toward Dr. Kozlov. Mysteriously smiling at the camera, she whispered into a microphone, "There is some exciting news that finally came to light. Let's hear it." She stretched out her microphone toward the information source in the spotlight.

It was impossible for the reporters to get anything out of those two who were communicating almost telepathically. Dr. Kozlov whispered something in his colleague's ear. Only the last two words caught the reporters' all-seizing nature: "right now."

The annoying microphones began to stab Dr. Kozlov's face. "Dr. Kozlov, what's 'right now'? Is there any activity in the Recolla department? Can we go with you?"

Stepping in front of the professor, Dr. Kozlov released him from the scene by gesturing behind his back for the quick escape.

Dr. Kozlov stood brave and tall, looking straight into the cameras. Promising silence filled the room. Reporters were ready to fetch a delicious piece of revealing news and throw back the bones of provoking questions into their next victim.

Dr. Kozlov took a deep breath. Microphones got closer to his face. Reporters' eyes and mouths became longer. Dr. Kozlov leaned toward the mics and sliced the air with his strong Russian accent. "Thank you for-r-r coming. We'll keep you in touch." Then he quickly disappeared in the hallway, leaving the press crew *cruelly supressed.*

Right after the nurse left the conference room, Tia rushed after her.

"Hi, I'm Tia Phrever, the Recolla Research Group assistant." She touched the identification card on her chest. "Before we reach the Intensive Care Unit, can you please update me on the happening?"

Paying zero attention to the girl, the nurse threw her tiny hand with wires of blue veins on it toward Tia. "Marge. The ICU nurse."

Short, skinny, fifty-year-old Marge walked very fast toward the Intensive Care Unit. Her tiny feet didn't make any noise and created the illusion of flying. Her silver-haired head was way ahead of her entire body, and her constantly moving appearance spoke of tough professionalism. She shot Tia with a quick look.

"Heard about you, Ms. Phrever. The way you dealt with a couple of patients…you're on the right life path." Parsimonious in wording and generous in action, Marge shared a few sentences with Tia. Her low-tone voice kept the happening clear and down-to-earth.

"Ofelia Rubio, twenty-three-year-old female. Admitted with head trauma a week ago. Fell into a coma. About half an hour ago, she came out of a coma with screaming, 'No-no…Noah…Noah…'"

"Noah?" Tia slowed down, which wasn't a very good idea at that time. The next moment, she caught Marge turning into the ICU. Tia sped off and found the nurse in an empty room, passionately discussing something with other nurses. Tia got closer to them.

Marge noticed Tia. "Ofelia disappeared. Nobody knows where she is."

Tia quickly looked around the room and, glancing at Marge, quietly said, "She's in Noah's room."

Without thinking twice, both ladies rushed to the Recolla Department.

A young girl dressed in a hospital gown was kneeling beside the bed where Noah lay. She buried her face in a blanket on his chest. Her long black hair scattered all over the bed and Noah's face, and little shoulders were twitching in a quiet cry. Time to time she was lifting her crying puffy eyes and looking at Noah's quiescent face.

Marge signed Tia to stay outside of the room and walked in with a nursing assistant. Talking to Ofelia, they helped her to get up and transferred her into a wheelchair. The nursing assistant moved Ofelia into the previous room and remained with her.

Tia was still standing behind the glass wall and observing the happening. Is Noah dead? She didn't want to think about it, but the answer was flying around the room. She saw Marge checking Noah's eyes, pulse on his wrists, neck, glancing at all monitors. Looking around the room without finding anything useful in order to run the additional tests, Marge slowly sat on the chair beside Noah's bed and lifted her tired eyes on Tia. The inevitable verdict was imprinted in them. It was unusual to see this tiny ball of energy being drained out so much.

"Ms. Phrever." The quiet voice of Dr. Kozlov interrupted Tia's thoughts. "You can come in."

Tia followed Dr. Kozlov into the room.

Noah lay in bed, still and utterly silent. Unusually pink cheeks and lips on his pale skin created the illusion of a healthy-looking young man resting in sleep. A peaceful smile was locked on his relaxed face. It seemed like he was taken away by some pleasant dreams.

Dr. Kozlov took out a stethoscope, touched Noah's chest, and listened to the emptiness that had taken the place of his heartbeat. He laid his fingers on Noah's neck. Vacant. He slowly took off the stethoscope and looked at the clock and then at Marge.

"Eleven fifty-nine. Please call Noah's guardians and the agency."

Dr. Kozlov and Tia left the room. Walking through the hallway in silence, they reached the Intensive Care Unit. Right before entering the unit's hallway, the doctor made an unexpected stop, faced Tia, and called her by the first name.

"Tia...are you alright? It's not mandatory to stay here. If you feel you need some time off, please do go home." Dr. Kozlov put both his hands on Tia's shoulders and looked into her eyes. "It's a little bit too much for the first day of work. Trust me, if you are willing to be part of our team, you'll see a lot of this."

"No…no. I am…alright. I can do it." Tia forced out a smile.

"You're stronger than I thought. My respect, Ms. Phrever. Again, if you feel you have to leave, don't say a word, just go. Promise?"

"Thank you, Doctor." Tia's next smile came out much more relaxed and sincere. She felt a sudden connection between this place and her, a professional connection. The lead doctor himself welcomed this raw graduate into his amazing team by worrying about her emotional well-being. *I am needed here. I'm on the right path.*

By the time Dr. Kozlov and Tia got into the Intensive Care Unit, Ofelia had been transported back into her room. Sitting on the adjusted hospital bed, she looked like a doll made of wax. Caramel-mocha skin turned into pale yellow, almost beige tone.

The liquid glass of sorrow filled out every artery of Ofelia's heart and hardened its last stratum upon the surface of her eyes. Screaming for the escape, her soul was brutally muted behind the glassy gate. Aloofness. Puffy hands of an innocent child obediently rested over the blue silence of the hospital covers. The conceived hope for happiness has been murdered unborn.

"Ofelia, do you need anything?" A nurse looked into Ofelia's eyes. "We're gonna do a blood test. Are you alright?"

Silence.

A thermometer was placed in Ofelia's mouth.

Dr. Kozlov checked her vitals. "She's dehydrated. The oxygen level is very low. Twelve hours IV and rest. Lab results to me as soon as possible."

Dr. Kozlov was laconic but specific with the nursing personnel. He liked the work being done with a high level of accuracy.

Tia noticed how people around immediately changed their

working technique when he was entering the unit. Everyone washed the relaxing smiles out of their faces and began paying extra attention to everything they were doing. A wicked ineptness tried to escape from every curve of Tia's lips, which wouldn't make the very positive impression on the first day of her work. Hiding under long eyelashes, her eyes were throwing gamine green sparks around the room. *I bet it's a great reference to work side by side with such a serious doctor.* She couldn't help herself and hid a smile beneath her lowered head.

Tia's little misbehavior was interfered by the soft but exigent wall speaker voice, announcing across the unit, "Dr. Kozlov, please proceed to the guest room number 5."

"Must be Noah or Ofelia's parents." The doctor glanced at his young companion. "More stress. If it's helpful, my advice—don't take it personally. Think of it like everyday work. Umm, well, try…"

For some reason, Tia felt that this tough doctor wasn't really tough with her. She sensed a great deal of insecurity coming from him when he spoke with her. *I hope it isn't personal because this is the last thing I need right now. I'll think of it like everyday work.* Proudly respecting her decision, Tia walked tall beside this brilliant doctor.

Nelly was sitting on the comfortable couch of the guest room and crying when Tia and Dr. Kozlov entered the room. Professor Kidd was standing behind her with a box of facial tissues in his hands.

Tia sat beside Nelly and slightly touched her shoulder. "My condolences, Nelly."

Nelly became quiet for a moment and blew her nose in a tissue. Looking nowhere, she said tiredly, "It was my fault."

Tia pulled back a little, giving Nelly enough space, and politely listened to her.

"My whole life…I tried to protect Noah from the cruelty of love affairs. I wanted him to be my little boy forever. Selfish old gal…" Nelly looked around interrogatively. "I didn't notice when he grew up…became a man. I denied all the girls he went with. They weren't good enough for my Noah, or perhaps, not good enough for me." She took a deep breath and, with a sad smile, continued. "One young girl I liked a lot. She was so adorable and crazy about my Noah. Ofelia... exotic beauty...But no! I didn't want to share my precious son with her. I didn't want to be number two in his life! So I've ruined it. I broke two hearts."

"Nelly, are you talking about Ofelia Rubio?" Tia exchanged a quick look with both doctors.

Nelly raised her empty eyes at Tia and nodded with the sad smile.

Tia wasn't sure if she could release medical information about Ofelia and threw a quizzical gaze at the doctors. Professor Kidd and Dr. Kozlov signed the instant yes at the same time. They were glad that this young girl took whole responsibility on comforting Nelly and granted the role of observers to them.

Tia got up and walked to the water cooler, giving enough time for Nelly to clean up her face and get ready for the upcoming conversation.

"Here's water, and chamomile tea's getting ready." With the quick look, Tia let the doctors know that she was expecting a certain work to be done around a teapot in the little kitchen corner.

Dr. Kozlov rushed to make tea. Professor Kidd remained where he was.

Tia placed a glass of water in front of Nelly and sat beside her. "Ofelia was admitted a week before Noah arrived. She had a head injury and fell into a coma. She woke up in the precise second when Noah...left us. The nurses who monitored Ofelia testified that when she opened her eyes, she screamed, 'No...no...Noah...' Then they found her in Noah's room, crying." Tia reached Professor Kidd for the box of tissue in his hands and picked a few for Nelly.

"She's still his soul mate." Nelly crumpled all the tissues and, sobbing, buried her face into them. "Noah loved me so much. He's sacrificed his happiness for me. I was supposed to step back...not him..." She hugged Tia and blubbered into her shoulder.

Tia stroked Nelly's back in silence. Then she put her palms on Nelly's shoulder blades and remained still.

Dr. Kozlov was about to bring a cup of hot chamomile tea and place it on the coffee table in front of Nelly, but Professor Kidd stopped him with his raised hand. Dr. Kozlov surprisingly looked at the professor and noticed that he was staring at Tia. The doctor redirected his attention at the same angle of view and immediately stepped back, spilling hot tea all over his shaking hand. Handling the situation without any noise, Dr. Kozlov put the cup on the floor and covered the burnt hand with his other hand.

Two medical professionals were standing side by side with the same expression on their faces. Their shifted-forward necks refused to hold together their dropped-down jaws. Wide open eyes were chasing the eyebrows that jumped after a few lines on both foreheads. That ridiculous look was caused by a very unusual color of Tia's eyes. They didn't have pupils and irises, but a solid gray tincture all over the surface.

It was hard to say how long those two were glued to the floor. Only the round clock on the wall behind them knew the exact time, but…it didn't care much about anything that usually happens in the guest room number 5. The clock was just doing its work, the work of walking each second to the past and check-marking their arrival with its obsessive clicks.

Tia slowly freed herself from Nelly's long hug and placed her hands upon Nelly's hands. Her gray eyes with amber rings around the pupils looked at the conciliated woman's face in front of her. "Nelly, do you have anyone to drive you home? I'll make a phone call for you."

Nelly looked at Tia with a tired smile. "Can I see Ofelia?"

The guest room door opened, and Marge flew in with her silent walk. She whispered something to both doctors.

"Impossible!" exclaimed the professor and rushed out..

Dr. Kozlov gave Nelly the permission to visit Ofelia and ran after the professor.

Tia knew that Nelly needed someone beside her right now and, with a comforting smile, said, "What if we have some tea?" She stood up, picked up the cup of tea left by Dr. Kozlov on the floor, and proceeded to the kitchen corner.

Nelly began to turn pages of the memory album. She didn't cry anymore because subconsciously, she was with Noah.

The two ladies were sitting in the quiet room, and only one was talking. Two cups of chamomile tea remained on the coffee table, and none of them were touched.

Dr. Kozlov and Professor Kidd were standing behind the glass wall of the room where Ofelia was resting. Both doctors looked confused going through the last test results and comparing them with the results of the first day and then a week after Ofelia's admission.

"What was the security report?" Dr. Kozlov took a deep breath and spread his hands in confusion. "It has to be something, Joseph. Don't you think that it was a little weird when she cried for Noah the second he died?"

Both of them quietly looked at the girl resting under constant control of the healing tubes and beeping monitors. Suddenly, they turned to each other with the same idea in their eyes.

"It's unlikely, Alex..." Professor Kidd whispered into his colleague's face.

"We have no choice. That might be the last right thing we can do before questioning Ofelia. Are you with me?" Dr. Kozlov, unlike his partner, seemed pretty determined with his idea.

"Okay. Even if the test shows positive, h-h-how will we explain it?" Spasmodically, Professor Kidd began to turn the pages of the patient's report on the clipboard in his hands, still looking for the nonexisting answer.

Dr. Kozlov, trying to comfort his friend, pressed the professor's unsettled hand to the clipboard and gave him a kind, warm smile. "My friend, we'll do what we always do—damn good work."

Professor Kidd stopped panicking and nodded through the smile. "Okay then...run the paternity test."

Dr. Kozlov immediately left his colleague. Professor Kidd entered Ofelia's room.

Ofelia slightly opened her eyes and stopped her absent look on the professor.

"How are you, my child?" It was almost impossible for Professor Kidd to fake a smile. Realizing that, he hid his eyes behind the clipboard pages, then assuming that it wasn't a very good hiding place, Professor Kidd cleared his throat and got closer to the girl. He sat on the bed beside her and took a deep breath. "I'm sorry for the loss of your friend, Ofelia." He touched her tiny hand while keeping eye contact. Noticing a tear rolling down Ofelia's cheek, he check-marked for the records that her mental health wasn't affected by a coma and the following stress, and she was capable to mentally process upcoming information.

"I know that it isn't a perfect time for you to talk, but there is something else you have to know about your well-being." Professor Kidd paused, giving some time for Ofelia to prepare.

Poor girl didn't show any interest and remained in the frozen eye contact.

"The last tests showed that you're two weeks pregnant." The professor paid extreme attention to her hand and facial muscles' activity.

A microscopic thrust of blood made Ofelia's hand twitch, and her heavy eyelids opened up a bit. Warm tears filled up her icy eyes and brought her face to life. Her lips moved in a smile and released streams of tears down her face.

"Do you have any idea how it happened?" Fully armed by the

unexpectedly positive reaction of his patient, the professor proceeded with the main question. "Do you know who the father is?"

Ofelia freed her hand, placed it on top of the professor's hand, and slightly squeezed it. She closed her eyes and nodded, just once. She turned her face sideways and fell asleep with a smile.

Marge entered the room. "Sir, Ofelia's family is here."

Professor Kidd turned his smiling face at the nurse. "Thank you, Marguerite." He got up and was ready to face the next phase of this unbearably difficult and significantly magical job on Earth.

Epilogue

Listen. That is all you have to know in order to concur your life—to listen. Not to pray for good luck or true love, but listen. Listen to the universe. Listen to yourself. Hear the voice of the energy that the universe cries for by touching every single cell of your body, testing every frequency of your soul. Identify this energy and devote your life to it because this will lead you toward the purpose of your life. Get along with the vibe you possessed in the moment of your conceiving. Generate this energy with every step of your journey, and release it back to the universe with the last exhale. Collect it again in the next life spin and make it stronger, happier, brighter, no matter what energy you were meant to stick with: great sorrow or betrayal, noble mind or a glorious warrior. Learn from your mistakes.

The ice-rounded moon sharpened the dark blue sky with its lofty alienation. There were three more nights left until it shines the perfection among the Earth. Majestic silence reigned between the moon and a woman on the tiny porch of a ramshackle house.

They stared at each other like mother and daughter after eternal separation. The woman's eyes were reflecting frozen flame of the moon when she mustered up her courage to speak. "You've been up there forever…alone. Some nights, you were barely seen, other nights, you were brighter than the sun, and still…alone. Tell me, how can you stand with such a loneliness and look irresistible?"

Silence.

The young woman made a step forward, keeping her eyes on the light, and stretched out her hand toward the majesty of the night sky.

"I am hopeless without my mother. I can survive physically, but the emotional pain…it's greater than the willpower to live." She stepped back and let the gravity take her body. She dropped on her knees and lost control over her exhausted arms. Her chin touched her chest. "Tell my mom…Rowena will see her tomorrow. You can't rise from the dead."

Four hundred years later, as an ordinary miracle, the moon was still doing its regular job of attracting people's attention and accepting their rhetoric questions. Anyway, that was the purpose of why the moon was created in the first place. Was the Creator happy with the job outcomes? Probably. And how can it be not, if every single person on Earth once in a while opens their very personal secrets to the moon without being asked to do so!

In a little town of Canada, on the back deck of some modern house, a middle-aged woman with an infant in her arms was standing still and looking up at the night sky. Silver-green moonlight found shelter in her big gray eyes. Exhausted by the constant tongue-lashing of her mother-in-law and an inappropriate weakness of her husband toward his manipulative mom, the woman was left with the only energy to stand and hold her baby. Her beautiful face features froze under the ice of disappointment of her family life. Without saying a word, she spoke to the moon, the only object in the whole wide universe that could understand her right.

"You've no idea how happy I am to see you tonight. Only two beings in the world could understand anything of me: you and my mom. Now, I have only you. One more night, and Earthy words will not find their best to describe your stunning perfection, and I will not be able to speak with you, but quietly enjoy your glory. Until then, please, help me out with something that I've given up any hope to understand. What have I done wrong in my marriage? You've made me beautiful with my heart and soul. I've learned to love my husband despite of our physical and spiritual differences that became such a mystery for others to understand our union. I work hard outside of my house and still take care of our baby and my husband's mother. I've dedicated my life to him. His friends envy him because of me and our beautiful baby girl. The family life is supposed to be perfect for us, just like you are tonight…Please, look down, find the answer. Why does he blindly follow his mother's commands to destroy his own happiness? Why did he choose his mother over his child and a wife? Why doesn't he want to be as part of our big happy family, including his mom? Where did I go wrong? Please, tell me the truth. Turn the Earth and my soul inside out and find the answer. You have my consent. Tell me what I have to do to save the family?"

She waited for a while with hope in her big eyes. Then she went back inside the house with confused feelings of disappointment.

Nicole refused to take another look to the sky, but if she did, she would see a huge aureole with almost all colors of a rainbow around the orb of the night. It was so bright, as if the sun itself was hiding behind the moon. A few hours later, the aureole became bigger and even brighter and expanded in all the directions far away from the moon. Its radiance touched the Earth. Yes, the moon has accepted the woman's request and sent its light down to begin the search.

Snowflakes peacefully twirled in a single waltz of tranquility.

They were circling down distancing from each other, guarding true, absolute silence out of the potential sound of any accidental touch of their pointy shapes.

With gravity's help, the snowflakes gracefully landed on the resting ground, on the deck of a house, and on the hair of a girl who was standing on that deck. She was looking up at the night sky. Her lips were slightly opened, but the warmth of breath couldn't dare to make a wave at the glorifying view. In the present moment, nothing seemed to be more important than the feeling of becoming a part of this unheard-of secrecy under the perfectly risen full moon.

"Every month, we wait for a night like this. Magnificent..." Marsha's voice broke the entrancement and made Tia to turn her head toward her mom.

She took a deep breath and, with a smile, came back to the view. "Mom...do you think people have a chance to be reborn? I mean, after they die...I know it sounds silly, especially when it comes from a medical research assistant. I don't know where this idea came from." Tia smirked at her mother.

Marsha touched the deck rail with one hand and hugged her daughter's shoulders with the other, keeping an eye on the moon. "There are no silly ideas under such an enlightening."

Tia paused for a few seconds and continued, "If we had a chance to be reborn, do you think it would be possible somehow...not to repeat the mistakes we've made in our previous life? I mean, to become more productive, clear with our life goals...without wasting time on some stupid arguments over nothing?"

"Just like the moon, every day more beautiful until it becomes complete." Marsha caught Tia's glance and held it with a meaningful smile. "You're thinking about your life, aren't you?" She slid her hand down to Tia's waist and slightly rubbed it, just in case, if her dearest one became cold. "Any regrets?"

"Actually, not," said Tia reflectively, gazing on a snowflake twirling through the air. "It's weird, but my life's being unfolded clearly in front of me, giving only a green light to anything I was trying to do. It seems like those little things of everyday life that make people miserable don't cross my way. If some of them do, I pass them by without any attention, and they don't come back anymore. It feels like I already know what I want and how I should proceed toward my goals. All the mistakes have been left somewhere behind, very long time ago. My life is clear like this full moon."

"You're saying, dear, that you have nothing to change in your life?" Marsha forced herself with a serious look, admiring the conversation. "What about those weird colors in your eyes? Are you alright with that as well?"

Green sparks in Tia's eyes immediately asked for permission to dance along with the snowflakes' flickering in the moonlight. "I've been thinking a lot about it and came to conclusion that I don't have to deal with that anymore!" Tia stated with a triumph.

Marsha stopped rubbing Tia's back and gave her a surprising gaze.

"Look at this miracle, Mom." Tia's dreamy voice and inexplicit smile tuned along with the silent music of the evening. "Does it seem like magic to you?"

Marsha got lost in her predictions. "Sure…It's beautiful…special." Her curiosity began to expand in all directions. She decided to be blunt in her words in order to give Tia all the freedom to express herself.

Tia continued, "And why do you think it's so special for you?" From out of the angled glance, she shot her mom with a bunch of prankish green snowflakes.

"Because…sharing a view of nature's sparkling dance in the moonlight with the dearest person in the world is always special and magical." Marsha completed the sentence with such an assurance, as if her answer were the only correct statement, and no other statements have ever existed. She didn't hide playfulness in her voice, just in case if her reply would go wrong. She sounded like she was making some sort of joke to avoid a possible embarrassment.

"Likewise, Mom." Tia smiled. The further she spoke, the more her voice began to lose the connection with the enchanting evening. "What about that man walking in the back alley? Looks like he is coming back from work because of his overalls, the backpack, and tired look. Do you think this evening is just as magical for him too? Probably not. It's just another regular night after work. Astronomers who observe the full moon as we speak won't find it magical either. For physicists, this waltzing music of snowflakes is just a reflection of the crystalized mist that's being pushed by the moving air from places with low atmospheric pressure into high atmospheric pressure back and forth."

"You're talking about different perceptions on the same aspect." Little by little, Marsha's amusement began to disappear. "How does it apply to your problem? I still don't get it."

"It's easy, Mom." Tia turned her full body toward Marsha. "I don't care what people think about the color of my eyes. All I care of is my own perspective on it, and…it's awesome. There is no difference between my eyes and someone else's eyes. They all change color in sickness, tiredness, happiness, excitement…you name it! Mine are just noticeable a little bit more in color, that's all. Very simple! Anyway, I am almost a scientist and know that everything is explainable. Believe me or not, I've proven it myself a couple of times at work. There is nothing in science that doesn't have an explanation. I study the brain, the most powerful part of human nature. The way this organ functions is still a mystery. I've been blessed with some extra abilities. This blessing opens the opportunity for me to study it, to collect more knowledge in human nature and expand its possibility. And I know that my new research will lead me to the theory that would explain the fact that there is nothing as wrong or right around us. There is no other side of the moon, but a wholesome creation. It means that any theory could be proven. You just need to know, and then…snowflakes will never touch the ground but waltz forever in the moonlight."

No words were said after the last statement, only contemplation of the ordinary magic.

Covered with a cozy winter blanket, the Earth was enjoying this grand show through the colorful view. On the opposite side of the sky where the full moon was showing off with all possible and impossible perfections, the aurora borealis began to play the night sky harp. Gently touching the strings of its green waves one after another, the northern lights noticeably accelerated the temp of tunes, throwing blue, gold, and red into the melody. Pouring into each other, colorful sounds created a new music. The flowing and pensive harp turned into a powerful, mind-blowing tuba. The colors began to sound sharper and captivating. The pulsing vibration grabbed its musical waves and, after pumping them in and out, released across the skies with myriads, shimmering in all colors of the rainbow, snowflakes, or stars, or glowing elements in the atmosphere. It was impossible to determine exactly what it was. One thing the Earth knew for sure: it has been for a while since the planet has witnessed such a performance in the night sky.

My insightful reader, prove me wrong, but I have feelings that the night sky description has suspiciously possessed you with the thinking of my next and very last part of this book. And like always, you were absolutely right.

"You have known how the project would end up even before you have had assigned it to me." A bright purple wave of the northern lights straightened up, slashed the sky in half, and faded in greens and grays.

Pulsing blue-gray-amber parabolas scattered randomly on the sky and united together around the fading purple.

"My dear Junntie, the ratio of a problem and the right solution is one to an infinite number. My solution would be favorable for the entire universe as from the Creator's point of view. You are a down-to-Earth creation, and of course, your way of decision-making would depend on the humans' well-being. You did well as well. Now the Earth is releasing enormous energy into the universe and beginning to balance itself."

Purple wave shimmers came out of the gray green.

"Correct me if I am hearing you wrong, Bohg. No matter what path mankind chooses unless they move forward. Is that what you are saying?"

The night sky turned into a huge moving rainbow.

"That is the correct answer, Junntie. It's all about energy. Good and bad is being accepted only on Earth because it is easier for mankind to understand rules of the universe. For you and me, it is an expandable balance that requires constant recharge for both energies. They don't exist without each other. Here comes our work—to keep the balance the way it should be. Even the brightest darkness of the night has to give way to the upcoming day. Then, so it be."